beachside kisses with my bodyguard

A SWEET ROMANTIC COMEDY

KRISTIN CANARY

This one's for any woman who has ever questioned her own worth. Hold your head high, because you are a true princess, you are loved, and you have immense value simply because you are you.

author's note and content warnings

Hi, friend! Thanks so much for picking up this book.

Just a quick note: The main characters in this story are from the fictional country of Kentonia, which I've described as "British-like." However, because I made it up ... well, I took a few liberties with some of their vernacular. While I mostly tried to keep their vocabulary similar to lovely real-life Brits, it may not be exactly the same. Basically, I reserve the right to say, "Well, that's how they'd say it in Kentonia!" Ha.

This book is intended to be a romantic comedy and therefore make you laugh and swoon. However, I always try to make my characters as relatable as possible. That means they are dealing with real issues, some of which might be triggering to you.

I want my readers to know what to expect when they pick up one of my books. Here are some topics that are touched on in this book:

- Death of a sibling (past)
- Unwanted media attention
- One very brief allusion to infertility

- Mention of the death of one or both parents (side characters, past)
- One scene in which a man attempts to intimidate and trap a woman (but nothing happens, and rescue is swift)

This book DOES NOT contain sex or swearing, and it DOES end with a happily ever after!

It is Book 1 in the Hallmark Beach Small Town Romance series and follows characters first introduced in my California Dreamin' series. However, you do not have to have read that series to fully and completely enjoy this book.

Happy reading, and welcome to Hallmark Beach!

Kristin

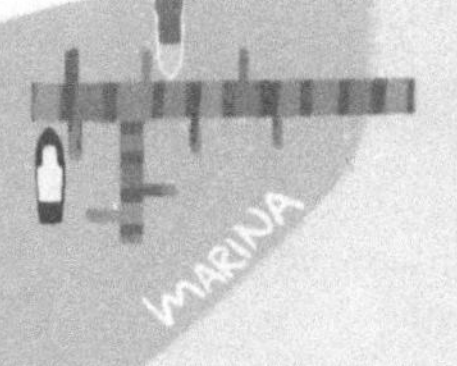

HALLMARK BEACH
hallmark beach
MARINA
THE PURPLE SEASHELL

Olive Paradise
The Bluestocking Bookshop
RAINBOW ICE
The Green Robin
Just Peachy Boutique
The Pink Rose
MAIN ST.

LEGEND
1: The Purple Seashell
2: Olive Paradise
3: The Bluestocking Bookshop
4: Rainbow Ice
5: The Green Robin
6: Just Peachy Boutique
7: The Pink Rose
8: The Black Hole
9: The Blackberry Muffin
10: Al's Grocery
11: The White Mocha
12: Something Blue
13: Red Sauce Pizza
14: The Golden Highlight
THE BLACK HOLE
Blackberry muffin
AL'S GROCERY
The White Mocha
Something Blue
The golden highlight
HIGHWAY 1

I never knew that freedom had a flavor.

But right now, it tastes like passion tea lemonade, chocolate pancakes, and a hint of sea breeze.

It tastes ... blooming brilliant.

"More lemonade?" The waitress—a smashingly gorgeous gal wearing her blonde hair back in a tie, *Lucy* printed on the name tag pinned to her purple T-shirt—holds up a pitcher of the pink liquid.

"Ooo, yes." I set my fork on my plate. "Please."

As the drink pours into my glass, my gaze lingers over the railing of The Green Robin's raised deck, at the boardwalk, sand, and Pacific Ocean waves below. The breeze rustles my long curls and welcomes me back.

When I came to Hallmark Beach, California, just last week —visiting with my brother's fiancée Lauren and her friend Shelby, who is getting married here in July—there were not this many other visitors. Oh, don't mistake me. The entire town is still charming, quaint, the kind of place with zero traffic lights and a million friendly smiles. But this time around, the board-walk is overrun with people.

Mums walking babies in prams. Runners taking advantage of the beautiful late-March weather. Friends gathering on the beach with coolers and netballs (or volleyballs, as my American friends would say). Lovers strolling hand in hand, not a care beyond being present with the one they love.

How I wish I had that luxury—but the man *I* fancy will never be mine. Still, if I can forget about that, about him, my whole being agrees that it's simply lovely in this town. The best part is sitting here, alone, no cameras in my face. Nobody watching, or judging, my every move.

Nobody caring who I am.

"I just have to say"—the waitress's voice breaks into my thoughts, and my gaze pivots back to her—"you look familiar."

Drat. People don't often identify me as the princess of Kentonia, but that doesn't matter to my parents or my lovable but slightly overbearing brother Topher who insist that I travel with a bodyguard for those times—like now—when I am recognized.

Can I help it that just yesterday, my bodyguard Tia had to rush home from where we were staying in San Diego thanks to a family emergency, leaving me completely free to do as I pleased? No, I cannot, though I probably could have stayed put. Instead, I decided to enjoy my freedom while I could, until my father or brother inevitably sends one of their favorite crusty old henchmen to become my shadow.

So, I came here—and I regret nothing.

Of course, I have a reason beyond the simple pleasure of improving my tan or window shopping. Before I can dive into that reason, though, two things must occur:

One: I have to convince Prince Topher that this is the best idea ever and that he should trust his brilliant sister who loves him more than her favorite pair of red Jimmy Choos. (Hint: that's a lot.)

And two: I need to convince Lucy here that I am not in fact the princess of Kentonia (even though I am) and that I don't deserve any more scrutiny than any other of her customers this wonderful Tuesday morning (which I really don't).

"I look familiar?" I smile broadly at Lucy. "Guess I just have one of those faces."

Lucy taps her delicate chin. The woman has excellent bone structure, and despite the fact she isn't wearing a stitch of makeup, her skin is flawless. "No, no, I remember now," Lucy says, a Southern accent floating around the edges of her words. "You were here with a group of girlfriends last week, right? With Shelby Phillips?"

Oh. Blowing out a breath, I nod. "Yes! You're so right."

Lucy's forehead scrunches. "I thought y'all left, but I must have heard wrong."

Maybe small towns are like palaces, where gossip rules the day. Hopefully they weren't talking about it because they know I'm a princess. Topher won't want me to stay here if that's the case—and *poof!* There would go my entire plan.

I pick up my fork and push my mostly eaten pancakes around on the plate. "People were talking about us?" I try to keep the question casual.

"Oh, not like that." Lucy turns and leans against the railing. I'm a wee bit surprised she's still talking to me, but it's the middle of the week and the restaurant is not terribly crowded at the moment. "My uncle Burt knows Shelby and I met her once before. And my aunt Janine owns The Purple Seashell—you know, the local inn?"

Oh, I know it, considering it's the only place to stay in town unless you count a few house rentals and condos. Thankfully, it's tasteful and adorable, and has a prime location at the northern end of Main Street, right on the sand where the boardwalk ends. "That's so fun that you've got family here."

"That's not always the word I'd use for it." Lucy's lips twitch at what's obviously a joke. "So are you alone, then?"

For now. I glance at my mobile on the table. It still hasn't buzzed—surprising, since I texted Topher at midnight last night upon arriving in Hallmark Beach. Asked him to call when he had a moment. Of course, being a prince who is training to become king keeps him very busy. Add on his upcoming wedding to American fitness instructor Lauren Everly and the man's hardly got two minutes to rub together.

This is the only potential wrinkle in my plan—Topher's ability to participate. And it's not exactly a *minor* wrinkle.

I realize I haven't answered Lucy. "My friends went home to San Diego. So did I, but I realized ..." Can I trust this woman? There's something completely open and golden about her, and typically I'm a fairly good judge of character. Learning to read people well is Politics 101 and essential for survival in the royal family. But I'm going to need someone's help if I want to succeed at my mission. Might as well be Lucy of The Green Robin.

Leaning back in my lime-colored chair, I twirl a piece of hair around my fingertip. "I realized that planning Shelby's wedding was not enough. I've decided to plan another wedding here, and on extremely short notice."

Lucy opens her mouth to say something else, but a beefy man who resembles the French chef from the cartoon *Little Mermaid* movie calls to her from the doorway that leads into the restaurant. "Lucy!" With his hairy arms, swooping mustache, and hulking stature—along with a scowl he's wearing like an accessory—he looks comically out of place underneath the bright and happy yellow-and-white-striped awnings, surrounded on either side by pink walls. But his clearly annoyed voice grates against the peace of the patio.

I hope I haven't gotten Lucy into trouble, but she just rolls her eyes with a smile. "Sounds like Tiny needs me."

A very improper and unladylike snort leaves my nose. "Tiny?"

"Right?" Lucy's eyes sparkle. "Okay, so you're planning a wedding. Have you talked with Rhonda over at Something Blue yet?"

"We met with her last week to discuss Shelby's wedding, but I wasn't able to connect with her yesterday." Which is when, in fact, I decided to drive the eight hours north from San Diego to Hallmark Beach. I'm not usually that spontaneous, but when you get a brilliant idea and you're free of a bodyguard for the first time in a good while, you jump at the chance to execute said idea.

Even if it's a bit of an outlandish one.

Lucy eases herself off the railing and holds a finger up to Tiny, who is now pacing in the doorway. The few patrons who are left on the patio eye him warily, but Lucy isn't fazed. "Oh, that's right. She's out of town camping with her boyfriend and doesn't have very good cell service."

With wedding season quickly approaching? That feels all kinds of irresponsible—and unfortunate for me. Looks like I'm going to be dusting off my party-planning skills, then. "Is there any way I can get a list of vendors here in town, especially venues?"

"My friend Elisse might still have a key to Something Blue. She used to work there part-time before her parents hired her on at their winery. I can check for you." Lucy frowns. "But to be honest, there aren't a lot of vendors around here. We've got one bakery, one florist, one inn. We host our share of weddings, but most people just hold them on the beach or at the inn."

Hmm. Topher wouldn't want public exposure like that. He'd want something tucked away, private. But surely there's a place around here that will suffice. I just have to find it. "I'll take any list you might have. When can I meet you to get that?"

Lucy moves toward the doorway that Tiny has finally vacated. "Let me talk with Elisse and I'll get word to you at the inn. But it might not be until tomorrow. I'm working all day here and then have a few things to help get ready for the festival this weekend."

"Festival?"

"The March Madness Wine and Art Festival." Lucy walks backward, her arms outstretched to match the smile on her face. "One of Hallmark Beach's finest. Have you noticed it's a bit busier than last week?"

"I thought it was due to spring break."

"That too." Lucy stops again, which earns her a growling *"Luuuuucy!"* from inside the restaurant. "The festival's Saturday and Sunday, but people who come every year like to spend the whole week. I'm surprised you got a room at the Seashell at all, to be honest."

Janine *did* say something about a cancellation when I arrived at the inn last night, but I was too tired to think much of it.

Another bellow echoes from inside.

Lucy turns. "I thought we talked about not growling in front of the customers, Tiny!" Then she pivots back to me and winks. "I'll let you know right quick about the list, all right?"

"Much obliged."

The woman ducks inside the restaurant again, leaving me to pay my bill and finish off my lemonade.

Yes, Hallmark Beach tastes of freedom, all right.

Freedom ... and hope.

And after I talk with Topher, maybe it'll taste of purpose too.

A quarter-hour later, I exit The Green Robin onto Main Street and breathe in another stitch of my independence. It smells like coconut sunscreen, like the earth after a rain. It's the juxtaposition of the beach on one side of Main Street, a dense grove of trees on the other. From what I ascertained during my visit with Lauren and Shelby, Main Street is an oblong horseshoe. It begins at the highway and travels west until it veers north through the downtown area and then heads east again and up a hill where it becomes Hillside Drive. This is where the majority of people live, in the section of town overlooking downtown and the beach.

I love how this town isn't just one thing. Yes, it's beach but it's also forest. And it's adorable with its happy pastel buildings that have colored-inspired names like The Bluestocking Bookshop, The Pink Rose Florist Shop, and The Golden Highlight Hair Salon. But then, between The Blackberry Muffin and The White Mocha is Al's Grocery—as if some old codger decided to buck the system.

Kind of like a princess who doesn't want to accept the way the media paints her, who seizes the opportunity to run off without a bodyguard, even if it's just for a day. I feel an affinity for this mysterious Al and want to promptly file into the grocery store to hug him.

But that would be strange—and decidedly improper—and though my mother was once a commoner and is the most grace-filled person alive, even *she* might think that was going too far.

I amble down Main Street in my jeans and favorite teal off-the-shoulder blouse and watch the town wake up. A teenage boy steps out from the grocery store and sweeps the steps.

Across the street, a woman sets up a display on the sidewalk outside the bookshop, and I glimpse the latest romantic comedy by Abigail Fox. If Topher doesn't ring me soon, I may buy a copy and read on the beach. There are definitely worse ways to fritter away the day.

But then, at last, the mobile in my back pocket rings. Sliding it out, I glance at the screen. It's a goofy picture of my brother and me. Well, of me. I'm squinting my eyes and making it appear as if my tall brother has ears like a rabbit. As for Topher, who has rarely been goofy a day in his life—until Lauren came into the picture, that is—he's standing there, arms folded, the barest hint of a smile on his chiseled face.

But he's not the one in the photo who holds my attention. I can't help but let my gaze linger on the man in the background. He's tall and strong, and there's no mistaking the laughter in his eyes.

I shiver at the sight of him—even merely the memory—but no, I've got to focus right now. The problem is that I've been waiting for this call, but suddenly, I don't want to answer it. Because I know how it will sound. I know Topher will probably pinch the bridge of his nose and sigh and ask me what in the blooming world I was thinking. He will say *there I go being Chloe again, not thinking things completely through before I race off into the unknown.*

But then I will retort that I only race into the unknown when I *know* that things will work out, and besides, he loves it when Lauren is spontaneous.

And he will tell me that Lauren drives him mad with her spontaneity but that he loves her anyway.

And I will say *You love me too, you big oaf.*

And he will agree.

And then, he will listen to me. Agree with me.

And I will finally prove to him—to everyone—that I'm not

just some joke. That despite spending the last several months lying around Lauren's house doing literally nothing while my bodyguard watched my every move (none of which were interesting in the slightest), I am not worthless.

That I have something of value to contribute to the world.

At least, I really hope that's what happens. It's completely possible he will tell me to get on a plane and fly back to Kentonia "where I belong."

Except, I *don't* belong there. Maybe I did when I was younger, when I allowed my family and the media to dictate who I was. But not anymore. The only problem? I'm not quite sure where I *do* belong. Because where in the world can a princess go to just ... be normal? Asking for a friend.

Oh, buck up, Chloe, and just do the blamed thing. Right. I sink onto a bench in front of The Blackberry Muffin bakery and lift the mobile to my ear. "Hello?"

"Chloe Huntington"—my brother's low voice rumbles from across the pond—"why on God's green earth are you back in Hallmark Beach?"

Darn the head of security who had the brilliant (and by that I mean *terrible*) idea to use a mobile app that's paired with a silver hoop I wear in my upper ear piercing to track my every move. I suppose it's better than injecting me with a tracker, but only just. I sigh. "Don't act like I'm doing something dodgy. I texted you so I could discuss this matter with you like the mature and civilized people we are."

He grunts. I can picture him sitting at the desk in his study, at home in the palace—which is really more like a large ancestral estate—surrounded by his shelves and shelves of books. Probably running a hand through his dark hair and wondering how he came to have a younger sister so completely his opposite. "That would require more than one of us to fit that description."

"Don't be rude, Christopher." Laughing, I sit back against the wooden bench, stretching my legs out in front of me. My polished pink toenails peek out from my white wedge sandals. "Of course I know all of this animosity is stemming from the fact you're worried about me, because you love me immensely. But just know that I'm completely fine."

"So long as Tia is with you, I suppose it's all right."

Wait. "Uh, I hate to inform you of this"—he has no idea how much, since it'll cost me my freedom—"but Tia left yesterday."

I can hear something slam shut. Perhaps his laptop. "What do you mean, *left?*"

"She didn't tell you about her departure?" This is a surprise, given how seriously she took her job the last few months. I mean, the woman wouldn't let me use the facilities without standing outside the door ... and that was inside Lauren's house, where I was perfectly safe.

"No." The word is tense enough to snap a wooden plank.

"It was a family emergency, so it's likely she was overwrought and forgot." I pause. "Don't give her the boot without allowing her a chance to explain."

"Fine," he grumbles. "But that doesn't change the fact that I need to send you a protection detail immediately. When they arrive, they can take you back to San Diego. Unless you'd rather return to Kentonia?" His voice lilts upward.

"Aw, you miss me, big brother?" I try to keep things light-hearted, to not let him see that there is no chance I'm returning to our country until I absolutely must. And that's not until the end of April, for his and Lauren's wedding.

Well, the *official* wedding, anyhow, if I get my way.

I hook my thumbnail under my front teeth. Blow out a breath. "Look, there's something I want to speak to you—"

"Chlo, honestly. Just come back. Lauren said you haven't

spent much time with her while you've been in California, anyhow."

"That's not true." I'll admit, I did spend more time with her roommate Kennedy than Lauren, but that was only because Lauren was always working or on Zoom calls with Felicia Butterflum (or Flutterbum, as I like to not-so-adoringly call her), the world's most obnoxious royal event planner.

In fact, Felicia is the whole reason I'm in Hallmark Beach now. Topher just doesn't know it yet.

I try again. "Can I just tell you—"

"Why don't you want to come home?"

And there it is—the question even *I* can't fully answer. Definitely not to him, and maybe not even to myself. Because it would mean admitting that I'm running away.

From royal life, yes. But also from an unrequited, ill-fated love that I can't seem to talk my heart out of. Sigh. I never fancied myself a runner, but here we are. It's really quite pathetic, isn't it?

I stand, because sitting isn't really my style either. "Christopher Alexander James Huntington, I don't care if you're a prince. Stop interrupting me. I have something I want to say."

Finally, blessed silence reigns on the other side while I turn and stalk across Main Street, veering down the alley between two buildings and out toward the still-bustling boardwalk.

Then, "What?"

"I want to plan a wedding for you and Lauren. One that happens before your official wedding. One that's all about you guys." And because I know he's going to be confused—and I don't want him to say no right away—I keep going, both my feet and mouth blasting forward. "Lauren's miserable, Topher. Flutterbum has taken control of your whole affair, and it's making her feel like she doesn't get a say in anything."

"I didn't think anything Flutter—I mean, Butterflum—was asking was terribly unreasonable."

I snort. "Really? Maybe Lauren hasn't told you everything because you're so busy." I don't mean to be accusatory, but if he wants examples, I'll give him examples. "First, Flutterbum told Lauren she had to wear a dress with long sleeves and lace. Can you really picture Lauren choosing that for herself?"

"I mean, she'll look beautiful in anything."

"That's not the point. A woman should feel gorgeously herself on her wedding day, but she told me she feels like a prissy poodle with all that lace."

"I suppose I can see that."

"But that's not all. Not even close. Flutterbum's also forcing Lauren to use our snooty cousins as bridesmaids, hold a bouquet that's twice the size of her head when Lauren wanted something simple, and serve lobster at the reception despite the fact Lauren hates it and her own mother is allergic."

"I—"

"And that's just the big stuff. There've been countless small 'compromises,' as Felicia calls them, that Lauren's had to make. But the straw that really broke her spirit happened last week when Felicia informed her that the two of you would not be allowed to share your first kiss during the ceremony because it's being held inside a sacred church—something you honestly should have told her about months ago, but I digress."

He groans. "What can I do? This is a royal wedding. There are certain sacrifices that must be made. And Lauren knows that."

"Don't you think she's sacrificed enough? She's already leaving all her friends, her life here in America, to live somewhere new—just to be with you, which, frankly I don't understand in the slightest." I end it all with a tease, because I know my brother's heart is for Lauren, and it's as soft as a biscuit soaked in tea. "I know you love her, and this is breaking her, Toph. Last week, when we were here in Hallmark Beach, Shelby got to decide everything about her own wedding day. And I saw Lauren visibly wilt before my eyes because she doesn't get the same courtesy."

He's silent on the other line. Maybe now I have his attention.

"Listen, it doesn't have to be this way. I know we can't stop the speeding train that is Felicia Flutterbum and the royal wedding, but what if we could still give Lauren a day that's all about the two of you? The way she would have planned it if she had the choice?"

"You think you could honestly do that?"

"Yes." I think. I hope. I will. "You know how good I am at planning parties." Maybe the only thing I'm good at, really. "And all it will take from you is three days cleared from your schedule and the ability to keep a secret from Lauren, because I want this to be a surprise for her. Can you do that?"

"Three days away? Chloe, you know I'm under immense pressure."

"I know. But this is *your* life. You already give so much to our country. I think anyone would understand you taking a holiday." I huff as my speed increases on the boardwalk, and I lap a pair of grandmothers with children toddling along in front of them. "Three days, Toph. A long weekend. That's it."

Rustling fills the receiver—presumably my brother's physical calendar he keeps on his desk like the positively ancient dinosaur he is—and my chest burns as I speed walk, bits of sand on top of concrete crunching beneath my sandals. Finally, "The first weekend of April. I can arrive Friday but must return Monday."

That only gives me little more than a week and a half.

But it'll be enough. It has to be.

So long as Topher sticks to what he's telling me and doesn't allow himself to be drawn in by duty and the crown. "Are you sure? You can honestly get away?"

"It's supposed to be my annual cabin retreat with Father to discuss matters of state. And life. But I think I can beg off, especially if I tell him what it's for."

"He likely won't approve." But I agree. Topher has to invite our parents, even if they say they can't come. Lauren's mum too, though she'd likely rather be at the official one.

"Probably not." Topher sighs. "I don't know about this, sis. There are already paparazzi circling here, trying to get the latest scoop on the wedding details. I'm frankly surprised Lauren hasn't been accosted yet, but I've got a man following her at long range just in case."

Why doesn't that surprise me? "I'll be fine. Nobody here's recognized me as royalty, not even on the last trip when I was here for a week." Of course, the three of us (plus Tia) mostly planned Shelby's wedding and hung out on The Purple Seashell's private beach, but I won't tell him that.

"If I agree to this, you can't tell people who the wedding is for. That would certainly draw extra attention."

Does the man think I was born yesterday? I'm only five years younger than him, but twenty-nine years of being held hostage by the media and their opinions have made me an expert. "Obviously." I slow down my pace, take a moment to step off the boardwalk, into the sand.

He's quiet for a long moment while I stand there, letting the sun soak into my skin, trying to breathe, to slow my heart rate. It's out of my hands now, but I realize that I need him to say yes. Not just for him and Lauren, but for me.

I need a reason to be here, away. I need to figure out what's next for me.

"All right. You win."

Squealing, I jump. A group of college guys eyes me appreciatively, whistling. If I did have a bodyguard nearby, I'd either be hustled away or those guys would regret their actions.

But for one blessed day, I'm still free, so I smile at them and start walking back toward my hotel. "You won't be sorry, Toph."

"Just be careful, Chloe. For goodness's sake, return to your hotel and wait for my man to arrive."

"Love you, brother." I hang up quickly, not wanting to make a promise I know I can't keep.

Because I have a wedding to plan—and not much time to do it.

FREDERICK

When the Prince of Kentonia texts you *Need you ASAP, mate,* you rush to his side immediately.

Unless, of course, you're in the middle of bench pressing more weight than you probably should on your own.

I mutter under my breath and strain against the barbell threatening to crush my chest as the mobile lying on the floor at my feet reads my text message aloud to me a third time. Annoying blighter.

Of course, I'm even more annoyed with myself. I probably shouldn't have added that extra twenty kilos, but sometimes all you can control in life is how much weight you place on your barbells. So you take what you can get.

Now, though, I'm regretting such actions.

Sweat drips down the sides of my temples as I push against the weight. I could probably call for help, but nobody else is in the small staff gym located at the back of the Kentonian palace. And even if there was someone passing by, I'd rather lose a limb than give the guys this particular reason to give me grief.

Imagine: one of the prince's bodyguards, stuck underneath a problem of his own making. I'm paid to be precise, to see the dangers in every situation—and yet here I lie, having severely overestimated my own capabilities.

There's a metaphor in there somewhere, but I don't have time to find it.

Instead, I grunt with the grunt of a thousand gorillas (gorillas DO grunt, right?) and manage to get the barbell up and secured onto the rack with shaky arms. Then I lean down, scoop up my phone, and haul it out of the gym in my T-shirt and athletic shorts, reeking of sweat.

But my prince—and best mate since our shared armed forces days—is in trouble. And I might be off duty as a body-guard, but I'm never off duty as a best mate.

After all, I owe Topher everything. If he needs me, I'm there. No questions asked.

I'm fairly certain at this time in the afternoon on a weekday, he's in his study, but while I careen around corner after corner —passing footmen who wrinkle their noses at my stank and a few maids who put their heads together and giggle as I jog by— I swipe open my mobile app to locate Topher, whose watch always tells us where he is.

Yep, he's in the study.

Feeling one of my customary migraines coming on, I leave the servants' wing, where I've lived off and on again for twelve years since becoming the royal family's youngest bodyguard at the age of twenty-two thanks to my father's intervention. Not that Topher needed much of a nudge to hire me after we'd spent four years in the Kentonian armed forces together and bonded like brothers.

Of course, the prince is not my actual brother—I'm nowhere near good enough to be royal. And my name is stained forever, thanks to the accusations leveled against my father a decade ago. But considering I no longer have a blood brother on this earth, Topher is the closest thing I'll ever have.

The palace hallways widen as I get closer to the executive level where the royal family lives and works. I know nothing about home decorating, but Queen Charlotte has managed to create a place that's both ornate and comfortable. There are pictures of the family everywhere, along with large pieces of artwork. Plants are tucked away in corners, and there's furniture that is actually nice to sit on.

Not that I spend much time here that isn't working. Topher invites me, of course, but I know my place. Even a best mate of the prince doesn't belong in certain wings of the house if he isn't on duty or also royal. My father—once one of King Johnathan's principal advisors—taught me that.

And I *really* don't belong here looking and smelling like I do, but that can't be helped at the moment.

Still, when I turn a corner and nearly run the queen and king down, I wish I'd taken just a few moments to shower off and change.

"Oh!" Queen Charlotte places a hand over her chest, her kind eyes crinkled in surprise—and amusement. "Training for a marathon, are we, Frederick?"

I instantly assume the pose of my station. Back straight, chest erect, hands clasped in front of my body. "No, Your Majesty."

The queen pats her dark hair, which is pulled back at the nape of her neck. She's casual today in a pair of trousers and a long-sleeved collared shirt with buttons. "At ease, soldier." She laughs, and her smile reminds me so much of Chloe, it hurts.

Chloe, who I haven't seen in months. Whose teasing laughter I can always count on to lift my spirits. Chloe, who brings light into every room she enters.

"What's the meaning of this?" King Johnathan is much more like his son as he frowns and narrows his dark eyes, his shoulders broad and unyielding. He's got on a full three-piece suit, which he wears like a badge, and his gray beard is closely trimmed like a bonsai tree.

"I'm sorry, sir. Your son rang and I came as soon as I was able."

The king grunts and turns from me. This is not how it always was between us. Before my father's trial, King Johnathan treated me like another son, welcoming me warmly and showing favoritism to me among all the bodyguards. (Of course, I'd have rather he didn't do the latter, but I do miss seeing his eyes bright with pride when they looked at me. Not ... this.)

But thank goodness for Queen Charlotte, the epitome of grace and forgiveness—even if there is nothing truly to forgive. "It's so good to see you, Frederick. How are your loved ones? Are they in good health?"

By "loved ones," she can only mean my parents, but even she can't bring herself to ask specifically about them. The Shaws are *personae non gratae* around the palace.

Around all of Kentonia, really.

It doesn't matter that Dad was innocent. People believe what they want to believe.

Which is why my parents moved to the mountains nine years ago. But not before my father gave me a speech that will forever be burned into my brain: *"After what he did for us, you owe the prince your life, your allegiance. No matter what they throw at you, you hold your head up and serve the crown well, just as the Shaws have done for over one hundred years. You cannot allow the tradition to be broken with me—with you. Do what I no longer can. Redeem our family name."*

What choice do I have in the face of such a request, especially when I'm the only Shaw left who can? If only Matthew was still alive ...

I clear my throat. "They are well, thank you, Your

Majesty." As well as can be expected, anyway. Thanks to the depression he's dealt with for the last decade, Father can no longer hold down a job, so Mum's had to work. I don't get to visit them as much as I'd like, but they get by.

In full view of her silent husband, Queen Charlotte places her hand on my upper arm, squeezes. "I'm glad to hear it." Her voice rings with conviction, so strong, so regal.

Just like her daughter, she is a force to be reckoned with.

"We won't keep you from Christopher now. Tell him his mother says hello. I hardly see the boy anymore, despite him living a few hallways down."

"I will, Your Majesty."

Once they turn from me—and I've officially been dismissed—I hurry toward Topher's study, where Stevens is standing on duty. He gives me a quick nod, indicating I can go in, so without knocking, I open the French double doors and head inside.

Topher is pacing—never a good sign—but when I enter, he stops. "Frederick." His shoulders sink with what I presume is relief. He places a hand on the wooden mantel above the fireplace that's helping to keep his large study rimmed with bookcases warm. It may be chilly outside these walls, but the palace is a bastion of coziness. "Thanks for coming, mate. I see I've taken you from a workout."

"Happy to bring my lovely gym aroma to your inner sanctum."

With just the two of us here, I can allow myself a tiny sliver of informality. While it's certainly safer for Topher and easier for me to do my job when he's inside the palace, it's rare for us to be alone here, to hang out as friends only, like we used to in the armed forces or when Topher was away at university and I was assigned to protect him there as his roommate and an undercover student.

I miss it. Being more than a bodyguard. Doing more than standing around waiting for life to happen, for someone to give me some directive. Making my own way forward.

Of course, maybe it's better this way. People tend to get hurt when I'm the one choosing the path.

Topher chuckles at my dumb remark, brushing his fingers down the sides of his dark beard. "I'll allow it just this once. The books will have to forgive me for subjecting them to your wretched smell."

I approach him, my trainers hitting the plush red rug covering the wooden floor, before I turn and flop into an over-stuffed chair near the fire. "And what about old Franny here?"

Some men name their cars. Others name their reading chairs. Look it up. It's a thing.

Topher shakes his head. "Only you, man. Only you would dare sit in Franny in your sweaty clothing. I should throw you in the dungeon for this."

"Topher." I tsk. "We all know this place doesn't have a dungeon."

"Not yet."

I stand and hold up my hands in surrender. "Fine. I'll leave Franny alone. But can you please tell me why I've hurried over here?" Then I clap a hand over my bicep and flex. "Muscles like these don't just appear out of thin air, you know."

But Topher doesn't smile back. Instead, he frowns. "It's Chloe."

My entire body stiffens, and I stride forward. "Is she all right?" I try—and am fairly certain *fail*—to keep the panic from my voice. "What's wrong?"

"She's fine, mate. I mean, she's gone mad, but what else is new?"

His words jumble in my brain, and I try to sort them out. "What's she done?" Chloe is beautiful and bold and unafraid, and she charms the absolute trousers off everyone she meets. And yes, she was once reckless, but she's older now. More mature. But of course Topher worries for her. He's her older brother, and it's his prerogative to do so.

"She's come up with a scheme to get Lauren and I secretly married off before the wedding in Kentonia." He explains Chloe's plan—and ridiculously short timeline.

I shake my head and laugh, because it's perfectly her. "So how can I help? Other than travel with you to your first of two weddings?" My lips quirk at the thought.

"Apparently Tia left her yesterday, which is when she decided last minute to drive the eight hours from San Diego to Hallmark Beach alone, so I need you—"

"Wait, what?" Now I'm the one pacing. Tia's a good agent —one of our best—but why would she knowingly put the princess in danger like that?

"I know. I got Tia on the phone after talking with Chloe. She apologized profusely, said her mum was in a car accident and she had to rush home to London."

"But to not even tell us?" I rub my left eye, which is twitching. "I'll have her head for this."

Topher quirks an eyebrow and takes me in. "While I appreciate your concern for Chloe's safety, that's my job, mate. I'll handle Tia."

I halt in my tracks. What am I thinking, showing him how upset I am over this? I force my body to relax one muscle group at a time. "Sure, right. I just can't believe one of ours would be so irresponsible."

"I understand. That's why I need you to go on ahead of the wedding and be my sister's temporary bodyguard."

If I hadn't already stopped, I'd be doing so now. As it is, I can hardly keep myself upright. Me, guard Chloe? Alone? I mean, I know he trusts me above anyone else. But this ... it's impossible. "I'm needed here."

"Chloe needs you more than I do. She's out there, where anyone might hurt her. Meanwhile, I'm stuck here, buried under a pile of paperwork every day. All you'll protect me from here is a paper cut."

"That's giving me way too much credit," I joke, still internally processing his request of me. "With the amount of reading you do, no one on earth can keep you from getting paper cuts."

He chuckles. "How true, how true." A quiet falls between us. Then, he continues. "So, will you go?"

My mouth opens to agree, because what other choice do I have? But if Topher knew how hard this was going to be, he'd never ask it of me. Maybe it would be better for everyone if I came clean of my admiration for the princess. Though simply calling it *admiration* feels like a betrayal of her somehow.

So instead of immediately acquiescing, I ask another question. "Why me?"

Topher doesn't hesitate to reply. "First, I know you loved California when we were there in November, and you hate the cold here. Here's a chance for you to see some sunshine."

I school my features, but his words are a surprise. Did he really notice how happy I was to be in California last year for American Thanksgiving—and the winter before that, when he met Lauren in the first place? It's my job to study him and know everything about him, but I suppose this is a good reminder that he knows me too. That we are friends first, and employer and employee second.

That's what Topher told me when I first became his bodyguard, and I guess he meant it.

After all, he knows how I devour travel books, and he's seen the map I've got plastered to my wall with pins in the places I long to travel. What's funny is that I've traveled more as a body-guard than I did in the armed forces—ironic since one of the main reasons I enlisted was to see the world. Well, that and it fit the plan my father had already laid out for me.

But even the travel I get to do these days is minimal. So having this chance to catch some fresh air, to experience a non-Kentonian spring ... it's everything.

"And second?"

"Second, I know you will do the best job of watching over her." He studies me for a moment, then leans forward and pokes the bicep I flexed earlier. "Can you imagine Jessup or Smith trying to keep up with her?"

I laugh, picturing the gray-haired guards who prefer desk duty trying to follow behind the vivacious princess. "Can't say that I can." I pause. "Is there a thirdly, or are your thoughts completed?" I can't help teasing my old chum, who is known for his logic and lists.

"Why, yes, in fact there is." But instead of laughing along, the furrow between his eyebrows deepens. "I know you love her like a sister too, and that I can trust you to respect her and keep her safe."

I swallow hard. "Right. Of course." Turning from the prince and pretending to inspect a book of Kentonian fairy tales on his shelf, I fight to keep my facial features neutral.

Because yes, I do love Princess Chloe Huntington. But what my best mate doesn't know is that I definitely do NOT love her like a sister. Never have, never will.

Not that it matters.

I lift my chin. "When do I leave?"

"Right away. Who knows what trouble she's already getting into."

It's not as if she's a child, though her family tends to treat her like one. Chloe's nearly thirty, after all, and she's long since outgrown her reputation as the partying princess. In fact, I haven't seen her even so much as buzzed since that night four years ago when I stumbled across her in the palace garden, so inebriated she could hardly stand.

But though I'm honest with my friend about a lot of things, I don't dare speak up on this matter. If I do, Topher's bound to hear the conviction in my voice. Bound to uncover my secret.

And then he'd never let me be her bodyguard, even for a few weeks.

It's probably a terrible idea, really, but I find that I can't say no. Don't want to say no, not when it means a chance to just be near her after so many months apart. And Topher's right. I don't trust anyone else to keep her safe. Tia was one thing, but we don't have many female guards (King Johnathan is a wee bit old-fashioned in that regard), and definitely not one who's available on such short notice.

So, looks like it's on me. I'll just have to put up extra precautions. Don't talk to her overly much. Keep things light. No joking or teasing as we've come to do. If I simply focus on the job at hand—keeping her safe—it'll be fine. Brilliant, even. A lovely vacation from the monotony of these palace walls.

I nod my head. "Right, then. Guess I'll go pack a bag."

Topher places a hand on my shoulder, blowing out a breath. "Thanks, mate." The guy carries the weight of the world—or at least, the country—and his family's safety is everything to him. "I'll rest easier knowing she's with you."

As I head for my room, his words bat around in my head. I know what he meant, but can't help wishing I could take them another way. That she could actually be *with* me. That I had the right to hold her, to keep her, to cherish her up close ... forever.

But being with her like *that* is impossible. I've taken an oath as a Huntington family bodyguard, and it's for life. At least, if I want to honor my family name. To rebuild it from the ground up. Because it's literally against the law, however ancient, for bodyguards in Kentonia to get married.

But that's not the only thing standing in our way. Even if the law was abolished, even if she somehow—miraculously—loved me back, even if Topher didn't depend on me and I didn't owe him my father's life ... being with me would be the worst thing in the world for Chloe.

And I would never do anything to harm her.

What I want doesn't matter so long as she's safe and secure.

three

CHLOE

"This place is completely adorable." I turn inside Something Blue, the wedding shop Rhonda owns just off Main Street.

Different sections of the store, the walls of which are adorned with framed photos of happy brides and grooms, nearly all of them posed with toes in the sand, have displays dedicated to a variety of wedding decor. Tiaras, shoes, garters, invitations, pens, bachelorette party sashes—for such a small storefront, it's got it all. That, combined with the smell of eucalyptus and lavender, makes my heart flutter and squeeze.

This is my happy place, especially when I think about all the planning that goes on within these walls.

"Isn't it?" Standing beside the front picture window, Lucy twirls the ring of keys her friend Elisse gave her last night. The late morning sunlight streams in and pools on the ground at her feet. "Rhonda's been in business for about ten years now. Before that, we really didn't have anyone planning weddings."

"Really?" I run the silk petals of a flower arrangement between my thumb and forefinger. "This town seems the perfect place for weddings. It's got so much character, and it's away from the big cities."

Lucy shrugs. Dressed casually once again in jeans and a three-quarters flannel shirt, she's still got on her name badge from the restaurant after working the morning rush. I know she's got to return soon for lunch service. "We've been trying for years to grow our economy. The festivals help raise awareness but there aren't a lot of places for people to stay. Besides, people are just kind of forgetful, you know?" She says this with conviction, like *she* knows even if I don't.

I can't say what I'm really thinking—that being so small, so anonymous, is a blessing. Maybe not for the businesses, but for the people. "Well, I know one thing for sure," I say. "I will never forget my time here, nor the amazing people I've met." Because where else can you go and get a stranger to let you into a wedding shop when the owner is away? Someone who doesn't know you're royal and is simply doing it out of the kindness of her heart instead of hoping you'll do her a favor in return, that is.

Lucy waves a hand in the air as if swatting a fly. "I may not have a love story of my own, but I enjoy watching others' come true."

Oh. Does she think I'm wanting to plan my own wedding? I suppose it's a valid assumption, and I haven't said anything to dispute the matter. But I should clear that up right away.

Before I can say anything, though, she continues. "Of course, for those of us who have stuck around town after high school, the pickings are slim. The guys are too young, taken, or too grumpy. Grumps are the worst."

"Unless it's a romcom novel."

"I don't know. Give me a cinnamon roll any day."

"Sometimes grumps make the best cinnamon rolls."

"In stories, maybe." She grins.

I know she's laughing, but I feel rather sorry for her and the other women of Hallmark Beach. Then again, it sounds wonderful to not be constantly hounded by men, most of whom only want to marry me for my status. I have my "pick"—and believe me, my father has tried to get me to choose one, going so far as to invite no less than four hundred eligible men from Kentonia and surrounding countries to my twenty-ninth birthday ball. Unfortunately for me, the man I want is the only one my father would never let me have.

And he himself wouldn't want me anyway. He's seen me at my worst, and he loves his job too much to ever leave it.

There are just too many things standing in our way. Which is why it's good that I'm here, and he's somewhere else. Maybe I have some sort of hope of getting over him. It hasn't happened yet, but it has to eventually. Right?

"Aw, you're wonderful, Lucy. You just have to have a little hope," I say, praying the same for myself.

"Eh, it is what it is. Love will come when we least expect it, right? At least, that's what my mom used to say." There's a sad smile on Lucy's face, and it makes me want to grab her hands, tell her it's all going to be okay. She walks farther into the store. "Come on. The vendor list you're wanting would be in the back office."

We pass two sofas and a handful of comfortable-looking chairs with a coffee table in the middle—probably where Rhonda meets with clients to discuss the details of their day— and duck into a small hallway.

Lucy unlocks the first of two doors, swinging it open and walking around the desk to sit in the chair there. Then she sorts through the keys. Apparently Rhonda feels her documents are worthy of Fort Kent levels of security. "Did you have any luck getting started on wedding plans yesterday?" She finally finds the right key and unlocks the desk drawer.

"Not quite." After breakfast, I decided a little uninter-rupted beach time would be all right, so I changed into my swimming costume (not that I went in the water—it's still cold even by my standards!) and hung about on The Purple Seashell's private stretch of beach. It's where Shelby's wedding will be held in a few months, and while it's beautiful, it would never work for Lauren and Topher's day if anyone got wind of them being part of the royal family. The media would have a field day with that, and the wedding would cease to become the private affair I'm hoping for.

I used the time to search the Internet for wedding ideas and pinned several before falling asleep in the lounge chair for a large portion of the afternoon. Must have been more tired than I'd thought from the drive up the day before. "By the time I got around to trying to check out the florist and bakery, they'd closed for the evening." Who ever heard of places closing by three in the afternoon?

Lucy laughs as she sifts through the file folders inside the desk. "Welcome to small-town life."

"Can I help look?" I move to sit in the chair opposite her.

"Sure." She slides a hefty folder out of the drawer and pushes it toward me. "So when is your fiancé joining you? And how soon are you hoping to do this? I know you mentioned it was short notice, but how short are we talking?"

My conscience pricks at her first question, so I ignore it for a moment and move on to the other. "I'm looking at two weekends from now."

Her head bolts up. "Today's Wednesday. So, like ten days?"

I flash her a grin. "Yep."

"What's the rush?" She glances briefly at my stomach, then goes back to examining the paperwork with wide eyes and pursed lips, like she's holding herself back from saying something more.

"Lucy." I can't help but laugh. "I'm not preggers, if that's what you're asking."

"What? Oh. Yeah. No." She stumbles over her words and her fingers slip from one paper to the other despite the fact she's looking at me. "Sorry." Her head falls to the desk, and she groans before looking up again, her features plastered with chagrin. "I didn't know if Brits were, like, still really traditional about having to be married first."

"Well, first of all, I'm not British."

"Really?"

Do I tell her the truth? Oh, why not? She doesn't seem the type that will go look up my country just because I mention it. Not unless she already suspects I'm a royal, which I don't think she does. "I'm from Kentonia, which is in Europe though."

"Sweet." She resumes looking through the stack of papers, her actions calmer, more fluid again.

"And while some in my country are traditional, others are not. I imagine it's the same here in America."

"That makes sense." She lifts an eyebrow. "So, *not* pregnant then? That's what preggers means?"

I laugh, my hair bouncing with the movement of my shoulders. "Correct." Then I place my hands on my stomach. "No baby here."

"I suppose you'd have some explaining to do if there was."

Blinking, I stare at the jumble of papers in my lap and freeze at the words spoken behind me. Did I imagine that deep voice tinged with humor?

But Lucy also must have heard it, because she looks up at the doorway behind me and smiles. "Oh, look who's here." She stands and holds out her hand as she passes me, approaching him. "I'm Lucy Reynolds."

"Frederick Shaw."

It's really him. But why? What is *he* of all people doing here?

Placing the papers back on the desk, I turn in my chair,

gripping the armrest as my head travels up the length of him. While not in a full suit, he's still got on trousers that are slightly rumpled and a black long-sleeved, button-up shirt that he's rolled to his elbows. The sight of the corded muscles of his tanned forearms that are normally covered by a jacket makes me shiver. My gaze works its way up his hard chest, the strong upper arms that no shirt can properly conceal, the shoulders made of lead, perfectly still as he stands stiff, at attention.

And finally, those piercing chocolate eyes that don't miss a thing. Those full lips. That white scar that divides his left eyebrow—marring the otherwise perfect symmetry of his face.

I think it's my favorite of all his features.

I swallow hard. Darn it all. In coming here, I'd hoped to cleanse my body's reaction to him from my system. Clearly, that did not work.

"Hi." It's all I can say, despite wanting to ask him why in the world Topher sent him of all people to protect me. Because clearly, that *is* why he's here.

His jaw flexes. "Hi."

"Well, that's a funny way to greet your fiancé." Lucy leans back against the doorway and watches us.

Fiancé ... wait. What?

Oh no. Lucy's made the worst possible assumption. I should have been clear with her earlier, that it's my brother getting married, not me. But Topher's words ring in my head: *"You can't tell people there who the wedding is for. That would certainly draw extra attention."*

And sure, I wouldn't have to tell her who my brother is. But I've already told her I'm from Kentonia. I've even told her my real name—my first name, anyway. If she got really curious, all it would take is her googling my name plus my country's and she'd be able to figure out who we are. Who Topher is.

The question is, is my instinct right? Can I really trust her?

And do I want to stake everything on that? Maybe, for now, I take the easy route. *Go with the flow*, as they say here in America. I can always tell her the truth later.

That is, if Frederick doesn't give it away first. Because right now, his eyes are narrowed, his brow furrowed. "I'm not—"

"Lucy's right," I practically yell as I twist and jump out of my chair. "That was quite a funny way to greet you. I just hadn't expected to see you today."

"Surprise." His voice is devoid of humor now, completely flat. Unreadable.

Lucy's still watching us, and I can tell by the way she's shifting from foot to foot that she's not quite sure what to make of all this. I don't want her to give it a second thought, to have any reason to be suspicious.

Which is why I hurry around the chair and fling myself against Frederick, wrapping my arms around his sturdy frame, tucking my head under his chin. "Hi, Muscles." The nickname slips out. It's the way I've always thought of him in my head, but have never said out loud.

I bury my head in his chest. Oh blimey, what must he think of me right now?

It takes a moment before those strong muscled arms wrap around me, and I can hear his heart beating beneath my ear. Is he just as affected by my presence as I am by his? Probably not. More likely he's wondering what in the world's gotten into his best mate's little sister, since this is the first time we've ever hugged.

"Um, hi," is all he says. Again.

I pull back and lift up on my toes—he's a good twenty centimeters taller than me—kissing both of his cheeks in our country's customary greeting. Of course, I'm never allowed to greet him like this at home, given our differences in status. So when my feet fully hit the ground again, my lips burning from their brief contact with his stubbled jaw, I'm not surprised to see the shock in his gaze.

I just blink up at him, unsure of what to say or do. What *am* I doing? He probably thinks I'm throwing myself at him. Which, okay, fine, I technically am. But I would never ... not in real life.

"Well"—Lucy's voice breaks through my confusion, causing me to jump and turn back to face her—"I'd better get back to work. The restaurant's owner will be leaving town for several months soon and I'm taking over management, so there's still so much to learn. But I think I found the sheet you wanted." She heads back to the desk and picks up a piece of paper, which she slips into my hands. Yes, it's a list of vendors, but it's painfully short.

My nose scrunches. Only a few venues are even listed.

Lucy's lips turn downward. "I know it's not much to go on. I really do think you'd be best off just going to the places in town and seeing if they have availability. A venue's going to be tougher. I'll put on my thinking cap for you, but there are a few out-of-town places on this list to get your search started."

I lower the paper. "Thank you so much."

"Hey, of course." She flashes me a smile, then directs one at Frederick, who is still standing stiffly against the wall. "If y'all aren't too busy with wedding planning, you should join a group of us tomorrow night for karaoke at The Black Hole just up the road."

"That's sounds fun. We might just do that." I take her hand and squeeze it. "Thank you, Lucy."

"No problem." She picks up the keys, shakes them. "I've gotta lock up, so unfortunately we need to go now."

"Sure. We'll probably see you at the restaurant in a bit. I'm getting hungry for lunch." I turn to Frederick, who is still looking at me with an inscrutable expression. I know I have a lot of explaining to do, but so does he. Why is he here of all bodyguards? I honestly cannot afford this distraction. The *only* good thing about Frederick being here instead of someone else is that he will blend in better as my pretend fiancé.

But only if he can get with the program and start pretending he's in love with me.

So, my heart dancing double time in my chest, I hold out my hand and look pointedly his way. "Ready to go, babe?"

FREDERICK

Babe?

What twilight zone have I suddenly entered wherein the princess of Kentonia is pretending like I'm her fiancé? I did understand that correctly, didn't I? The massive migraine I've been nursing all morning isn't causing my brain to malfunction?

But no, she's standing there, hand extended, one perfect eyebrow arched over those pleading blue eyes.

Waiting.

And while I don't understand *why* she's doing this, I trust her. So I take her hand in mine, twining our fingers together. Mine is large where hers is small. Mine's calloused and rough, hers smooth and soft. This is every fantasy come to life, simply strolling through the store and out the door with her.

And it is the sweetest torture, knowing it's only for a moment in time.

The woman who was helping her, Lucy—who looks harmless enough, but whom I'll still be doing a background check on later—locks up behind us and yells goodbye before looking both ways and crossing the street. I turn to Chloe, whose eyes are following Lucy. Her hand is still tucked in mine, and she's nibbling her bottom lip, an action that drives me absolutely mad with the desire to kiss away whatever's causing her concern.

Normally when I feel this way, I avert my eyes, count to one hundred slowly in my head, bring myself back to equilibrium. Normally, I can't follow her when she inevitably rights herself and moves on to the next thing, the next room—wherever. Right now, though? It's my job to follow her.

There is no escape from my desire. But I can still count to one hundred. Can still hold myself from her. So I drop her hand accordingly. "You need to tell me what's going on."

Her gaze shoots to me and gone is the far-off look in her eye. "It's quite obvious, isn't it? I'm guessing Topher informed you about why I'm here. Lucy thought I was planning my own wedding, and that you were my fiancé. So I went with it for the time being. I actually think it's brilliant." Chloe folds her arms over her chest, and she retreats into herself a bit. It's not often that she lacks confidence, but in this moment I can read her like one of her favorite romantic comedy novels. "Now it's your turn to tell me what's going on. Why did Topher send you?"

"To protect you."

"Well, yes. But why *you*?"

I'd normally tease her and ask whether I should be offended that she didn't want me around. But there can't be any teasing. Not today. Not until Topher and the rest of the security detail arrive in nine days. "He thought it would be best."

I could go into more detail, sure, but this isn't the place for a discussion. We are standing on the edge of the sidewalk, and there are people milling about everywhere. I don't like this. She's too exposed. I haven't had a chance to assess the dangers of this community, and the wrong person could overhear us.

"Let's go." Taking a step toward the crosswalk, I then turn to make sure she's following me. She's not. "Come on, Princess."

"Muscles, you can't call me that here."

I flinch at the tease in her voice, the use of that nickname for me, and rub the bridge of my nose. I need to stay focused on the task at hand, which is getting her to a less busy location and figuring out what kind of situation she's gotten us into. "I said, we need to go." I pause. "Please."

She looks me up and down, sighs. "All right, all right." Thankfully, she follows, and I do my best to veer around the midday bustle of tourists and locals alike traversing Main Street. Some are stopping at the windows, looking inside, and exclaiming over whatever wares are inside. Others are charging forward, sure of their destination. But all of them are in our way as I get us from Point A to Point B—the beach.

I don't even take the time to remove my socks and loafers, just plow through the sand until we're standing close enough to the water for the sound of it to drown out what we are saying. Despite the nice weather, the beach isn't as crowded as the street (likely because it's a Wednesday), so the nearest grouping of people is a good fifteen meters or so down the beach.

Chloe stops beside me and whirls, hands on her hips. "Why are you acting so strange?" She's breathing a bit heavily and I suddenly feel guilty for making her rush.

"I'm not acting strange." I definitely am. But I have a good reason for holding off on our usual camaraderie, because these are anything but usual circumstances. Other than that night in the garden four years ago, I can't remember a time when the two of us were truly alone like this, no other family, or friends around.

Not only does that mean I need to be extra cautious—on alert for anyone who might wish to harm the princess—but it also means that there are no buffers between us. Our jokes and our teasing are normally very brotherly and sisterly. They've had to be, with so many eyes on us.

But now? Not only does she want me to ignore the fact that it's just the two of us here, but also pretend she's going to be my wife. At least, I assume that's what she was implying with her brief explanation of what happened back in that bridal shop.

The idea is honestly like a stab to my chest. Of course, *she* doesn't realize that. It's not like she thinks of me the way I think of her. She's royalty, for goodness' sake. So far above my station in every way that she'd never even consider me—even if her father *would* give consent. Which he won't, thanks to my father's reputation.

"You most definitely are." Her back to the sea, Chloe cocks her head. "Look, I know this seems ... unusual. And I wouldn't want to make you uncomfortable. But, Topher said we have to keep a low profile here. That's why pretending like this is *our* wedding we're planning is perfect. Then there's no risk of exposing the real bride and groom to the paparazzi or any other curious intruders." Her blonde hair reflects the sun's rays and flows down her back as she lifts her chin, and gone is all the self-doubt. She doesn't even realize how regal she just naturally is, even in jeans and a blue sleeveless top that matches her eyes. How beautiful.

And she definitely doesn't realize how much I want to step forward, lean in, and kiss the perfect ridges of her smooth, tanned shoulders—

Easy, mate.

But it's no use. My mind is rebelling, spinning out of control, wanting to accept Chloe's idea of a fake engagement for selfish reasons, so that I finally, at long last, have an excuse to touch her whenever I want, to hold her the way I've always craved.

And see? This is exactly why it's a rubbish idea.

But once Chloe Huntington gets a notion in her head, it's nearly impossible to get it out. After all, this is the same woman who, at age seventeen and despite the protest of all of her father's advisors—my father included—invited one of the country's poorest tenements to the annual Christmas ball, supplying the women with gowns from her very closet.

Very pig-headed, this one. Charitable too. And completely lovely in every way.

Still, I have to *convince* her that it's rubbish ... but how? I can't very well explain that I have a difficult enough time burying my love just being near her. That holding her hand, pretending to be engaged to her, would send me over a flippin' cliff.

Blowing out a breath, I run a hand through my hair, though there's not much on top thanks to the close-cropped cut I've kept since my armed forces days. "Chloe ..."

She bites that full, beautiful lower lip yet again. "Frederick, I want this day to be perfect for my brother and future sister-in-law. I've seen this wedding planning taking a toll on them both. Flutterbum doesn't listen to a thing Lauren really wants, but *I* know what she would like because I know her. And that means I could help give them the best day of their lives. Why wouldn't you help me do that?"

I've been around countless dignitaries and politicians, and Chloe is even better at getting what she wants than they are. Some might find it manipulative, but I know she's not seeking this for her own benefit. She's just speaking from the heart, and her passion and love for others shines through. She's fully Chloe, fully authentic, and I love every fiber of her for it.

Frankly, she inspires me to be better.

Still. "I don't know." I huff and frown at the ocean, which darts toward the sand then recedes like a dance. "I'm here to protect you. That's my main priority. How am I supposed to do that if I'm playing the part of adoring fiancé instead?"

She gives a little hop and a grin. "That's the best part of this plan. Even though I still maintain that I don't need a body-guard, don't you think you can protect me even better if you have a reason to be near me every waking moment? Nobody will suspect you're an agent, so if I'm actually ever in danger—and let's face it, I never am—they won't see you coming."

The woman should have been a barrister. I stroke my chin, find several spots I missed shaving this morning—well, yesterday morning, really. After hopping a red-eye when Topher gave me my new assignment, I arrived in Los Angeles at three a.m. and slept in the airport until the car rental desk opened at six. Then, after slamming three cups of coffee, I drove the four hours north along Highway 1 to Hallmark Beach.

I've never taken a more beautiful drive—all cliffsides and crashing waves below—but I couldn't fully enjoy it because I only had one thought. To get to Chloe, who had been without a protective detail for nearly two days.

Should have known she wouldn't even want a bodyguard in the first place, though. Perhaps that's part of the reason she's come up with this scheme—to feel somewhat normal. It can't be easy having someone follow you everywhere you go. And she's right. The royal Kentonian family isn't all that well known here in America. It's a small country, after all.

Still, risks do exist, and I'm not willing to expose her to them, even if it wasn't my job.

I sigh.

She steps closer, placing a hand on my forearm and looking up at me with those blue eyes that match the waves just beyond. "Please, Freddy?" Her whisper fills the space between us, and for a moment, I forget what she's even asking me.

Please? Yes, of course, I'd do anything for you.

And honestly? I would. Even rip my own heart from my chest and feed it to the wood chipper—which is essentially what I'm doing in agreeing to this plan. "All right."

She squeals and throws herself at me again, this time without abandon. My body envelops her petite frame and I'm a man lost, but before I can garner too much pleasure from holding her, she pulls away and casts her eyes to the sand. "Sorry. I got a bit carried away there. I'm just really grateful."

Doesn't she know she need not apologize? But yes, it would be better for us both if she kept our physical touch to a minimum.

How likely is that *when you'll be going around town pretending to be engaged?* my brain taunts. *You're going to have to, at a minimum, hold her hand.*

I silence my doubts and force a smile. "No problem, Princess."

"I told you not to call me that here." Her finger prods my stomach, but then she stops. "Although I guess it could be like a cute little pet name, right?"

It's how I've always meant it, but of course I can't tell her that. "Sure."

A grin blooms on her face, and her cheeks redden ever so slightly. "Okay, then."

"Okay, then," I echo. Then I think of something. "Shouldn't you have like, I don't know. A ring or something?"

"Ooo, good point." She holds up her hand and flips it so I can see the ring she wears on her right ring finger. It's simple—white gold with a large circular diamond and nothing else. "Will this work? It was my grandmother's."

"Seems like it would."

"Great." She slips it off her right hand and hands it to me. "Want to do the honors?"

No, absolutely not. "That's all right. You can."

Shrugging, she pushes the ring onto her left ring finger. "Voila! We're official."

"Great." I draw out the word. My stomach chooses that moment to rumble. Good. I need a distraction from staring at her hand, with that ring ... and what it supposedly symbolizes. "Don't suppose you've had lunch yet?"

"I haven't. Let's go to The Green Robin where Lucy works. There's a bacon cheeseburger on the menu that I've been eyeing."

Have I mentioned how attractive I think it is when a woman has a healthy appetite? "Sounds fabulous."

"And then after that, maybe we can visit some of the wedding places to get the planning started. Hopefully find a venue. That kind of thing." The distracted look is back on her face. She's even twirling a piece of her hair around her forefinger. Chloe's in planning mode, and it's a brilliant sight to behold. "Yes, lots to do." Now she's talking to herself, a trait I find completely adorable.

"Let's get to it, then." After all, her schedule is my schedule and I follow where she leads.

For better ... or for worse.

CHLOE

It's only been mere minutes, and I'm already questioning what I've gotten myself into.

As we walk the busy boardwalk toward The Green Robin, I peek at Frederick. He's scanning the landscape, this way and that—probably assessing for threats, just like his training dictates. The initial confusion over what's happening has apparently worn off, and he's back in full bodyguard mode.

My heart aches just watching him.

I was so focused on Topher and Lauren's day, on having the perfect "disguise" by pretending to be the bride, but I forgot to factor in one little thing when I went along with Lucy's misunderstanding and concocted this harebrained idea.

How hard it would be to pretend to be engaged to the man I love—when he has no idea I love him.

Yeah, if you haven't guessed yet, I'm completely mad for the guy. Have been since the moment he found me oh-so-gracefully hurling into a rose bush in my slinky dress and heels after yet another party and, instead of scolding me as my brother might have, simply helped me to my room.

Sure, I'd thought him handsome all my life, back when he

was just Mr. Shaw's son who I'd see at the annual Christmas ball, or even Topher's royal army buddy when they were back during leave. But being five years older, Frederick never looked at me as more than a little girl playing dress-up.

So I kept my crush a crush, directing my attention toward guys my own age who didn't deserve said attention, but who were more than willing to see me as a woman. Guys like Troy.

But that night in the garden, Frederick didn't just see Kentonia's "partying princess." He saw *me*, and what he said changed my life. Changed how I felt about him too. Infatuation turned to love.

And he doesn't even know it.

Can't ever know it, either. Because it was the spark in the powder keg that led to my greatest mistake—falling for a man I can never have.

Thankfully, the next week and a half are all about pretending. I grit my teeth. Yes, we can do this. We have to do this. For Topher and Lauren.

We've arrived at the restaurant and Frederick opens the door, peeks around inside. "All clear."

Oh, boy. This might be more difficult than I imagined. Because what I need right now is a fiancé, not a bodyguard. "Thanks, Muscles," I tease with eyebrows raised. Maybe he needs a reminder of what we're doing here.

His tight jaw flexes and he's silent as I sigh and turn to the hostess, a young twenty-something who's sitting on a stool behind the greeting podium and staring at her phone. It takes Frederick clearing his throat for her to look up, and when she sees him, she does a double take.

I understand, birdie. I do.

"H-hi," she stammers, standing abruptly and dropping her phone to the ground.

Frederick swoops down and collects it for her.

"Oh my goodness, thank you so much." And now she's looking at him like he's her knight in shining armor. She fluffs her red hair, and her small nose piercing glints from the sun streaming in through one of the restaurant's skylights. "How can I help you? Table for ..." She glances at me, her eyes dimming slightly. "Two? Or are more joining you?"

"Just the two, thanks."

I think the girl is going to become a puddle right there on the floor, and who can honestly blame her? Between his good looks and that rumbly voice, it takes a long time being around Frederick Shaw to build up even the tiniest bit of resistance to his charm. Ask me how I know.

"O-okay," she says as she fumbles the plastic menus she's taken up from the podium. "Do you prefer indoor or outdoor seating?" She's still only addressing him. I'm a non-entity. Which is kind of amusing, and refreshing, considering how things normally are.

Frederick glances at me, a question in his gaze. I know he's probably thinking it will be safer inside, that he can more easily watch over me tucked away in one of the corner booths. And while the inside of the open-concept restaurant is charming, it's got nothing on the deck and the natural beauty of the outdoors.

"Outside, please," I say.

He frowns slightly, but nods.

The girl finally looks at me again, then lowers her gaze to the ground. "Follow me," she mumbles as she walks through the mostly empty dining room to the back door leading out to the patio.

We emerge again into the salt-tinged air, and I've got the strongest sense of déjà vu, having just been here this morning. But this time I'm not alone.

And there's Lucy, once again standing and chatting with the only other customers, a couple around our age. A young boy of around four or five with red hair and the cutest freckles ever runs around the rest of the deck with a foam sword, swinging it (unsuccessfully) at a few seagulls perched on the railing.

The hostess leads us to the table next to the couple. "Does this work?"

Lucy glances up with a smile and a wave. "Hey, guys! So good to see you again. Here, Lynette, I've got this."

"Okay." Our hostess hands us our menus and scurries away.

"I want to introduce y'all to some friends of mine," Lucy says, indicating the couple in front of her. "This is Jordan and Marilee."

Jordan, a well-built bloke with white-blond hair and a golden tan, gives us a friendly wave, as does Marilee, who's wearing her brown hair up in a messy bun piled on top of her head, stylish black glasses perched on the bridge of her nose, her cheeks dusted with some sort of white powder. "It's so nice to meet you," she says. "Lucy was just telling us all about you."

Hmm, maybe I was right to not trust Lucy. But within seconds, that notion disappears, because I can tell by the friendly smile Marilee flashes me that whatever Lucy said about us was completely innocent and non-malicious. Hmm. I'm not used to that, but it endears me instantly to them all.

"Lovely to meet you both as well," I reply.

Marilee gestures to the empty spots across the table from them. "Would you like to join us for lunch?"

"Yeah, please sit," Jordan says.

Beside me, Frederick frowns, opens his mouth—probably to say no. What's his deal? Is he just grouchy because I sprang all of this on him? He doesn't like when his job becomes more unpredictable than usual. Probably doesn't get paid enough for these kinds of shenanigans either. But I know he cares about Topher and Lauren, and if we have any hope of making this wedding a success, we are going to need the locals' help.

Plus, I love people, and this particular couple seems lovely.

"We'd love to, right, hon?" I say, batting my eyes up at Frederick.

He grunts but follows my lead. "Sure." Then he pulls out a chair for me, and after I slide in, he plops down beside me.

Lucy says she'll give us a few minutes and heads back to check on something in the kitchen.

I set my menu down, already knowing that the cheeseburger pictured on the front has my name on it. "I'm afraid to ask what Lucy said about us."

Frederick is silent, pretending to peruse the menu, though I can tell he's actually sizing up Jordan and Marilee. Jordan, meanwhile, has his eyes on the boy, who is yelling "Arrr, matey" from somewhere behind me.

Marilee laughs. "Nothing bad, I promise. She just mentioned that there was a foreign couple in town planning a last-minute wedding."

"She also asked if you had time to bake the cake." Jordan eases back in his seat as his eyes find Marilee. His gaze is soft around the edges even as his voice presents a gentle challenge.

"Oh, I don't know." Marilee takes a quick sip of her dark soda, her cheeks pinking. "That's Marla's specialty."

"And she's left you in charge of the bakery for the next few weeks." He pokes Marilee's upper arm. "You're totally capable, Mar." Jordan turns to us. "The cake she made for Ryder's birthday was out of this world awesome." Grabbing his phone off the table, he flips his thumb across the screen and then turns it to us, revealing a photo of a cake in the shape of a wooden pirate ship. There are three masts with sails, a ship's wheel, and kraken legs coming up out of the blue water and wrapping around the body and foremast of the ship.

"It's incredible. The detailing—wow," I say. So many people out there have amazing talents, ways they contribute to and make the world a better place. And while I wish I had something equally beautiful to give, I am choosing in this moment to be grateful just to witness others' beauty. "It looks like it belongs on one of those 'is it cake' television shows. Completely brilliant."

Jordan sets his mobile down and nudges Marilee. "See?"

My heart dances at this revelation. "I was hoping to stop by the bakery today—The Blackberry Muffin, right? So you work there?" Maybe the dust on her cheeks is flour. That's adorable.

Marilee nods shyly. "I'm the assistant baker. Marla, the owner, is simply wonderful to work for and has taught me what she knows. I'm not as good as her, but I do my best."

"And your best is amazing." There goes Jordan again, gushing over his woman's accomplishments. It's clear the chap is mad about Marilee.

And then there's Frederick next to me, who has abandoned his menu and is sitting with his arms crossed over his chest. His brow is furrowed. It's the look he's normally got when on duty —the look I've dreamed of wiping off his face when he's standing against a palace wall. How many times I've thought of approaching him and seeing if I can get him to break character, but like the guards at Buckingham Palace, he's too much of a professional. Especially if my father is anywhere in the vicinity.

I know Frederick feels like he needs to prove himself extra to my father after his own was first accused and then acquitted of treason. I don't know everything that happened back then, but I do know it changed Frederick. He can still be the most charming, silly guy at times, but there's an extra weight he's carrying.

I want him to know that while I respect what he does—

devoting himself to defending the crown—he's not invisible. He's not *just* a bodyguard. Not to me.

I want to see him smile, laugh. Let loose.

But maybe that's expecting too much from him right now, when he's being subjected to his best mate's little sister's schemes. He's made it clear that, if he had a choice, I'd simply let him do his job, let him fade into the background until Topher and everyone else arrive.

And yet. If I allow that, then these people are going to see right through our farce and wonder whose wedding we are in fact planning.

I can't let that happen, so I do something about it. Reaching down, I take Frederick's hand and loop it around my shoulders, then pinch his knee. His fingers press my shoulder, not a friendly *hey there* squeeze but a *what are you doing* squeeze. I pinch his knee again and hear him hiss through his teeth.

Before Marilee and Jordan can say anything about our strange behavior, I continue the conversation right where Jordan left off, addressing Marilee. "I'd love to hire you to do the wedding cake if you've got time. We don't need anything as complicated as a pirate ship," I assure her. "Could we schedule a cake testing sometime soon?"

"Um." Shifting in her seat, Marilee tucks a free strand of hair back into her bun. "Sure, yeah. How about Friday? Say, around two?"

"Sounds great. Right, Muscles?"

Frederick grunts. "Yeah, thanks." He lifts a hand and rubs at his temple. Oh no. Poor guy. Does he have a headache? That could explain his strange behavior. His migraines have plagued him for years and the silly man won't even take medication for them. Says he doesn't want anything to dull his senses even a smidgen. And I believe him. I don't think it's about appearing weak. He truly doesn't want to let Topher down. Being a bodyguard is, to my knowledge, the only thing he's ever wanted to do.

If only there weren't that ridiculous Kentonian law preventing bodyguards from marrying. Not that that would keep my father from his disapproval. Or keep Frederick himself from viewing me as anything but the little sister he never had—and that's a direct quote, thank you very much.

An internal groan passes through me again. I can only pray he sees the necessity of what we are doing here, that he wants to protect my brother and sister-in-law's privacy as much as I do. Because the thought that he might believe I'm using these circumstances to hit on him is ... well, frankly, mortifying.

Lucy returns with waters for me and Frederick and takes our order before flitting back to the kitchen. A few more customers have been seated around the deck—I guess we aren't the only tourists with an appetite at this time of day—and one of them exclaims when Ryder trips.

Jordan immediately jumps out of his seat and goes to the boy, who stands right back up and starts running again. But now that there are others here, Jordan hauls him up and over his shoulder. "Hey, Mar, I'm going to take him down to the sand to run around for a few. Text me when the food's here?"

"Absolutely," she says with a wave, watching them go with the hint of a smile on her lips.

They are the absolute cutest, and my stomach twists with happiness for them—finding each other in this vast world—and sadness for myself.

Knowing I can never have what they have.

Because I'm destined to marry some prince or dignitary. Sure, my father has given me my time here in America, but when I do return home for Topher's (official) wedding in Kentonia next month, the king's sure to resume his attempts at matchmaking.

Eventually, I'll have to do my duty and give in.

I mean, to be honest, I'm not even sure I want children. Not if they're going to be subjected to the media like I was. It would be so hard to protect them from that. And I've seen how devastating it can be on a person's psyche. Maybe I'd be more open to the idea if I could establish some sort of normal life. But that's about as likely as my bodyguard here falling in love with me.

So yeah. Not worth focusing on.

Frederick leans close to me, interrupting my thoughts. "I didn't get a chance earlier to do a perimeter check," he whispers low enough so only I can hear. "Normally I wouldn't leave you, but since the deck is raised, I should be able to see you from the ground. That all right?"

I can hardly focus with his warm breath tickling my neck, but I manage a "Yeah, of course."

He glances at Marilee. "Sorry, I'm not feeling great at the moment." It's not a lie—I see the strain behind his eyes—even if it is a convenient excuse. "I'll be right back."

"Oh, I'm sorry to hear that." She cocks her head in sympathy. "Of course, take your time."

Frederick taps my mobile on the table—a signal to keep it close in case he needs to call me and give me any directive—and I nod back. Yes, I know the drill. He gives my shoulder one more squeeze, this time a bit friendlier, before sliding his arm off and whisking himself away.

I feel the loss of him immensely and sigh. All of these months away from him, I'd almost convinced myself to let him go. It was easier being an ocean apart, not facing the daily reminder of his strength, his entirely too manly scent, his loyalty, and goodness.

This week and a half just might be the end of me.

But I will soldier on, because this isn't *about* me. It's about giving my sister-in-law—someone who hates being in the public spotlight, but is willing to do it for the sake of love—the chance at having a normal wedding.

And about making someone else happy.

Even if the path to that is part misery for myself, taunting me with a glimpse of what *could be* ... if things were different.

I'm already dragging from this never-ending day, and it's only half past five. I can't believe it was only this morning that I arrived in California. It feels like I've lived a lifetime already.

If I'd have told early-this-morning Frederick that he'd be fake engaged to the princess of Kentonia, or that he'd have spent the afternoon first at the florist then at the hair salon to book wedding-day appointments for the wedding party, he'd have told me I was barmy.

And he certainly would have laughed in disbelief at the image of me and Chloe in the small lobby of a bed and breakfast one town over from Hallmark Beach, about to receive a venue tour for our "wedding." Would have told me there was no way I could survive the experience of holding Chloe's hand —of being zapped with those electric touches over and over again—without weakening in my resolve to keep her at arms' length.

And he'd be right.

But this is a mental game and I'm mentally tough. I simply need to keep playing the part of stoic grump. I'm hoping others will just believe it to be my personality and not try to read into what it says about me and Chloe as a couple.

"Mr. Shaw? Ms. Marie?" A tiny woman approaches with stiff shoulders, her black hair slicked back and tucked so precisely into a bun it nearly looks like one solid, removable piece. Like a helmet she takes off at night. She taps her short, buffed, and unpainted nails along the back of the clipboard she's holding. "Welcome to the Moon Bay Inn," she says in a rather monotone voice. "I'm Betsy, and I'll be giving your tour today."

It feels like she's shouting, but I know from experience that's just the migraine talking. I must not have had enough water on the flight over, and my body is paying for it now. But I do my best to keep a neutral expression so no one knows that it feels as if tiny gremlins have taken hammers to the sides of my skull and the back of my neck.

At least we only have this one appointment standing between us and some sleep. After lunch—while I called and spoke with my parents, letting them know I'd be out of the country for a few weeks in case they needed me—Chloe contacted the other two venues on the list Lucy gave her. Unfortunately, they were booked for next weekend. But the Moon Bay Inn actually had availability, so she snagged us this appointment.

"Oh, it's wonderful to meet you, Betsy." Chloe—aka Ms. Marie, since we decided it was smarter to use her middle name instead of her real last name—reaches out with her free hand to shake Betsy's. She flashes a warm smile her way. "I can't tell you how excited we are to be here, and that you had an opening on our preferred wedding date."

"Yes, that's extremely lucky. We book out years in advance." Head cocked as she studies Chloe, Betsy removes a pen from the top of the clipboard. Clicks it as if to remind us that she's in charge here. Then the woman turns on her heel and begins walking through the lobby, which boasts some tasteful nautical decor and is painted blue. Chloe could probably tell me the exact shade, but that's not really my forte.

My forte is keeping her safe, and so far, thankfully, nobody we've encountered today has seemed to know who Chloe is. But I need to always be alert, always be prepared, especially considering the large influx of newcomers Hallmark Beach is scheduled to get tomorrow and Friday ahead of the wine festival this weekend.

Betsy tells us a bit about the history of the inn as she leads us out to a walled-in garden space. Chloe asks intelligent questions and Betsy answers them, her body language growing more and more open the longer they speak. That's no surprise to me, though.

Because Chloe is clearly in her element. Everywhere she goes, Chloe makes people feel special, giving them her full attention. She commands respect but not in a way that makes people feel degraded or less than. It's a gift few royals possess. Even Topher intimidates people without meaning to. But just like Queen Charlotte, Chloe becomes best friends with everyone.

It's both a gift and a curse, because it makes it more difficult to keep her safe. Much more difficult than hermit-like Topher, whose favorite place is the library.

Still, I wouldn't want Chloe to live any other way.

As Betsy drones on about what the inn offers for weddings —something about tables and place settings and flowered wedding arches—I move into the garden and walk the perimeter so that I can examine the venue. Even I have to admit the space is beautiful, its stoned walls lined with bushes that are teeming with flower buds and open flowers alike in a variety of species that I can't name. Under the vibrant blue spring sky, with just a nip of a breeze in the air from the ocean a short jaunt away, this would indeed make a right proper spot for a wedding. A beautiful one too.

But beauty isn't enough. I need to examine the venue also from a protection detail standpoint.

From what Betsy has said, with such a small wedding invite list, we could hold both the ceremony and reception here. Because the inn is three stories high and right on the beach, we could station agents at each entry and exit point, as well as along each of the public balconies that overlook the garden.

The only thing that makes me nervous is not being able to book out the entire place. But at this late stage in the game, that's impossible. We'll just have to prepare as best we can and keep the other guests away from the wedding during the ceremony and reception.

"What are you thinking?"

I glance up to find Chloe there, no Betsy in sight. "Are we alone?"

"Yes, I told Betsy we needed to look around a little more and chat, but Freddy, I think we found the place." She clasps my hands in hers, and shakes them like she's trying to hold back a squeal. The joy in her voice—and on her face—is a shot to my heart.

I want to tease her about her optimism, about wishing things into being, but instead I keep my face devoid of emotions and nod. "I believe it should work for the security team as well." Then, because no one is watching after all, I gently extricate my hands from hers and fold them behind my back before I begin walking again, this time toward a large stone fountain that's gurgling. The sound of water hitting water is rather soothing, though it does nothing to relieve the pounding in my head.

Nothing but sleep does that.

But I can't—won't—tell Chloe that, because then she'll insist on going back to the hotel when she needs to be doing stuff for the wedding.

"Hey." Her soft voice is beside me again and I look over. Clouds have rolled in where there was once sunshine in her eyes. Did I do that to her by walking away? The last thing I ever want to do is hurt her, though I'm not sure how my actions would have done that. Maybe she's just worried that I'm going to give away that we aren't really engaged.

"Hey." I sigh and sink onto a stone bench beside the fountain, feet spread wide and head hanging down. "Look, Chloe, I'm sorry I'm rubbish at pretending. I'll ..." But do I really want to promise I'll do better? Rubbing the side of my head, I press on. "I'll *try* to do better."

She lowers herself beside me. "I'm sorry it's so hard for you." Her whisper floats between us, nearly smacking me. I want to scream the truth—that it's not hard to pretend to love her. It's hard to pretend *not* to love her *while* I pretend to love her.

Blimey. That makes my head hurt even worse. I knead my temple more furiously.

"But I do appreciate you trying."

All I can do is grunt in reply. I'm not sure rubbing my head is actually helping. In fact, it feels like I'm doing more damage. But massages are like that, aren't they? You have to get a wee bit hurt in order to experience the healing on the other side.

If only this fake engagement was like that too, but I have a feeling that it will only end in disaster.

I breathe out through my nose, fighting the pain piercing my skull. "So, what's next? Just sign some paperwork and pay the deposit, I wager?"

"I think so."

"Let's do it then." I stand quickly, but black dots flash

around the corners of my vision and I thud back onto the hard stone bench. My head sinks into my hands and I try to breathe steadily through the pain and waves of dizziness.

"Whoa there, Muscles." Chloe touches my back, my shoulder. "Come here."

Come ... where?

I glance up, the light of the sun making my stomach roil. She's scooted to the end of the bench. And she's patting her lap.

"No." I shake my head and wave her off. "I'll be fine."

She snorts. "Stop being so stubborn and lie down. I'll be your pillow."

My *pillow?* "You're a princess. I'm not using you as a pillow."

"How can you keep me safe if you can't even stand up? Come rest for a few moments and then you can go back to saving the world."

I groan. "Stop using logic to sway me."

"It's working then?" Her voice holds a smile.

"Chloe, it's just not appropriate." Then again, neither is this entire situation.

"Look, I understand that you see these definitive lines between us as royalty and bodyguard. But in this moment, just until your head is better, can we simply be Chloe and Freddy, two friends who are helping each other out?"

I feel myself giving in. But I have to throw one more jab, one more attempt to be strong. Sure, my eyes are still shut and I'm cradling my head like a baby, but if my father saw me right now, he'd tell me to man up and do what I came here to do— protect the princess. Reclaim the family name.

He'd tell me not to jeopardize twelve years of loyal service to the crown by being improper with the princess.

"How is me lying my head on your lap helping *you?*"

"For starters, it would be far more convincing if you laid

your head on my lap than if we continue to sit a whole meter away from each other looking like we're having a row," Chloe says. "Especially because at this very moment, Betsy is watching us from the balcony."

"That's not dodgy or anything." This joking response pops out, and Chloe's giggle confirms her delight that some of the teasing between us is back.

I sigh. I'm weaker than I thought. Maybe if I can just get rid of this flippin' headache, I can get things back on track. "Fine. You win." And then I shift and stretch out my legs on the stone bench, placing my head in Chloe's soft lap. My feet dangle over the side—it's bound to happen when you're as tall as me—but instantly, I am more comfortable.

Until Chloe begins to run her fingers along my forehead, my temple, down the line of my nose, over my closed eyelids. I nearly leap up from my spot, but Chloe places a hand on my chest. "Stay put, Muscles, and that's an order." It's probably my imagination, but her hand seems to linger right over my heart, and then it's gone, all ten of her fingers going to work again on my head.

"Yes, Your Royal Highness."

"That's a good chap."

It's relief like nothing I've ever felt. Her touch—first gentle, then firm—soothes away the tension, chases the pain. It's better than any medicine, any pack of ice, any rest.

I'm not sure how long I lie there. In fact, I'm fairly certain I fall asleep under her ministrations, because when I finally open my eyes, they're a bit gritty like they are after a nap. I blink up at the darkening sky, only to find her beautiful face hovering over mine. "Hey," she says again. Seems to be our thing lately. "You feeling any better?"

"I think you cured me, Princess."

She smiles softly, but her eyes alert me to something amiss.

I sit up, groaning at the effort. My muscles are stiff, my rear end tender from the hard bench. "What's wrong?"

"I was worried about you." She takes her hair and threads it through her fingers, chewing her lip again.

"There's more."

"Ugh, yes." Now it's Chloe's turn to stand. Arms crossed over her chest, she stares into the fountain for a few moments before twirling back to face me. "Betsy came by while you were napping since she was about to head home. I told her we would love to book the venue and she said she'd draw up the paperwork."

"That's great." So why does she look like someone disappointed her?

"Yes, except when she returned with the paperwork, it had our wedding date at the top. But it was for one year from now."

Oh. "That's not good."

"No." Chloe laughs in a self-deprecating way. "And when I informed her of the mistake, she told me that it was ridiculous to think I'd find a proper venue with only ten days to spare. I don't know." A pause. A tremble of her lip. "Maybe it *is* ridiculous. Maybe *I'm* ridiculous for thinking I could do this."

I hate sitting here and watching her come undone without being able to pull her into my arms. But since we don't have to play the happy bride and groom in this moment, there's no excuse for me to do so. With my headache abated, our time being just Chloe and Freddy has ended.

But even if I can't offer a hug, I can still offer her words. "It's literally been one day of looking. This is the only place you've tried so far."

"But there weren't any other venues listed on Rhonda's sheet."

"So you'll ask around and find somewhere else." I spear her with a look, trying to infuse the confidence I feel into her own veins. "Look, Chloe, I don't know anything about planning a wedding, but I know you. You're one of the most determined people I know. If anyone can do this, you can."

It's several long seconds before she responds, but she's looking at me in a way that unnerves me. Studying me as if she can peel away the layers and see what's underneath.

Blimey, I hope she can't.

She swipes away a single tear, nods, then lifts that gorgeous chin. "You're right. I *can* do this." Chloe straightens her shoulders. "*We* can do this. I believe in us."

I don't know about that, but I do believe in her. "I'm with you." Even when I don't agree with her methods.

"Thanks, Freddy. For being here."

"Always." The word is out before I can stop it, and I wonder if it surprises her as much as it does me. So I rush forward with more words, to undo any harm the first might create. "It's my job, after all."

She freezes, nods again, looks away. "Right. Yeah. And you're very good at it."

That I am. Sometimes, maybe too good.

So perhaps Frederick's standoffish behavior *wasn't* due to his migraine.

Because the entire drive back from the Moon Bay Inn, he's been sullen, quiet, giving me one-word answers when I try to engage him in conversation about ... well, anything, really.

It's got me wondering if he actually finds me annoying. Perhaps he's only been nice to me in the past because Topher was around.

I grip my stomach at the thought and turn to stare out the window as we coast into Hallmark Beach. Frederick slept for quite some time on that courtyard bench, and I confess that I didn't mind one bit. It allowed me the rare opportunity to watch him without worrying he'll catch me. And I know that sounds completely creepy, but there's something about sleep that just brings peace to a person who's so clearly burdened.

The worry lines in his forehead that are constant companions ... gone.

The tense and focused gaze that makes him so good at his job ... goodbye!

His body seemed to melt as I touched him, and at first I

thought that perhaps it meant something. That maybe my touch set his skin on fire. The reverse was certainly true.

But now his mood resembles that of the moon overhead, casting shadows around the clouds onto Main Street as we drive toward The Purple Seashell, which I haven't seen since I left my hotel room this morning. We've been going nonstop with planning activities and haven't had a chance to check Frederick in, but hopefully Janine will have another room available for him.

I sit up straighter. How has it taken me this long to realize this might be an issue? What did Lucy say? That I was lucky to get a room before now?

Oh no.

If Frederick has hated the idea of pretending to be engaged to me, he's definitely not going to like sharing a hotel room. Although I suppose if Tia had been here, she would have stayed with me.

What's the protocol here? Maybe I'm making too big a deal out of this. As a bodyguard, is he allowed to let me out of his sight—even if all I'm doing is sleeping, tucked safely away in my room for the night?

I swallow down my doubts and pray for a cancellation. Yes, some space would be good for both of us.

After traversing down a busy Main Street, we pull into the car park at the small two-story, gabled, lavender-painted inn. We unload and snag Frederick's bag out of the boot of the car, then head up the inn's front steps, which face the boardwalk. A sweeping patio juts out to the left and wraps around the inn, offering an unparalleled view of the ocean. I'm tempted to linger a moment, to sit in the swinging bench hanging from the patio roof, to take in the white sand and breathe in the salted air.

Anything to keep Frederick from discovering our predicament. The guy is already exhausted, despite his migraine nap. I don't want to test his patience any further.

But perhaps it's better to get it over with. To see what our fate holds.

I follow as Frederick eases open the screen door, which squeaks a hello as we step through it and past the heavy oak door that's been propped open. The lobby is small, but flows into a pleasant living room with a table and four chairs—which are currently occupied by a family playing checkers—as well as a couch and chairs in one corner, a fireplace, and a few book-shelves. Topher would be in heaven, and I could easily see myself curling up there and reading an Abigail Fox novel.

Not that I'll have any spare time on this visit.

At the reception desk, a heavyset woman with gray-streaked hair smiles up at us from behind a gossip magazine. "Hello, Chloe dear. Having a good afternoon?" She pauses as her eyes light upon Frederick. "And just who's this tall drink of water you've brought with you?"

I laugh and once again take Frederick's hand in mine because even if he finds me annoying in real life, the show must go on. "This is Frederick." I hesitate only a moment. "My fiancé. Freddy, this is Janine Reynolds—Lucy's aunt."

"Fiancé? Hot diggity dog, he's a looker."

Frederick flashes her that charming grin I know he's capable of (despite evidence to the contrary so far). "It's a plea-sure to meet you, ma'am."

"Ooo," she squeals, fanning herself with a meaty hand. "And will you also be staying at our lovely establishment?"

"I will indeed."

"Fabulous, fabulous." Janine swings her chair around to a box and pulls out a white room key card. "I'm a bit sad that a beauty such as yourself is taken, Chloe, love. Would have liked to introduce you to my son, Garrett. He's not in town at the moment but plans to come home later this year to give me a break from running this place so I can travel a bit with my church group."

She says all of this in one breath while running the key through a machine and typing something into the computer. "But I can see why you fell for this one. Woo-wee, that accent! Although he speaks the same as you, so I guess you know him from back home—wherever that is. Where did you say you were from, dear?" While looking at me, she hands Frederick the key.

"Oh, a small country in Europe," I say. "You wouldn't know it."

"Try me."

I look to Frederick for guidance on whether to answer fully, but he's staring at the key in his hand. "Sorry, ma'am, but how much do I owe you for the room? I'll be staying up until the wedding."

"Wedding? We're having a wedding? When?" Janine sits forward and grabs a pen, twirling it between her fingers. "I do so love a wedding."

"Er, right. Well"—I look between Frederick and Janine—"we're hoping to find a venue available not this weekend but the next. I know it's short notice, but we just can't wait any longer." I turn to Frederick, smile, and touch the top of his fingers. Here goes nothing. "I love this man with my whole being."

Oh goodness, I hope he believes me to be acting.

Because for a moment, something flashes across his face—disbelief, maybe?—and he just stares at me. Like, really stares at me. In my dreams, he'd toss that key aside, jerk me into his arms, and kiss me long and deep.

In reality, though, Janine sniffles and sighs, breaking whatever that moment between us was, if anything. "You two are as sweet as blueberry jam, that you are. Now, as far as wedding venues, honey, well, I've got the beach here, but I believe we have an event booked that weekend. Then again, that's just one evening and I don't rightly remember which, so we might have some availability. You'd have to ask Kelsey Loveland. She's my assistant manager, but she's already gone home for the day."

"You are so sweet," I say. "We've got a few other things in mind, though." Even though we don't. Oh, how I hope we can find other venues to try. But even if it wasn't so exposed, Topher is not a beach wedding kind of bloke.

"That's right perfect." Janine claps her hands and picks up her magazine, which she shakes at us. "Well, go on, git. I'm sure you're wanting to spend some time alone together now that you're reunited."

I don't miss the waggle of her eyebrows. Nor the way my stomach plummets to my toes. I glance at the key in Frederick's hand, then back up at him.

His eyes widen. He's realized what's going on here.

Reaching for his wallet, he grabs his credit card and holds it toward Janine. "Here. For my room."

Janine just laughs. "Your little lady already paid, silly. Unless you want me to switch the card on file?"

He chuckles, but it sounds like some sort of animal is being strangled. "No, no, you misunderstand. We need two rooms."

"Reeeee-ally?" She stretches out the word and leans forward again, steepling her fingers as if Frederick's is an outrageous request.

"Yes," Frederick says with a hard edge to his words.

Janine sighs. "I'm sorry, but I've only the one room. Chloe was lucky to get it, with the festival this weekend and all."

I've never seen Frederick so pale. Perhaps he's thinking of what Topher will say. Maybe he's considering what a wind-up it will be to share a room with me.

I don't really know what he's thinking, to be honest.

But I *do* know that if we don't get out of here now, he's going to blow our whole cover to pieces.

So with a quick, "It's not a problem—thank you!" to Janine, I tug on Frederick's sleeve and lead him out of the lobby, up the stairs, and down the hall to the last door on the left.

Straight for a one-bed situation that would make Abigail Fox very proud.

FREDERICK

One room.

One. Room.

The words bang around in my skull, and I blink as Chloe fumbles with her key against the door she's led me to.

Okay, okay. One room isn't all bad so long as there are two beds. Most hotel rooms have two beds, don't they?

She finally gets the green light and opens the door. We step inside and all breath leaves my body. My vision narrows and blurs at the corners, and my headache returns in a flash.

This room is tinier than the military bunk I shared with Topher.

Oh no. Topher ...

If he saw us here, sharing a room like this, he would absolutely murder me. Especially if he saw the singular bed taking up most of the space. I mean, sure, it's tastefully decorated with a seashell-shaped headboard and light olive-colored comforter, flanked by two side tables. The walls are painted a lavender hue, and there's a private en suite bathroom. In any other circumstance, I'd consider the room to be quite cozy.

But *cozy* is the furthest thing from what I want when I'm sharing a room with a princess I can't have.

"I know it's not ideal," Chloe says from somewhere behind me, "but think of it this way. At least you can keep a closer eye on me here than you could from next door. Every waking moment." She laughs, and I can tell it's just as forced as mine was earlier. "Every sleeping moment too."

Blimey. I shut my eyes against the thoughts that pervade my brain. Watching Chloe when she's awake is hard enough. But seeing her at her most vulnerable in sleep?

Forget Topher. He's the least of my worries. My biggest concern is not going completely mental before the wedding arrives. Because it will take every ounce of restraint to keep myself from revealing to Chloe Huntington how much I completely worship her, body and soul, before the week is up.

But there's no alternative. Nowhere to retreat to, no bunkers to hide in. *Time to man up, mate.* Reopening my eyes, I say, "It'll be fine." Then I roll my luggage around the bed and set it beside Chloe's behemoth suitcase. The contrast would make me smile if my brain wasn't still sending painful shock-waves through my head.

Chloe closes the door to our room and hangs her handbag on a peg to the right. Then she studies me. "Relax, Muscles. I'm safely tucked away for the night. We'll figure this out, okay?" After a few beats, she yawns. It's fake as anything I've ever seen on her, but I know she's trying. This isn't her fault any more than it is mine. We are victims of our circumstances, and I need to get my head on straight.

"You're right. Your safety is my number one—my only— priority here." All of this fake engagement and wedding stuff is secondary to that. And I can't forget it.

Chloe rounds the bed and pulls back a gauzy white curtain

hanging alongside the window behind one of the side tables. "We have a great view of the marina. Come see."

"I'm fine here, thanks."

She looks at me over her shoulder, and my mouth goes dry at the sight of her framed in the moonlight that's streaming down from the heavens, encircling her. "So stubborn." Then she yawns again, this time for real.

Her yawn is contagious, triggering one of my own, and I take the moment to kick off my trainers and stretch my arms over my head.

Chloe's eyes flit down to my stomach and her irises seem to darken, briefly becoming a stormy Black Sea instead of the usual clear blue Caribbean. What in the world? Glancing down, I realize the bottom of my shirt has ridden up to expose my lower abdomen. Quickly I drop my arms, the skin at the back of my neck flushing with heat.

Did she like what she saw?

Irrelevant, dude.

I clear my throat. "We should probably—"

"—get some sleep. Right." Chloe averts her eyes and squats in front of her luggage, tugging at the zip.

The unzippering fills the silence in the room and then Chloe pulls an article of clothing from her suitcase. I catch a glimpse of something pink and silky, and steel my jaw as she stands and heads into the restroom.

Blimey. I was so focused on the bed situation that I forgot to consider the sleepwear situation. Surely the princess is too proper to put on anything scandalous. Right? Then again, she didn't count on having a roommate.

Determined to focus on something else, I begin internally counting to one hundred as I assess the possible places for me to create a bed on the floor. There's minimal space between the foot of the bed and the TV stand-slash-dresser, and I'm not sure my large frame would fit there without massive discomfort. Besides that, I wouldn't be able to get an easy visual on the princess if something were to happen in the middle of the night. The bed is also closer to the restroom than the room's entrance, so I finally opt for the space between the main door and the bed. If someone were to attempt to come in at night, he'd run into me first.

That decided, I rummage through the dresser until I find an extra pillow and blanket. Then I kneel to make a nest on the floor. I suppose it's pointless to wish that carpet would magically appear beneath my knees rather than hardwood, but I close my eyes briefly and reopen them anyway. No luck.

I hear the door to the restroom squeak open. Glancing up and over the side of the bed, I see the upper half of her—blessedly covered in a long-sleeved, button-up pajama top with the initials CMH on one side—as she brushes her long hair.

A few seconds later, she marches my way, swinging around the bottom edge of the bed and placing her hands on her hips when she sees my homemade sleeping bag. "Frederick Shaw, what are you doing?"

My eyes nearly bug out of my head at the sight of the rest of her PJs—shorts that are by no means indecent, but provide far less coverage than I'm used to seeing on her. Her long, toned, tan legs are nearly my undoing, but I fling myself onto the floor and inside the extra blanket. "Just about to go to bed. Why?"

"You are *not* sleeping on the floor."

Here we go. "I am, Princess."

"But it looks so uncomfortable."

"Looks can be deceiving."

Chloe laughs, staccato and disbelieving. "You aren't even ready for bed."

She's got a fair point, but now that my body is prostrate, I'm not sure I could stand. It's certainly not worth doing simply to change into an undershirt and pair of athletic shorts—which is not normally how I choose to sleep, mind you, but clearly is how I'll be sleeping for the next week and a half until I get my own room and can go back to wearing jockey shorts to bed.

"I'm fine," is my only response. "You get some sleep, all right?"

"Freddy, honestly." She huffs. "After all your travels, you should be sleeping in a real bed tonight. I can take the floor."

"Absolutely not." What does she think I am, a monster? No flippin' way would I allow Chloe to sleep on the floor like some commoner. "Besides, it just wouldn't be proper."

"Oh, forget what's proper." She moves closer and I turn to see what she's up to. I wouldn't put it past her to lie down on the floor in an attempt to force me to the bed. Thankfully, all she's doing is sitting on the bed's edge, staring down at me. "Do what's practical."

"I can't."

"Why?" There goes that bottom lip nibbling again, and I'm undone. I can hear the exhaustion, the frustration in her tone. "I feel bad enough about all of this. If I hadn't come here, you wouldn't have been forced into this rubbish scheme of mine. And you'd have your own room at Lauren's where you'd be able to get a decent night's rest. Instead, here you are, lying on the floor literally at my feet."

"That's where I belong, Princess." I try for a tease, but perhaps the words ring with too much truth for her liking, because if I didn't know any better, I'd think Chloe might cry— but she's far too spirited for that, isn't she?

"Stop it, Freddy. I mean it."

How can I explain this in a way she'll understand? "I'm a soldier, Chloe. A little hard ground for the night doesn't frighten me."

"But you shouldn't have to endure it for my sake."

"I'd endure a lot more for your sake." As soon as the words leave my lips, my stomach flips.

Chloe's lips part, eyes going round.

I rush on. "You're my princess, after all. And"—I force the distasteful words from my mouth—"like a sister to me. Besides, however innocent sharing a bed would be, I wouldn't be able to sleep knowing your brother might pop out from my nightmares and murder me."

She smiles, but it doesn't quite reach her eyes. "Right. Of course." Then, after remaining quiet for a few long moments, she lifts her chin, determination clearly renewed. "But Topher isn't here, so you shouldn't lose sleep on account of him. And if I'm your princess, I can boss you around, right? Isn't that how this works?"

There she goes, challenging me again. She's too smart and too stubborn to accept the act I'm trying to put on with her. Even if she doesn't understand why I've been treating her with less camaraderie than normal today, she knows we'll never just be subject and princess.

And I can't do it, can't keep up this kind of battle with her, because she's just going to keep advancing, keep pushing back on the walls I've erected. It's no use. I have to revert back to our normal gregarious interactions. At least when we're sparring light-heartedly, I can use my charm against her. Tease her into seeing things my way.

I stretch my arms behind my head and close my eyes. "What's that? I can't hear you from my extremely comfortable bed for the night."

She snorts—a sound I love. Because as regal, as elegant, as much of a fashion icon as Chloe is, she's also not afraid to be herself. "All right, wise guy." There's glee in her voice, like she's actually won. And maybe she has. "I'll respect your decision."

I crack one eye open. She rounds the bed and climbs in on

the other side, pulling the covers over her. Giving up? That's not very Chloe of her at all. "What's the catch, Princess?"

At that moment, a pillow flies across the room and whacks me in the face.

"Hey!"

"Oops." Facing me, she props herself up with an elbow so I can see her in all her gorgeous glory. Doesn't matter that her face is scrubbed of makeup. Chloe's still the most beautiful woman in the world. Especially when she's looking at me like this—eyes teasing, lips quirked to one side. "It slipped. Can I get it back?"

How did I ever think I could hold this woman at arms' length, stiff and unyielding? She's way too much fun to tease. "I didn't hear a please."

"Please, Muscles?"

And don't get me started on her silly nickname for me. I'll go to the grave pretending it doesn't make me want to strut and preen every time I hear it. "Hmm. Tempting. But no." I snatch up the pillow—it's one of those frilly, bulky ones that's just for decoration—and tuck it on top of the other pillow currently under my head.

Her laughter is the best music. "Fine. I didn't want it anyway." With that, she reaches up to her lamp and shuts it off.

I smile and let my eyes drift closed again, no longer able to hold back a yawn. My entire body sinks into the floor—and blimey, I may as well be sleeping on a craggy rock. I move to my side, trying to find a comfortable position. How tempting it is to join her up in that soft, comfortable bed, but I know then sleep would be nigh on impossible.

Eventually, my body gives up and my buzzing nerves finally settle.

But my brain doesn't, bringing me a torturous night of dreams about *her*—and what can never be.

CHLOE

Well, *that* was one of the worst nights of sleep I've ever had.

Groaning, I blink up at the ceiling, my eyes roaming over the smooth white surface that's now flooded with light coming in through the window behind me. My hair is strewn in every which direction and I quickly push up with my elbows so I can finger comb the strands back into submission. Then I run my hands over my lips and chin, breathing a sigh of relief when I don't find any drool there.

Because Frederick might only see me *like a sister* (as he reminded me last night), but I would still like to disabuse him of the notion. I mean, I'm not asking for him to love me the way I love him, but come on. He could at least see me as a woman.

I thought, for a moment last night, perhaps he did. When he saw me in my PJs, and averted his eyes ... but likely that was simply a sign of respect.

Whatever the case, his reaction was in direct contrast to mine, when his shirt lifted, and I couldn't help but freeze up like a person under hypnosis after glimpsing the tan sliver of skin and the glorious physique Frederick's hours in the gym have most certainly honed. As my American friends might say —*Holy abs, Batman!*

It was only for mere seconds, but I feel forever changed by the experience. Makes me wonder what else he's hiding under that shirt.

Ugh, I need to get a handle on my emotions, considering he's lying on the floor just a few meters away. But when I lean across the bed to see whether he's also awake, I simply see a neatly folded blanket topped by two pillows—one that was thrown at him. I grin at the memory.

At least I have my Freddy back—the joking, teasing version, not the stoic, silent grump I was subjected to for much of yesterday.

Hopefully that's who I'll see today as well.

I purse my lips together and glance over at the restroom, but the door is wide open, and no one is inside. That's when I notice a note stuck to the shade of my lamp. It says, *Running out to get some proper tea and breakfast. Please do not leave the room. I'm counting on you to BEHAVE.*

His message is followed with a winking smiley face and his sign-off: Muscles.

Snatching the note up, I place it against my beating heart and sink back into my pillow like a lovesick lunatic. *Oh, girl, you're in trouble,* my mind baits me.

Don't I know it. I've been in trouble for years. But I've never been in such close proximity to him—and alone, at that— for such a long period of time.

At that moment, the door opens, and I scramble to stick the note onto my side table before sitting up in bed and watching Frederick slide inside, a tray with two lidded cups and a green bag featuring The White Mocha logo in his hands.

The scent that's all him—woodsy with twists of verbena

and cinnamon—wafts into the room, and mmm, he looks as good as he smells. His jaw is shaven clean, and a black Henley stretches across his broad shoulders, hugging his biceps and chest, leaving nothing to the imagination (okay, probably some things still). His medium-washed jeans sit low on his hips, and he's got trainers on his feet.

Back home when he's in protection mode, he wears a suit. And even though he looks smashing in that, I much prefer the casual look. It makes me want to stand up, round the bed, slip right into his arms, and find a home there.

He smiles when he sees me. "Good morning, Sleeping Beauty."

Oh, yay. My Freddy just might be here to stay. I flip my hair in an exaggerated manner. "Why, hello, good sir. Have you procured me my breakfast?"

"Indeed I have, fair princess." His eyes sparking, he maneuvers around the bed and hands me the pastry bag, which is warm from whatever's inside. "Though if you don't eat it soon, it will be lunch."

What? My eyes shoot to my phone, which tells me it's currently two minutes till eleven. "You should have woken me." I still have so many things on my to-do list for this wedding. Yesterday we didn't even begin to make a dent. And besides all that, we've a venue to find with no viable leads.

"You looked far too peaceful for that." He sets the drink carrier down on the side table and takes a cup in hand. "Besides, my job is far easier when you're asleep. Can't get into any trouble that way."

I stick my tongue out at him—a habit my father abhors—and then dig into the bag, pulling out a few sandwiches wrapped in foil-lined paper. Unwrapping the first, I peel back the thick white bread and find four slices of bacon. The smell alone is enough to make me sigh with pleasure, but when I see the bread is slathered with butter and ketchup, I squeal. "How in the world did you find a bacon butty on a menu in America?"

"I didn't." Frederick takes a quick sip of his drink. "In fact, the cashier thought I was barmy when I described it to him, but the cook said he'd be happy to try making it."

"Well, if it tastes anywhere near as good as it smells, I'm a fan for life." I scoot my legs back a bit so he can take a seat on the end of the bed, since it's that or the floor.

After a moment of hesitation, he sits with one leg pulled up, one flat on the ground. Taking out the second sandwich, I pull the wrapping halfway down before handing it to him. He balances his drink on the flat square post on the footboard of the bed before taking the sandwich from me. "Thanks."

"What inspired you to ask for this?" Does he know it's my favorite breakfast in the world? He's observant, but surely he doesn't know *that* about me.

He shrugs. "Traveling is wonderful, but I thought we could both use a little taste of home." His voice is wistful, and his eyes are looking out the window behind my side table. What's he thinking about now?

As I take a bite, I highly agree with his assessment and likely communicate that fact with the low moan in my throat. "Oh my goodness, I think this rivals the ones Chef makes at the palace." Grabbing a napkin from the bag, I wipe the edges of my mouth. "Just don't tell her I said so."

"My lips are sealed." He bites into his own sandwich and looks up at the ceiling, eyes closed, while he chews. I am far more fascinated with his Adam's apple as he swallows than I probably should be, and I'm not sure if I dart my gaze away quickly enough when he suddenly looks my way again.

"What?" He takes a napkin and swipes his chin. "Is there something on my face?"

Oh, drat. "Yeah, you've got something right there." I point to his nose.

He takes another swipe. "Did I get it?"

"Nope." I grin. "You've also got something here"—I point to his mouth—"and there." His left eye. "And there." His right.

He stops wiping, then purses his lips down. "Really, Princess?"

"You asked if you had anything on your face." Taking another bite, I laugh again.

He snags my foot through the thick comforter and pinches it, wiggling it before letting go. "You're impossible."

"Why, thank you." I pretend to bow, before sipping my drink. He's brought me an English breakfast tea with a dash of cream—again, just the way I like it. We both continue eating and drinking, and then his contemplative look returns.

Instead of wondering, this time I ask. "What are you looking at?" Twisting in bed, I gaze out the window myself. The same view as last night greets me. Boats of all shapes and sizes bob in the Hallmark Beach Harbor located on the north side of the inn. "The marina?"

"Something like that." Polishing off his sandwich, Frederick balls up the wrapper and tosses it into the rubbish bin across the room.

"No, don't do that."

"What? Prove how great of a basketball player I would make?" He flashes me a grin.

That grin does all sorts of things to my insides, but I can't let him see that. So I ball up my own wrapper—which I've picked clean of any leftover bacon bits, thank you very much—and throw it at his head. Unfortunately, I miss and knock his cup clean off the bedpost. Gasping, I climb out of bed at the same time he does and scramble right into him.

We go down in a heap on the floor, him flipping at the last moment so he takes the brunt of the fall. I gaze down at him, my hair burying his face. "Oh my goodness, I'm so sorry! Are you all right?" I try to dig through my hair and find him, but it's a tangled mess at this point.

"Can't. Breathe. So. Heavy."

I gasp again. "I am not." Then I roll off of him and smack him in the arm from where I lie next to him as he laughs.

His laugh turns wicked and he clutches his stomach, then rolls toward me, his eyes turning serious. "Are *you* all right?"

"Me and my heavy self are just fine."

"Oh, come now, Princess. Surely you know I was joking. You weigh as much as a feather."

"Only slightly more." I roll my eyes at the ceiling. "But yes, I'm okay. Just more worried about Janine's floor if there was a lot left in your cup."

"Nah, I was almost done." He sits up, then gives me a hand too, and we both peer toward the cup, which has kept its lid on and hasn't spilled a drop. "See? All good."

"No, we are absolutely not all good."

Folding his knees up and placing those strong arms around his legs, he lifts an eyebrow in my direction. "And just why not?"

Am I prying too much? It's already enough that he's pretending to be my fiancé, right? He deserves to have his private thoughts about things. And while we've always been friendly, I can't exactly call him my closest confidante. After all, he's more Topher's friend than mine. But maybe he'll indulge me. "You're not getting out of answering my question."

"And what question is that?"

"What were you looking at?"

He frowns and his hands make fists, his forearms tightening with the movement. "Just the boats."

"And what were you thinking about?"

"It doesn't really matter. So, what's on the agenda today?"

"I thought we could stop at the dress shop and then we have to look around for a venue. But don't change the subject." Tentatively, I reach out a hand and squeeze his. His skin is warm, and I wish I could hang on, but I don't. "What you're thinking about matters to me."

His brow bunches and he shifts on the ground a bit. I'm guessing it would be more comfortable to move back to the bed, but I don't want this moment gone, broken, and I'm afraid any movement might make it flit from my fingertips.

Finally, he answers, his voice low. "I've always thought a sailboat would be a brilliant way to see the world."

When he doesn't say any more, I prod with gentle words. "And that's something you'd like to do? See the world?"

"I mean, yeah. Who wouldn't?"

"There are a lot of people. My brother, for one." I cock my head. "Where would you go?"

"Everywhere," he answers in an instant. "Other than Kentonia and the foreign nations Topher's had to visit as part of his duties—and one other time as a kid—I haven't seen much."

"And knowing Topher, all you've seen of those other countries is the airport and palaces, eh?"

"Maybe a famous monument or two." His eyes wander back to the window. From our spot on the ground, I'm sure all he can see is the cloudy sky above, but maybe he's imagining the boats again. "But yeah, I'd love to immerse myself in a place. Maybe backpack through Europe, see more of the States than California. Just go, no plans, no responsibilities. Simply ... discover where the road takes me next."

"Sounds lovely." And it does—the idea that that kind of freedom could ever exist.

"I've got a whole map with pins of places I'd like to see. Books dog-eared and highlighted and abused. Topher would be horrified." He chuckles.

I laugh too, then ask the question burning in my brain. "So, why haven't you? Traveled more, I mean?"

Frederick seems to shake himself from whatever trance he's been in. "My job doesn't really allow for that."

"Have you asked? I'm sure Topher would give you the time off. You're his best mate. He wants you to be happy."

There his lips go flat-lining again. "I'm happy serving your family. It's my honor and privilege, and something I plan to do forever if he'll let me."

I look down at my stomach to see if the knife I feel twisting there is real. Okay, well, it may be imaginary, but it feels the same. That word ... *forever*. It's the culprit. Taking a breath, I steady my voice. "You plan to be a bodyguard forever? You ... you never want to get married or have a family of your own?"

I don't know why I'm torturing myself with these questions. It's not as if he'd choose me even if he was free from that stupid law that says bodyguards can't marry.

Because my life comes with strings. Marriage to me wouldn't let him travel all that much either. And I would never want him trapped like that.

And yet ...

His eyes are on me, like he's trying to understand something. "I ..." He pauses, swallows. "I think I *would* like those things. Especially after seeing my parents' strong love for each other. I can't help but be inspired by it. By the way they held each other together after Matthew died. The way my mum has stood by my dad all these years."

This is the first time I've ever heard Frederick mention his older brother, who died in a freak accident in Peru when he was barely out of high school. I was only seven when it happened, and hardly remember anything about it except that I was forced to wear itchy stockings under my dress at the funeral.

And Frederick's tears. It's the only time I've seen him cry, and he was only twelve, but *that*, I remember. What a tragedy it must have been.

And then, to make matters worse, there came the arrest, the trial. I was only nineteen, and Topher (along with Frederick) was away at university when Frederick's father was accused of treason against my own, so I didn't get an upfront view at how the whole affair affected him. But I do remember admiring Mara Shaw as she courageously spoke out against the imprisonment. She never stopped believing in her husband's innocence, never stopped petitioning, never stopped yelling to anyone who would listen for justice. It wasn't until my own brother stepped in and helped prove Martin's innocence—despite the media storm and public fury that came against him—that he was acquitted.

But it had all started with Mara and her tireless efforts. "She was amazing."

He smiles, and it's soft, sweet. "Still is." Then he sighs. "Even after he was found not guilty, he wasn't allowed to resume his position. Too many naysayers for that. So she had to start working again as a schoolteacher. They struggled financially, had to downsize their home. Lost all their friends. And when Dad drifted into a depression, she was the only one who could dig him out of it."

The way his voice gets all choked ... I can't breathe with wanting to pull him into my arms, to offer him a sliver of comfort. But my presence here with him will have to be enough. "I'm so sorry they've suffered so much. That you all have."

He's silent for a long while. "Thank you, Chloe."

"But ..." I hesitate, not wanting to say too much. Not wanting to push my luck. Because I've only just begun to peel back the layers of this man, and I can't help but want the whole blooming onion. "I guess I still don't understand why you wouldn't want that kind of love for yourself. Someday, I mean."

He shifts his knees closer to his body. "Being an executive protection agent for the crown is the path that was chosen for me, and I've accepted that."

That's news to me. "I thought you loved it."

"I do, to an extent."

"Who chose it for you, then?"

"It's what my father always wanted for me. And sure, there were a few years in the beginning when I considered begging off to do other things. But after the trial, after T—" He trails off.

After ... what? I lean forward.

The muscle in Frederick's jaw flexes and he shakes his head. "Suffice it to say that I'm content, Chloe. Can we please just leave it at that?"

No. Because I want to know more. So much more. Like what makes this man tick. What makes him so good? Why is he so loyal to my family after everything we've put him through? Even I can see that my father holds him at a distance. He could have saved his old friend a world of pain and hurt by re-welcoming him into the palace after the trial, but I think a part of him doesn't believe Martin was actually innocent of selling secrets to the spies who then plotted his assassination.

It's a wonder Father's allowed Frederick to stay, honestly. But Topher wouldn't stand to have his best mate thrown out into the streets, and my father—who can be strict when he wants to be—doesn't desire discord with his son, the future king.

So that answers the question of why my family has allowed Frederick to stay on as a bodyguard—but it doesn't really say why Frederick has done so.

However, I sense he's said all he's willing to right now, so I dust off my hands and stand. "Sure. We can leave it at that."

For now.

ten

FREDERICK

I still don't understand how Chloe's gone months in America without being recognized. After all, she draws attention wherever she goes, especially today in those trousers that hug her hips and that pink top that's an innocent tease with the way it cuts straight across her body, leaving her shoulders bare.

Not that I blame the bloke who's rubbernecking as we pass him on the boardwalk on our way to the dress boutique, but I give him a death stare all the same.

He holds up his hands in the universal "sorry, man" gesture and continues on his way as we saunter south, past Rainbow Ice and The Green Robin.

Meanwhile, Chloe just keeps talking on the phone, unaware of anything amiss. But that's what I'm here for, after all, and so far, it hasn't been too difficult to keep her safe. Hopefully that continues.

"Oh, I'm so glad you thought of that, Shelby." Chloe's voice is filled with excitement and much more confidence than yesterday. Of course, this afternoon's search hasn't yielded any more promising leads on a venue, but I'm thankful she seems to have her pep back. "Yes, that's perfect." A pause, then a nod.

"Good. Yay! This is working out so well. Just be sure to bill me for it, okay? No, no excuses. This was my idea and that's going to be my wedding gift to them." She laughs again and her whole face—or what I can see of it from the side, anyhow—lights up.

I know I should focus on the surroundings, including the late-afternoon beachgoers lounging on the sand, playing their music and tossing discs around, but I allow myself three seconds to just watch her.

She brightens the whole town more than the sun, which finally decided to show itself about an hour ago.

"Okay, and the guys ... did they agree to do the thing? Yes? Ooo, Lauren is going to love it so much. Topher is on board, though he says I'm ridiculous for asking." She nods, grinning. "Mmm-hmm. Yep. Okay, bye!" When Chloe hangs up, we've arrived at the back of the Just Peachy Boutique, where apparently Chloe will be trying on dresses to find something that will work for the wedding. The ladies—that is, Chloe plus Lauren's friends from San Diego—all decided to get their own bridesmaid dresses in whatever color they wanted because Lauren is spontaneous and "will love it."

"Good news?" I ask as I open the door to the aptly colored peach building.

"Shelby remembered a wedding dress Lauren loved when they were shopping for Shelby's dress. At the time, she wouldn't try it on, but Shelby thought it would look perfect on her. Last night she went back to the shop, and they still have it—and in Lauren's size." Chloe kisses her fingertips and flings them in the air. "It's fate!"

"That's great."

We step inside the boutique, which is small-ish like most of the shops on Main Street, but well lit and clearly organized, every inch of space used well and clearly marked, with everything from trousers to shirts to dresses, mostly for women. The formal gowns—including a handful of wedding dresses—are in a separate space, hanging from a rack in the back corner of the store, where there's also a bank of mirrors and a raised dais overlooking two chairs, likely for the token male who inevitably has to accompany a woman inside.

A few other female customers browse the casual section, but thankfully no one is currently in the back section. Fewer eyes mean less attention on Chloe.

"Hi, there. I'm Stephanie." A short woman approaches. She looks only slightly older than us, with dark spiked hair and a casual dress paired with trainers, and she's wearing a large smile. Much more approachable than Betsy from the Moon Bay Inn, I dare say. Her eyes study Chloe and widen slightly. Is that recognition I see there? Hmm. But then her grin moves to me, and she continues as if nothing is amiss. Perhaps I imagined her reaction. "How can I help you today?"

"Hi, Stephanie!" Chloe chirps as she slides her hand into mine like it's the most natural thing in the world. "I'm here to look at some of the formal gowns." Then she leans her head on my shoulder and rests her other hand on my upper arm.

"Awesome. Any special occasions?" The woman rubs her hands together and raises her brows.

Chloe just laughs. "A wedding."

"Yours or someone else's?"

Chloe leans closer. "I'm not here to look at traditional wedding dresses, but ..." She holds up her left hand, wiggles her fingers, and winks.

"Lovely. Always happy to meet a bride. Though I have to say, I'm not used to seeing many grooms in here. Some would say it's bad luck to see the bride in her dress before the wedding."

"Oh, we don't believe in all that," Chloe says with a laugh. Then she glances up, those crystal eyes fixed with an adoration

I can't help but wish was real. "I want to make sure Frederick thinks I look perfect in whatever gown I choose."

Is she kidding? "You look perfect in anything you wear." The answer's out before I can stop it. But it's the kind of thing a fiancé would say, right?

Chloe's lips settle into a soft smile, and her cheeks tinge pink.

"Aw, you two are just adorable." Stephanie claps her hands and points to the back. "Okay, so you'll find all the formal gowns there. Our entire stock is on the floor, but if you find something you like, I can order your size for you. Feel free to use the dressing room behind the mirrors and then come out to the dais so you can see the dresses from all angles."

"Oh, that's perfect. Thank you so much, Stephanie."

"Of course." The woman starts to turn, then stops, mouth half open. Closed. Open again. "I have to say, you just look so familiar. Have we met?"

I stiffen.

Chloe's thumb swipes down the length of mine. "I don't think so."

"Hmm. My mistake then," Stephanie says. "Let me know if you need any assistance."

"We will."

Once Stephanie heads back to the register, which is to the left of the entrance, Chloe tugs on my hand, but I don't move. "We should leave," I say.

"What? Why?"

"I think she knows who you are."

"Don't be silly, Muscles." Chloe gives me another tug. "Lucy recognized me too when I first arrived, and it was simply because I was here with Shelby and Lauren last week. I'm sure Stephanie and I passed on the street. It's not exactly New York City."

"Maybe." I frown, but against my better judgment, walk with Chloe to the dress section, where she begins browsing what's on the rack. Turning, I face the bulk of the store and stand, hands clasped in front of me.

"Freddy," Chloe laughs from behind me. "You look like a bodyguard."

"That's what I am."

"Well, yes, but you're being *obvious* about it."

Oh. Right. "Sorry. This is my first fake fiancé gig."

"I forgive you." I feel a poke in the back. "Now turn around and help me."

Obliging, I pivot and watch her flip through the hangers on the rack, metal on metal scratching as one after another scrapes across the surface of the rod. "What exactly am I supposed to help with?"

"Help me decide what to try on. This is my brother's wedding, after all." She pulls a gown out enough to examine it without pulling it off the rack. "I have to look smashing."

Impossible, this one. "I meant what I said, Princess." And yeah, maybe I shouldn't have said it, but surely she knows it's just an objective fact. I'm not saying something a million other men wouldn't say.

"Really?" She peeks up at me from the corner of her eye. A cheeky grin overtakes her whole face. What's she got up her sleeve? Then she whips a dress off the rack and holds it up against her body. I don't know a thing about fashion, but even I can tell this is one of those dresses that is in a magazine somewhere as an example of the year's worst fashion state-ment. A hideous shade of orange in a stiff-looking material, it's poofed up in all the wrong places. "You think I'd look perfect in *this*?"

Somehow, some way, I don't let out the chuckle that's bursting for release inside of me. Instead, I lift my chin, stroke my jaw, and pretend to consider what she's proposing. Then, "I stand by my previous remark, Princess."

"All right, then, Freddy. Challenge accepted." Turning, Chloe whisks around the corner and toward the dressing room, which is just a room with three solid walls and a blue curtain hanging on a rod. When, on instinct, I start to follow her, she holds a hand up to my chest. "Whoa there, Muscles. Not even a bodyguard is allowed back here when I'm changing."

"Of course." I wince. "I wasn't thinking."

"I know you just can't wait to be wowed. Now, go sit."

After she disappears behind the curtain, I finally allow myself to laugh. She's utterly ridiculous, and I love her for it. Chloe Huntington is the complete package: caring, beautiful, generous, and silly.

She's going to make some chap very lucky one day.

I grunt.

At that moment, she sticks her head out of the curtain, concealing everything from the neck down. "Muscles!" She's laughing. "Go!"

But I'm frozen at the sight, telling myself to close my eyes and stop wondering ...

Don't be a creeper, mate.

Her eyebrows lift with an amused tilt, and the motion shocks something in me.

"Right. Yeah. Sorry." I turn on my heel and rush to one of the two seats. My heart pounds and I pull at the collar of my shirt, tugging it back and forth in rapid succession to create a breeze because WHEN DID SOMEONE TURN UP THE THERMOSTAT IN THIS PLACE? My breath shudders and my knee bobs as I wait for her, finally remembering that I should be paying attention to our surroundings. A quick scan of the boutique shows it's just us and Stephanie, who is busy on her computer behind the desk.

She glances up, finds me looking her way, and waves.

I give her the guy head nod of acknowledgment and turn to find Chloe coming around the bend. And see? I was right. She's perfection, and it has nothing to do with what she's wearing.

Somehow, she makes the ugliest gown in the world look like it was made for royalty. The fitted bodice and high neck only serve to accentuate her curves, hugging her in all the right places.

"It looks like a peacock and a fox had a baby." Chloe turns and shows off a long zip. Orange and yellow ruffles that resemble "plumage" trail from her waist down to the ground, where they drag a good meter behind. Then she wiggles her rear and all the ruffles sway, making it appear as if orange water is trailing down her person. "What do you think, Freddy?" She poses, a hand propped on her hip, the other in the air as she sweeps her nose up to the ceiling.

"He's in utter awe, Princess."

I jump from my seat at Stephanie's voice behind me and twirl to find her standing there, phone in one hand, the other clasped against her chest as she smiles. Did she take photos?

"Sorry," Stephanie squeaks when she sees me advance toward her. "I'm a gossip rag queen and I could have sworn I recognized you, Princess Chloe. You're my favorite princess of all the princesses out there." She loops down into an awkward bow.

Clearly, she's not a threat—at least, physically. But if she leaks the photos I'm sure she took, then she could do some major damage, nonetheless.

I glance back at Chloe, who is gripping the full skirt of her gown as she leaves the raised step and heads this way. "That's so sweet of you, Stephanie." When she reaches us, she places another calming hand on my arm but keeps her gaze on the shopkeeper. "So, can I tell you a secret?"

"Of course you can." Stephanie flips her phone between her two hands.

"Well, here's the thing." Chloe smooths a strand of hair behind her ear. "This wedding is supposed to be a secret, and we came all the way here, to Hallmark Beach, because we'd hoped for some privacy."

"Oh, I won't tell anyone you were here. Not at all." Pressing her finger and thumb together, she moves them across her lips. "I promise."

"I'm going to hold you to that, Stephanie. Because Frederick here is actually a bodyguard, and if I don't get your absolute solemn vow that you won't tell a soul about this until after the wedding is over, then I'm not sure I can keep him from confiscating your phone as a matter of national security."

Oh, she's good. Both charming Stephanie and threatening her all at once—but without being obvious about it.

I fold my arms over my chest and steel my gaze to back up what Chloe said. It's not as if I have any jurisdiction here in America to take people's property, and Chloe knows that.

But Stephanie clearly doesn't, because her head bobs up and down and she holds up three fingers. "I absolutely promise." Squinting at her own hand, she changes which fingers she's holding up. Looks a bit longer. Then nods. "Scout's honor."

Then, much to my chagrin—and Stephanie's delight—Chloe pulls Stephanie in for a quick hug. "Thank you, dear. You've made me so happy." She pulls back. "Now, I'm going to finish trying on dresses. Is that all right?"

"Oh, more than. In fact"—Stephanie continues—"I'm going to close the shop while you do that. You know, to ensure you have more privacy."

"You think of everything, Stephanie. Thank you."

"You just let me know if you need anything else. Anything

at all. A slip. Champagne. My Social Security number." Stephanie laughs, a bit of a nervous edge bubbling up.

I get it. It's the Chloe Effect.

That doesn't mean I'm fully convinced that Stephanie won't blab to everyone she knows about this encounter. But we've done all we can do, and Chloe's safe from harm. We'll just have to see how the rest of it plays out later this week.

Stephanie flutters away and gives the door lock a click, then flips the sign on the front door to CLOSED, flashing us a thumbs-up afterward before heading back to her desk.

"I know what you're thinking, Muscles, but I really think she'll keep her word."

"You have more faith in people than I do."

"We're both good at reading people, Freddy. Just in different ways. You can see what people intend, especially when those intentions are bad. And me ..." Chloe shrugs. "I can see what people want." She tilts her head, and her hair flows with the movement. "Most people, anyway."

Then, before I can understand her cryptic meaning, she flounces away, grabs a few more dresses off the rack, and heads back to the dressing room.

Moments later, I hear her call out. "Freddy, a little help!"

Instantly, I'm on my feet. I should have trusted my instincts and gotten Chloe out of here when we first arrived. Stephanie hasn't left her desk, but what if there's someone else here I didn't account for, didn't see because I was distracted by all things Chloe?

If anything's wrong, if anything's happened to her ...

I skid around the corner toward the curtain, which is still closed. "Chloe?" My voice is ragged, threadbare, because I'm hardly holding it together here. "I'm coming in there." Then I fling open the curtain—and find her alone with her dress half unzipped.

It makes a V from her shoulders all the way down her back, showing off the impossibly long swath of her skin in between.

I blink. She did call for help, didn't she? I didn't imagine it?

She glances over her shoulder. "Oh, good. Thanks for coming. The zip's stuck—I think the ruffles got caught in the track. Can you help? I can't seem to get it."

And there's no guile in her eyes, no proof that this is a scheme of any sort, but saints alive, what a way to give a man a heart attack. I'd almost rather have found a perpetrator in here. *Almost*—except that would mean Chloe would have been in danger. But at least then I'd have something to hit, somewhere to put this electric energy pulsing through every vein in my body.

"Sorry, hope this isn't too weird. It's not like I'm indecent, though."

I nearly scoff. She clearly has no idea the effect she has on men. At least, on me. Then again, this reminds me very much of the backless dress she wore to her eighteenth birthday ball. Every time her hair swayed and exposed a tiny hint of the skin beneath, I nearly chased her down to ask for a dance—even though I was working at the time.

Didn't help that Topher was there, his eyes boring into me. That's the one and only time he said the word "off-limits" to me. I understood, and we never spoke of it again.

"Freddy?" her soft whisper fills the tiny space, which I close off with the curtain for her privacy.

Of course that leaves us alone in a confined room, making this moment even more intimate, even more tempting. Even more like the dreams that plagued me last night.

"It's fine, Princess." Of course it is. It has to be. *Get ahold of yourself, man.* "I'm at your service."

She's quiet as I squat and try to work the ruffles loose from the zip. Several times my fingers unintentionally graze the soft skin of her back, and they twitch to do more than that. Every time we make contact, her breath hitches. Perhaps my fingers are cold?

Finally, I manage to pull the material loose, which allows the zip to slide up and down—nearly to an inappropriate spot.

Time to go.

"Will there be anything else?" I ask, moving my gaze to the ceiling, where there's a fluorescent light just overhead.

"Nothing, thank you."

And with that, I take off out of the room, nearly stumbling over my own feet like a gelding that's just been born. I've got to get out of my head. Protecting Chloe is all that matters.

Anything less than that, and I've failed her.

CHLOE

Given what happened earlier this afternoon with Stephanie recognizing me at the boutique, a crowded bar is the last place I know Frederick wants to be.

But this is our chance to talk to some of the locals all at once. To see if any of them know of any venues I haven't come across in my research. Because I'm failing hardcore at locating somewhere for my brother to get married. And without that, my entire plan will fall to pieces.

We step inside The Black Hole, and my fears are confirmed. Because while the pub isn't seedy by any stretch of the imagination—it's actually fairly clean as far as bars go—it's dimly lit. Not only that, it's a complete crush inside, over-flowing with twenty- and thirty-somethings. Rock music pumps through large speakers on either side of a small stage and the dance floor is a lesson in differences, with some people slow dancing sweet and close, and others gyrating in a manner that would make many of my royal relatives turn up their noses in disdain.

A bar stretches down one long wall, and two female bartenders in sleeveless shirts pull shots and clean highball glasses as they chat up patrons on stools. There are booths lining the opposite wall, with high-top tables and chairs scattered throughout the rest of the space.

"Do you see anyone we know?" I call back to Frederick, who is close on my heels (my Louboutins, to be exact—I've been dying for an excuse to wear them).

He steps closer and momentarily leans in, placing one hand on my lower back in a way that makes me shiver while pointing with the other. "There, in the back corner."

Of course he *would* spot everyone before I do. He probably already knows where all of the exits are and how he would get me to each one should the need arise (which it won't). I squint in the direction he's pointing as my eyes adjust to the dark and take in the sight of Lucy, Marilee, two more women, Jordan, and one other guy in a cowboy hat.

"Ready?"

Frederick purses his lips for a moment. "Are you sure about this, Chloe?"

"Of course I'm sure."

He just stares at me, and I sigh. "Nobody is going to recognize me. Look how many people are here. I'll be fine. Safety in numbers, right?"

"Total misnomer. But fine." Then he holds out his hand. The fact that he's the one to initiate our pretense this time around ... well, he's holding up on his promise to try, and I can't really ask more of him than that. Especially after I thought I'd scared him away when I asked for his help with my zip a few hours ago.

I loop my fingers through his and we walk toward the booth, weaving through the crowd and around the booth where people are in line to sign up for karaoke, which is supposed to begin soon. Despite already having a beer in one hand, a tall man is heading toward the bar, bobbing to the beat when he bumps into me. "Whoa, sorry!" His drink flies all over the floor —thankfully not on me—but instead of jumping away, he just kind of slumps, using me to hold him up.

He towers over me, as tall as Frederick though with a wider girth, but in an instant, Frederick is hauling the guy away from me like he weighs nothing. "Get off of her." His voice is low and menacing, and to the untrained eye, his body appears relaxed as he faces the guy and pats his shoulders. But I've seen him relaxed before, and right now, his body is poised to strike if need be. He's like a big, graceful cat who may decide to chase that gazelle—if he deems it's worth it.

It's extremely sexy, if I'm being quite honest.

"Touch her again, and we're going to have a problem, mate."

Thankfully, the big lug just blinks at Frederick before grinning, throwing an arm around his shoulder, lifting his mostly empty beer in the air, and screaming at the top of his lungs, "No problem here, *mate.*" He slurs the last word, then saunters off toward the bar.

"Idiot," Frederick mutters so softly that I only know he said it from watching his lips. "Sorry about that," he says to me. "You all right?" Shaking out his hands, he then loops one arm around my waist, holding me firmly against his side.

All right? I might faint right here on the dance floor. Either that or float away. Not only because my side is about to spontaneously combust at any moment, but because standing like this is a declaration to the world—*STAY AWAY. This woman's mine.*

If only it was real. Still, I'll take any contact he'll give me. I'm like a junkie, and my drug of choice is Frederick Shaw.

"I'm fine, Muscles." Understatement of the year. "You know, you're handy to have around in a place like this."

"I mean it, Chloe." Though I didn't know there was still

any sort of space between us, he pulls me closer. "We can turn around and leave right now."

"I trust you to keep me safe."

Frederick frowns, then nods, and we walk toward our new friends in the large round booth that's a step up from the ground, where Lucy waves and smiles as well as any royal. She climbs over Marilee and Jordan and gracefully lands on the floor before throwing her arms around me. "You're here! I'm so glad." Pulling back, she does a once-over of my outfit—a green pleated A-line dress in chiffon—which is probably too dressy given the fact she's in cowboy boots, jeans, and a plain long-sleeved shirt. "And you look amazing. Girls, doesn't she look great?"

She's completely interrupted the other members of the booth, but nobody seems to mind as they toss us friendly waves and lift their drinks in greeting. "Gang, this is Chloe and Frederick. You guys already know Mar and Jordan." She points to the new guy and two brunettes who look like twins across from Jordan. "And this is Kelsey and Elisse Loveland—their family owns the winery. Oh, and Elisse is the one who gave me the keys for the wedding shop, remember? And this is Landon Bennett. His family's land is next to the winery, and he works there with the Loveland boys. Poor Kelsey and Elisse have six brothers—can you believe that?"

Frederick, who let go of my waist when Lucy hugged me, grabs my hand and squeezes. Is he as amused at Lucy's gift of gab as I am?

"Nice to meet you, everyone." I smile. "Mind if we join?"

"Absolutely not." Jordan squashes up against Mar and Frederick and I pile in next to him, while Lucy remains standing. "And help yourself to some food. We always get a bunch and then split the tab."

The table is littered with greasy-looking appetizers of all

kinds—egg rolls and sliders, wings and nachos. "Brilliant, thank you," I reply. "Is it always this busy here?"

"Not even close," Landon says as he takes a swig of his beer. He tilts up the brim of his cowboy hat. "Festival and spring break have this whole town crawling with crazies."

"What kind of crazies?" Frederick pipes up.

"Oh, just your usual hot heads and brainless beach bimbos," Elisse (I think?) says.

Landon smiles around his sip of beer before setting down the bottle. "I was more thinking about the old rich folks who yell at you if you park in what they think should've been their parking spot."

"That only happens to people who drive pickup trucks as big as their ego," Elisse spits back with a grin.

"Don't be saying mean things about Jessie."

"And don't get me started on that name!"

Everyone laughs at their friendly banter. "How do you all know each other?" I ask.

They exchange glances.

"It's a small town." Lucy shrugs. "Everyone knows every-one. But we all went to high school together, and we're the ones who stuck around." She points at Jordan. "Except for him. He left, but knew what was good and came back to us."

Jordan playfully tosses a crisp at her. "Of course I did. All my favorite people are here." He nudges Marilee.

They are just the cutest. Taking a thick pretzel stick from a small bucket container in front of me, I turn to Jordan and Marilee. "So, parents' night out, eh, you two? I love that you guys take time for that."

Their brows knit together, and silence descends on the group before they all burst out laughing. What did I say that was so funny?

"Oh!" Lucy is finally the one to stop laughing first. "You

thought Jordan and Mar were a couple? I can totally see how you'd think that since I never said any differently when I introduced you."

Huh. I scan my memory and indeed, no one ever said anything about them being married. "Sorry," I smile sheepishly. "I just assumed."

Marilee chuckles again and elbows Jordan. "You're not the first to ask. We've been friends forever."

"But not *best* friends"—Lucy interjects, waving her finger in the air—"because that title belongs to me."

"Always." Marilee winks at her. "But yeah, Jordan is a great dad and hates to leave Ryder at home. We have to force him to come out with us."

I notice Jordan isn't laughing anymore, just crunching on some crisps like he hasn't eaten anything in ages and crisps are his favorite food in the world. Then he downs his entire glass of water in one long gulp.

Interesting. I'm tempted to ask if he's married to someone else, if Ryder's mom is in the picture, but maybe that's better left to another time.

"Well, sorry for the mix-up."

"Don't think anything more of it." Marilee steals one of Jordan's crisps and he slides his entire plate of nachos in front of her. "So, how did your first few days of wedding planning go?"

"Well, we got a few things marked off of our list." With some effort, I break the pretzel in half. I could really use a drink right about now, but I haven't seen a server at all. Maybe we have to order at the bar? "But the biggest obstacle is the venue." I fill them all in on the drama of finding a venue only to be let down. Everyone groans for me and promises to think about alternative options we could check out.

"That's a very quick turnaround, though eloping is definitely romantic," Kelsey (the other twin) says. "How did you two meet?" She seems quieter than Elisse, more contemplative. If I remember correctly, she's the one who works for Janine at The Purple Seashell. Perhaps I'll see her there later this week.

I'm so busy thinking about this that I forget to process what she's asking. Drat. We can't very well say that Frederick is my brother's bodyguard, can we now? How did we not consider what story to tell everyone? "Um," I begin.

Frederick places a hand on my knee and squeezes. "Her brother and I were in the armed forces together, and are still best mates." His thumb rubs circles on my skin, making it hard to focus. Does he realize he's doing that? Likely not, but you won't hear me telling him to stop. He continues with the story. "After we both got out of the service, I visited his home, and it happened to be Chloe's eighteenth birthday."

Ah, I see what he's doing. Taking pieces of the truth, not revealing their full extent—like the fact that we'd known each other, at least as acquaintances, long before that, since his father had worked as an advisor for mine. In fact, his entire family line has served our family's in some capacity for over a century.

I'm curious where he'll go next, because I well remember the night he's talking about. My parents put on a smashing coming-of-age bash and invited the royalty and dignitaries of all our surrounding countries. I wore a black gown that I'd had commissioned from a little shop in downtown Kellerton. The front of the dress had been rather conservative and plain, with a sweetheart neckline and long sheer sleeves, so that any official photos of me would show the world I was someone to be taken seriously. After all the undeserved chatter to the contrary, I was determined to change my public image.

Of course, I hadn't been able to resist adding a bit of rebellion by asking the designer to make the gown completely backless. I wore my long hair down, so it wasn't readily apparent to all, but I'd hoped that if any of the handsome gentlemen Father had invited were really paying attention, they'd notice. It had made me feel secretly powerful in a way, with some semblance of control in a world that seemed to control me more and more every day.

Frederick's really selling this, because everyone's attention is fully on him. Lucy's got her elbows on the table, leaning over with her chin settled on top of her fists. Despite his insistence that he's rubbish at this, it appears there is no *try* with Frederick.

"So anyhow, my mate invited me to hang out at his sister's party—he was required to attend and is a bit of a recluse when it comes to crowds and parties. Well, I took one look at Chloe all glammed up in this stunning gown and I just knew. She was it for me."

I freeze. That sounded so ... genuine. Could it—could he actually have real feelings for me?

No, no, no. He wouldn't have been able to hide it all this time, right? Perhaps he's actually not a rubbish actor at all. That's a much more likely explanation, considering that I've never seen a hint of true flirtation from him. Maybe his military training included lessons in subterfuge.

Elisse lifts an eyebrow. "And your friend didn't care that you went after his baby sister?"

"It's so romantic," Lucy croons.

Kelsey and Marilee both sigh, hands over their hearts, and I fully understand the sentiment. Somehow, of its own accord, my hand finds Frederick's on top of my knee, and I run my fingertips over his veins, tracing each one up and down, slow, steady—the exact opposite of the rhythm of my heart in this moment.

His eyes dart to me, surprise flashing in them before he pulls his hand away and wraps it around my shoulders instead.

A proper admonishment then—just like at the Moon Bay Inn courtyard yesterday when he pulled his hands away from me.

Watch out, Chloe, my brain says. *Your feelings are showing.*

My cheeks flush. And now I *really* need that water. "I'll be right back." Before he can protest, I inch out of the booth and leave him to finish answering the barrage of questions. He won't like me being away from him like this, but he should still be able to see me across the room with his super spy eyes.

Cutting through the crowd on the dance floor, I nearly slip on a puddle of something sticky, but right myself just in time. Bodies press against me on all sides, but no one gives a care or extra consideration to me. I suppose this is what it feels like to be normal, eh?

And maybe what it feels like to have a broken heart too.

What does it take for a girl to get a drink around here?

I've been waiting an eternity (okay, fine, more like ten minutes), but still haven't been served by the bartenders. It appears they only want to chat up the male clientele. Sighing, I slump onto a stool and glance back at our table. The others are still talking, laughing, but Frederick's gaze is narrowed in on me. He gestures at me to come back and starts to get up, but I put up my hand in a HALT motion.

I need my space, and I'm hoping he respects that.

He hesitates a moment, then gives me a nod. But his eyes never leave me. If our new friends see him, they'll likely think he's of the jealous sort, the kind who doesn't want his woman going off without him. I should probably go back there, save our cover. After all, I want them all to like us.

But at the moment, I just don't care.

So I flip back around in my stool and face the bar, awaiting my turn to grab a blooming glass of water.

Two hands alight on my back, skimming down toward my waist—but they are *not* Frederick's hands. And it's not Frederick's voice in my ear. "Well, aren't you just all curves and sweetness. Want to get out of here, Pretty Lady?"

My hands grip the counter as I whip around and find the "jolly" giant who ran into me on our way in. His eyes are now completely rheumy, his long black hair is greasy and tangled, and he's grinning at me like I'm a prize steer he's trying to rope.

"Hi, sorry, not interested." I say this in a gentle but firm way, because I have no wish to make him angry. Who knows what the result of *that* would be, given his obvious inebriation.

"Oh, come on now, sweetheart. Give old Ricky a chance." His words slur but his movements are surprisingly quick as he leans both hands on the counter, trapping me on the stool. I don't really want to touch him but in trying to duck away, my nose smacks his meaty arm.

"Please go away."

"You like it, sweetheart, don't you now?"

How does nobody around us seem to notice what's happening? But karaoke has begun and most everyone's attention is on the stage where someone is massacring a beloved 'N Sync song.

Still, I have bigger problems with this bloke's face getting closer every moment. "I have a fiancé, and he's not going to like this."

"I don't see him anywhere."

My heart rate kicks up a notch and I open my mouth to scream for help—

"I'm right here, mate." Before I know what's happening, the

guy is wrenched away from me and Frederick is there, his eyes flashing with something I've never seen before. Controlled rage pools and lingers, just itching for an excuse to leak out. "And I thought I told you not to touch her again."

Seeing him like this … it's both terrifying—and exhilarating.

Ricky staggers for a moment and punches right then left, but Frederick easily outmaneuvers the overgrown idiot without laying another finger on him. The big guy finally gets so dizzy that he falls to the floor.

I lean down to see if he's okay, but then Frederick has me by the arm and is tugging me down a dark hallway toward an Exit sign I never would have seen or known existed. To my knowledge, nobody is pursuing us, but Frederick doesn't stop, slamming his palm into the door's crash bar and pulling me into the alley behind the bar, which is backed by the forested side of Main Street.

We round the corner, and he presses me up against the building, covering my body with his own in a protective stance —his palms flat against the wall on either side of my head—as he glances around the bend.

"Frederick?"

"Shh."

I purse my lips together, waiting, and somehow my hands find their way to Frederick's waist. And it is a firm waist, let me tell you. I force myself to be perfectly still. Yeah, no. Not working. This position does nothing to keep my frazzled breathing at bay or calm the crazy racing of my heart.

Frederick's face is still fixed on the exit, and I can almost read his mind, like I'm a student in Bodyguarding 101 and this is a pop quiz. We aren't leaving yet because he wants to know why the guy attacked me. Did Ricky somehow know I was a princess—like Stephanie earlier today—or was he simply a drunk idiot?

He didn't say anything that would lead me to believe the former, so I have to conclude it's the latter. "Just a drunk idiot," I whisper under my breath.

"What?" Frederick finally tilts his face downward and *oh my*. His nose nearly touches my own. I smell the mint on his breath, the woodsy cologne that clings to his clothing. Would I be able to smell it on his skin too if I pressed my nose against the throbbing vein in his lower neck?

He blinks. "Are you all right, Princess?"

"Hmm?" I jerk my eyes back up to his face and pray he can't see my thoughts plainly there.

"I said, are you all right?"

He's asking in an official capacity, I know. But oh, how I wish there was a different reason he had me up against this wall. How I wish he would lean in and—

Thinking about that is not going to do you any favors, Chloe. This is not one of Abigail Fox's books.

Sigh. My brain is correct.

"Chloe."

I jolt. "I'm all right. Come on. Let's go."

But he doesn't move. "I don't know if I can keep you safe in this town." His gaze trails over my face. "I tried to get to you the second he approached, but the dance floor was crowded. There wasn't a path. I had to make one. And the whole time, I was ..."

He was ... what? My fingers flex against his stomach. "It's not your fault, Freddy."

"It absolutely is. It's my job, and I shouldn't have left your side."

"I left yours, remember?" I attempt a tease, but he's still lost in his guilt, in his thoughts.

"In many ways, smaller towns are harder because you ... you just stand out far too much. I know you don't want to hear this, but it might be too risky to stay in Hallmark Beach, Chloe."

No. "You've done a great job of keeping me safe so far."

"Yeah, that's why a woman probably has pictures of you in a ridiculous dress that she could sell to the tabloids for thousands." He swallows hard, and his nose lowers a fraction more, barely brushing my own. "That's why a drunk idiot had the chance to get his hands all over you."

"I had it handled."

His lips quirk. "I'm sure you did." Then he grows serious once more. "I know you don't want me to, but I need to tell Topher—"

"Don't tell him anything. Please, Freddy."

A beat. Then, "Why does this mean that much to you? I know you want them to have their special day, but neither of them would want it to be at your expense."

A breeze tickles my cheek, a reminder that we are still outside, still in this alley, in the dark. But my whole being wants nothing more than to stay right here, for all of eternity. "Because." I don't want him to see me as weak, but honesty is the only route I've got. "I know our country doesn't think much of me. I know I'll never be good at giving public speeches that rouse a crowd, or outmaneuver a political opponent, or do much more than set fashion trends. But one thing I *am* good at is planning events, and if I can use that talent to bless the people I love the most, then ..." I shrug, at a loss for more words to explain.

He's silent for a while before speaking again. "Okay, then."

"Okay ... what?"

Frederick sighs and straightens, finally easing off the wall— and away from me. Boo. "We'll stay. But if anything else happens, I'm pulling the plug on this operation."

"All right." I shake out my hands. "Done."

"Good. And—"

The alleyway door slams open, and Frederick pushes me back up against the wall, covering my mouth with his hand.

"Chloe? You out here?"

We both breathe easier at Lucy's voice. Before Frederick can pull away, Lucy giggles. "Well, well, well."

Clearing his throat, Frederick steps away from the wall and I turn my head to find my new friend with hands on her hips, looking pointedly our way.

"I told everyone that you were fine after stupid Ricky went after you—he's a drunk bozo who hits on anything that moves. But Jordan said we should all go looking for you guys anyway."

The door opens again, and footsteps crunch in the gravelly alley. "They're here, guys," Lucy calls. "And they are a-okay. Making out, just like I said they would be."

Whistles and jokes follow, and our new friends head back in after we make our excuses and leave for the inn.

"Well, one good thing came from tonight, I suppose," Frederick finally says as we take to a very deserted Main Street.

"And what's that?"

"I think we convinced everyone we really are a couple."

"I'd say so."

He reaches for me again, brushing his fingers against mine under the glow of a streetlamp. "I think you were right."

I cock my head to the side and flash him a grin. "Ooo, go on."

"Cheeky." He smiles, shakes his head. "But I'm serious. Acting like a couple may be the only way to keep you safe right now. To act like"—his smile stretches and thins—"we're completely mad for each other."

Throat suddenly dry—I never did get that water, after all—I nod. "That way nobody is suspicious enough about our intentions to investigate why we're really here."

"Right."

We start walking again, our feet finally hitting the board-walk that leads to the inn. "There's just one thing that's bothering me," I say. "I hate lying, especially to Lucy. She's been so helpful, such a good friend already ..."

"I know what you mean. I suppose just try to think of it like we're going undercover. Lying for a purpose, and for only a short time." Frederick kicks at a pebble. "I'm not particularly worried about her, or Marilee and Jordan, to be honest. Their background checks came back clean, and my instincts tell me they're good people. The others we met tonight seem like it too, but I haven't had enough time to assess them." He drops my hand. "We got lucky with Stephanie at the dress shop today. Not everyone is as easily charmed as that."

"So what you're saying is, I'm charming." I try for a joke, but it falls short as we climb the steps of The Purple Seashell. Most of the windows are dark, though the lobby inside is warmly lit, welcoming. But I'm not ready to go inside yet. I lean against one of the porch posts and sigh. "Do you ever wish ..."

He copies my position at the opposite post, facing me. "Do I ever wish what, Princess?"

"For a normal life. Tonight, I was so ... I don't know, envious of those people in there. Able to go wherever they pleased, alone. I mean, not that I really mind having you here, but that's because it's you. If it was any other bodyguard ..." I blink an unexpected tear from my eye. "I know I've been blessed with wealth and privilege and a good family who actu-ally loves each other, and that I don't have it difficult compared to so many people suffering out there. But ..."

"But that doesn't mean your heart doesn't also wish for something so badly it hurts sometimes to breathe?"

How does he know how to put into words what I'm feeling? "Yes. Exactly that."

I bite my lip as I try to make out his features, but the porch itself is too dark for that. Somewhere behind Frederick, the ocean laps against the shore, its usual white noise diminished by our distance from it. That's how it is here, in Hallmark Beach. I know the roar of the media and the pressure that comes with my royal life is out there. It still exists. But this place, these people, have a way of diminishing their power.

Is it wrong for me to want to latch onto that for as long as I can?

"Am I ungrateful to feel this way, Freddy?"

He takes a step toward me, and his large hand cups my cheek, whisking away a tear I didn't even know had fallen. "No, Princess. It's good to dream. To think about what you want, especially after this, once you've got this wedding planned. That's important too." His words hover, like they're incomplete. He's so close, and I want him closer, but I'm afraid to move. Afraid he will remember that this is not how a bodyguard is supposed to act toward a princess.

Times like this, he treats me so differently than any other man ever has, even Troy, who I dated for two years. It's purely platonic, I know, but there's a respect, an admiration there. Fredericks's the guy who sees my hidden tears in the dark when others ignore them in the light of day.

"I sense a *but*," I whisper.

"But"—he emphasizes the word, a smile in his voice—"even if you weren't a princess, you would never be normal, Chloe Huntington."

Before I can process the absolute sweetness of his words, he steps away and holds out his hand. "Now, if you don't mind, I'd like to get some sleep. I have an incredibly comfortable blanket fort calling to me and I just cannot wait to lie down."

I snort and roll my eyes. "Your back is going to hate you by the end of this trip."

"Anything to keep you safe, Princess."

Oh, my heart. Because I know something he doesn't, and it's ironic in the extreme. It's not the Stephanies and the Rickys of the world that are the most dangerous to me.

It's Frederick Shaw, and only him.

FREDERICK

Sometimes, back in my armed forces days, I would wake up in a new, unfamiliar place, and it would take me several long moments to remember where I was.

But I think here, in this hotel room, that will never be the case, because all night long, I'm aware.

Aware she's only meters away.

Aware of every breath she takes.

Aware that it's only been two days, and I'm already failing in my resolve to keep her safe. Both from any dangers lurking out in the world ... and from the ones inside of me.

Other than the horrific sight of Chloe's eyes filled with trepidation as a large man blocked her in last night, there is nothing more torturous to me right now than lying in the same room as Chloe and not holding her while she sleeps.

Nothing.

I curl my fingers into my blanket and blink at the ceiling, counting to one hundred for the thousandth time since I woke up. It's early morning—the sky outside the window is dim but not dark. Given that the sun rises in March around seven, I'd estimate the time to be around six or possibly even earlier.

Oh, rubbish. There's no use. I sit up, because my mind will not allow me to go back to sleep. I keep replaying my conversation with Chloe last night, her words about wishing for normalcy. It had the same wistful tone I'm sure my own voice did when we discussed my love of traveling. Or my love of the idea of it, anyhow.

I used to think that it would be the best job in the world, to be a travel writer. To journey, find adventure, to just ... go. But I did always imagine a family to come home to as well.

Things, unfortunately, don't always work out the way you hope. And whenever I try to get the things I want, someone always manages to get hurt.

But Chloe—I wish things could be different for her. She deserves that kind of freedom, that kind of life.

I stand and peer down at her, the dim glow from the stars and moon allowing me to take her in. The comforter has been tossed aside, and she's lying on her back, arms and legs spread wide, taking up nearly the entire bed. Her hair is strewn across her pillow in a haphazard way she'd never allow in wakefulness, and long eyelashes brush her high cheekbones. That mouth I love to watch pouts in the most delicious way, and I ache to know what she dreams about.

Before my eyes can skim over the rest of her—including her bare legs—I turn away and head toward the restroom. But a buzzing breaks through the quiet of our room.

My mobile is vibrating.

I hurry around the bed and locate my phone plugged into the wall behind my pile of blankets on the floor. While clicking the side buttons to stop the vibrations, I glance at the Caller ID: Topher. Makes sense. After my initial arrival in Hallmark Beach, I've texted but haven't chatted with him. He likely wants an update.

I let it go to voicemail, then type in a text letting him know

I'll call him back in a minute. Once I locate a zippered jacket from my bag, I toss it on, slip on a pair of sandals, jot out a quick note to Chloe, and take my phone and my room key out the door, down the stairs through the empty lobby—guess it's too early for staff to be here yet—and out onto the front porch swing.

It's a beautiful morning, with the first rays of the sun just beginning to peek over the horizon in the pre-dawn hour. My mum once said it was the sun's way of gently nudging the moon aside, letting it know it's his turn to take a rest for the night and the sun's time to shine. The breeze coming off the ocean nips at my face, my ears, so I pull the hood of my jacket up. My athletic shorts won't do much to keep me warm, but I don't expect to be out here long.

Lowering myself onto the swing, I pull up Topher's name in my contacts and place the call.

He answers within seconds. "Hey, Fred. Everything all right? You never ignore my calls."

"Yeah, no, I just didn't want to wake Chloe—" And that's when I realize that a lack of sleep and not having my caffeine this early in the morning have done me a grave disservice. I wince at what I know is coming.

"What do you mean, wake Chloe?" Topher's voice is steel. My best mate is a rather serious chap, though Lauren has softened him greatly. Still, he wouldn't hurt a fly—not unless that fly messed with his baby sister.

Of course, I have to tell him the truth. Probably should tell him the entire truth, about the fake engagement. All of it. After all, I owe Topher my father's life. He risked his own reputation to prove my father innocent all those years ago. His own reputation and prospect as future king suffered as a result. So I owe him nothing but honesty in return.

And yet. Chloe's asked me not to say anything. And for

now, there's not a reason Topher has to know the rest, other than the fact he might be upset if he finds out later and I wasn't the one to tell him.

"I can explain, mate." I lean forward in the seat, the phone still pressed to my ear. "When I arrived, there were no other hotel rooms available. There's this festival in town, and well, I didn't really have any other options." A pause. "And of course, I'm sleeping on the floor between the bed and the door in the safest defensive position. Not that I expect any trouble while we're here." Tapping one foot against the wooden porch floor, I feel a pinch in my gut at the lie of omission. I should tell him about Stephanie. About Ricky.

But then, he might tell us to cancel the whole thing. To come back to Kentonia right away. That would crush Chloe. And it honestly is my professional opinion that those things were both flukes. We need to be careful, yes, and that will mean continuing our pretense, but I do believe Chloe can pull this off.

I don't want her feet cut out from under her—the freedom she's enjoying, however temporary, stolen from her—before she's had a chance to prove it to herself.

I can practically *hear* Topher thinking from across the pond. The silence is louder than a herd of elephants in a stampede.

Finally, "If it was any other man sharing her room, I would be on the next flight over to make sure he never walked again. But it's you, so I have no need to worry." A pause. "I *don't* have any need to worry, right?"

"Of course not." That he would even have to ask whether I would ever take advantage of the princess is almost insulting— especially given how well he knows me. And hopefully my tone of voice, which would likely be considered insubordinate except for the fact right now we're talking as friends, demonstrates that to him.

"Good."

There's more he has to say. I can feel it.

I stand up and pace—both to get the blood pumping warmth through my veins and to give me something to do other than wait. "Well? Get on with it."

"It's just ..." A grunt comes over the line. "When I told Lauren that I'd sent you along as Chloe's bodyguard, she found it amusing."

I freeze. "Amusing, how?"

"She has some ridiculous notion that you care for my sister."

"Of course I do. You know that."

"No, not as a brother would. Like a man would."

I can't tease out what he's getting at—does he *want* that to be false? True? Would he care? Would he be hurt if I told him the truth after keeping it inside after all this time? But he's the one who told me "off-limits" over a decade ago, so I assume he's just feeling out the situation, analyzing every angle with that big brain of his, trying to compute what this could mean if I truly do care for the princess as a man and not a brother.

Also ... how does Lauren know? I thought I'd been so careful to hide my true feelings. Perhaps I've been a fool, let my guard down somehow.

All I know is that confirming my feelings will do absolutely no good. Topher will likely pull me from duty, Chloe will no longer have a fake fiancé cover story, and Lauren and Topher won't get a dream wedding that's personalized to them and their tastes.

But still, I hate the idea of lying. So I go a different route. "You know me better than anyone, Toph. Do *you* think I have feelings like *that* for your sister?"

"At one time, I might have." He's careful, slow, with his words. "But no, I haven't seen any evidence of that." Then he breathes out an audible sigh.

Of relief, I presume.

My stomach flips over. Is he relieved because the idea of Chloe with *me* is so terrible? Does he think so little of me as a man of honor? Or does it have to do more with my family's reputation and how being with me would mar Chloe's?

That's what I suspect, given the fact that he trusted me enough to send me here, after all. As a bodyguard, at least, he thinks I'm good enough.

But as a potential husband for his sister? No. He likely thinks she's destined for more than being dragged down by an association with a Shaw. Even though he himself helped clear my father of all wrongdoing, the prejudice against my family still exists in our country a decade later. Documentaries have been made. Conspiracy theorists have entire podcasts related to the attempted leaking of the king's secrets to Russia and how they believe my father to be the ringleader. There have actually been signed petitions calling for me to be removed from my position in the palace because some assume I'm there to carry out the rest of my father's dastardly plans.

Topher doesn't care about any of that. He doesn't care how that gossip might affect him. And thankfully, many years later, he's managed to get the people on his side again. But his sister? He'd never want her reputation blighted by mine.

And neither do I.

"Glad we cleared that up," I say, resuming my spot on the bench and leaning back, one arm lying casually across the back of the swing. "Now, tell me how things are going there. And don't leave out a single sexy detail."

He chuckles. "Nothing sexy here, I'm afraid. My day started with a meeting with Parliament—"

"Ooo, tell me more."

"You're ridiculous."

"Just here to keep you laughing." And anything else he—or anyone in the royal family—needs.

Even if it means being the best darn fake fiancé the world has ever seen.

thirteen

CHLOE

Like all of the shops and restaurants on Main Street, The Blackberry Muffin is just as adorable inside as out, with its checker-patterned floor tiles in black and white, its bright yellow accent wall behind the register and display case, and small yellow tables adorned with silk flowers. Music floats down from somewhere over our heads, and I can't quite make out the lyrics, but the soft beat makes it feel like something romantic.

Patrons take up the tables, snacking on delectable-looking treats like muffins, donuts, American cookies, and more. A young woman, probably in her late teens, greets us, flashing her braces with a smile. "Welcome to The Blackberry Muffin. What can I get you?"

"Oh," I begin. "We're actually here to s—"

"Chloe, hi." Marilee breezes in through the swinging door behind the cashier. "You guys can come on back here."

I start back, Frederick on my heels, and when we reach the door, he pushes it open with one hand and places the other on my lower back. The contact burns right through the camisole I'm wearing, and I stupidly stop in my tracks and glance up at him. Our faces are much closer than I thought they'd be. "Thanks," I whisper.

He just looks at me for a moment, something in his gaze I don't recognize. Then he blinks and it's gone, replaced with amusement. "It's just a door, Princess."

But he knows it's more than that. He knows I'm thanking him for playing along. For not pulling the plug last night. Does he also know I'm thanking him for the chills chasing each other up my spine?

I sure hope not.

Marilee's waiting for us at a large yellow kitchen island with three black stools. "Take a seat," she says, a slight tremor in her voice. Given the fact Jordan had to prompt Marilee to tell us about her cake-making skills, I gather she's nervous for our cake-testing appointment.

I fully understand, because she's kind of our only option as far as cake-makers goes. Especially with only a week before everyone arrives.

Of course, if I don't find a venue, none of this will matter. You can't eat wedding cake or have a wedding without a place to get married.

But that's a problem for another hour. Right now, let us eat cake.

I slide onto one stool, but instead of taking the other one, Frederick stands behind me and places his hands on my shoulders. Maybe he feels like he can protect me better from this angle, his eyes on the gleaming kitchen knives stuck to a metal backsplash behind Marilee. Though if he is expecting Marilee of all people to go stab-crazy on us, I might start to question his judgment.

"I'll be right back," Marilee says as she heads for what looks to be a walk-in refrigerator.

Meanwhile, Frederick steps closer to me, his chest pressing

up against my back as he leans his hands on the counter on either side of me. Except for my front, I am completely encapsulated by him—a peninsula surrounded by the Ocean of Frederick.

It's nearly the same position I was in with Ricky last night at the Black Hole.

But it does *not* feel the same. At all.

"Is this okay?" he breathes into my hair, and every brain cell I have completely evaporates.

Okay? Okay? What is *okay* ...?

"Earth to Chloe," he teases, and it takes everything in me not to turn fully on my stool, grab his face with my hands, and kiss that saucy mouth of his into silence.

"It's okay," is all I can manage, my voice shaky. "Is it okay with you?"

His low chuckle reverberates in my ear, setting it on fire. "Just playing the part you assigned me. Am I doing well, Princess?"

Oh goodness, I am not responsible for my actions in this moment. It's his fault for being impossibly sexy. "I could think of a few ways you could improve your performance." Who even am I right now?

"Yeah? I'm all ears."

"You sure you can take a critique?" Since when did my own voice get all throaty and—dare I say—sultry? I mean, we did talk last night about upping our game when it came to convincing everyone we are together, but I did not expect him to play so hard. Not that I'm exactly complaining. "Wouldn't want to bruise that ego of yours."

"A *real* man can take critique."

I shiver at his words and open my mouth to go what will likely be one step too far, when Marilee returns with a covered platter.

"Sorry, that took longer than it should have," she huffs, struggling with the weight. She is a wisp of a thing, and the glass platter does look heavy. "I think my helper rearranged things back there this morning."

"No problem." Frederick leaves me and hurries over to help her with the platter. And while I love that he's being a gentleman, I kind of hate that it means he's gone. After he sets the platter down, he sits on the stool beside me. "Those look delicious," he says, eyeing the cakes as Marilee unwraps the options and arranges them on a cute little cake stand.

"Thank you. Obviously these are just the flavors. You can select your style from a book I've got lying around here somewhere." She frowns and glances about, then pushes her glasses up the bridge of her nose. "I swear, I'd lose my head if it wasn't attached to my body. Feel free to get started on the cake samples and I'll go take a look around." Then Marilee flits off toward a back hallway, presumably toward some sort of office.

The cake has been sliced into tiny square bites and labeled with their names. There appear to be six options ranging from chocolate and some sort of strawberry to a white cake and one that's more yellow in appearance.

"Shall we?" Frederick picks up a tiny square piece of cake, and that's when I notice Marilee forgot to give us forks. Or maybe we are intended to eat them without, since they're cut so small.

"Sure." I reach across the counter and grab the same light pink cake he's holding. "What's this flavor?"

He reads the label. "Strawberry champagne."

"Sounds divine, and like something Lauren would appreciate." Holding up my piece, I click it lightly against his like we're toasting. "Bon appétit."

"Bon appétit," he agrees before downing the cake in one bite and groaning. "Oh, that's delish."

I follow suit, popping my piece into my mouth. Moist and tender, the cake seems to melt against my tongue, its champagne flavor just subtle enough to be unique without overpowering the berry icing. "Ooo, you're so right."

Frederick selects the chocolate one next, eats it, and exclaims. "That one's even better." After snatching up another piece, he turns on his stool and his knees bump against mine. "Here, you need to try it." He holds it up toward my lips.

Like magnets, we both move slightly closer to each other. Our legs are like jigsaw puzzle pieces that fit together perfectly, sliding one every other, so I'm now both facing him and surrounded. The skin on my legs is fully covered by my trousers, and yet I feel his skin pressing against my own, burning through the jean material like it's made of flames.

He seems to realize our closeness at the same moment I do, and he doesn't look entirely unaffected—a pretense, since Marilee might come strolling in again any moment? Can a person fake the darkening of eyes that are already a delicious shade of chocolate? Or am I just seeing the reflection of the cake in Frederick's hand, the one that's still extended and hovering close to my mouth?

I blink, one, two, but he doesn't lower the cake, so I lean forward just enough to catch it in between my lips. Unfortunately—or fortunately, perhaps—I misjudge how small the piece is and end up with the tips of Frederick's fingers brushing against my mouth.

His eyes widen, but he doesn't move his hand and I don't move either, fully immersed in this dream world of our making. Any second, the episode will end, the reality will become unsuspended, but for now, in this moment, I am tasting the combination of chocolate cake and Frederick's touch.

And it is heady.

As I swallow the cake in one bite, his thumb swipes up and

across my mouth, snagging on my bottom lip for a split second too long.

I cannot breathe, not with how he's motionless and staring and leaning in to—

"You had some icing there."

His words snap the suspension of disbelief between us, grounding me on this stool. I've got whiplash upon landing, especially when he twists back in his seat and continues sampling the cakes as if nothing extraordinary just happened.

Perhaps, for him, it didn't.

What are you thinking, Chloe? Of course it didn't mean anything to him. He probably wonders why you're acting so strange toward your brother's best mate.

No, I'm not tipsy in high heels, but there I go, embarrassing myself again in front of him like I did years ago.

We finish off the rest of the samples in silence, and he finally turns and asks which one was my favorite. I want to scream CHOCOLATE at the top of my lungs, but that would be a dead giveaway.

Besides—I remind myself AGAIN for the millionth time— this is not really a cake for my own wedding. It's about Lauren. And Lauren would like the strawberry one best.

When I tell Frederick as much, he nods and stands. "Very good, then. All that's left is for you to select a cake style. Ah." His shoulders sink with what appears to be relief as Marilee comes waltzing in, binder in hand. "If you don't need me for this part, I'm going to go find the loo. I'll be right back."

Before I have a chance to answer, he flies past Marilee toward the back hallway.

She whips her head around to watch him go, then turns back to me. "Everything okay?"

I blink at his retreating back. Something is off—and it's probably the fact I was an idiot.

He knows how I feel about him. He's got to.

But I keep my back straight and just smile at Marilee. The only thing she can help me with right now is cake. "Yep." I rub my hands together. "Now, let's see what gorgeous design you're going to make for us."

"Will do." She slides the binder in front of me. "But first I wanted to tell you that I thought of somewhere you might hold the wedding."

"What? Where?"

She removes her glasses, which have flecks of white powder on them, and attempts to clean them with her also dusty apron. "My neighbor, Greta Graber, has a beautiful house on top of the hill with a decent-sized yard that overlooks the ocean. She's rented it out for small business events before and might be willing to help you out if it's available."

My heart nearly stops. "Are you serious? That sounds perfect." Secluded but beautiful. "We don't need anything big. We've got thirty, maybe forty, people coming, tops." I don't know if Father and Mother will make an appearance, but if they do, they'd bring an entire entourage as Father naturally has a much bigger security team than me or Topher.

"That should work." Marilee places her glasses back on, but even I can see the smudges reflected with the light from above. She keeps them on her face, though. "I'll give you Greta's number, but you might have better luck catching her at the festival on Saturday. She's best friends with Lucy's Aunt Bea and they'll probably be at the booth for Burt's Auto Shop since Burt is Bea's husband."

Wow. I'm having a little trouble keeping all of Lucy's relatives straight. "Why is there an auto shop booth? I thought it was a wine and art festival."

Marilee pops open the front of the binder. "That's Hallmark Beach for you. They'll cluster together the art and wine booths—wineries from all over West Coast come to represent—but every shop on Main Street will also have a booth. Nobody wants to feel left out." She shrugs. "Burt says the vendors get the best seat in the house, a chance to people watch and interact with them. Have you met him yet?"

"I don't think so."

"Oh, you'd know if you had." Marilee chuckles. "He's a character. But a good man too. He and Bea took Lucy in after ..." She shuts her lips. "Well, that's her story to tell. But just know that if you can't get ahold of Greta before tomorrow, you should find her at Burt's booth."

"You're a lifesaver, Mar. Thank you so much."

"I'm so happy to help. Oh, one more thing." She flips past the binder's first page and any nerves I had over Marilee's ability to deliver a beautiful cake are squashed with the picture in front of me: a cake made to look like a present, with lace, pearls, and flowers instead of a bow up top. "Elisse and Kelsey are having some ladies over tonight for appetizers and wine. Their brothers will be busy loading up and prepping the wine for the festival tomorrow, but Elisse and Kelsey's parts are done until the actual festival. So would you like to come hang out with us?"

How is it that I have lived in Kentonia my whole life and, other than Lauren and her friends, have never felt included and welcomed into a group so quickly? The fact they don't know I'm a princess and just know I'm Chloe squeezes my heart all the more. "I'd love to." But drat. "I'd hate to leave Frederick behind, though. He doesn't know anyone else here ..."

Marilee smiles. "I could see if Jordan's free." Then she snaps. "Oh shoot, I forgot he's got a thing with Ryder's other grandparents tonight."

Other grandparents? Oh. The parents of whoever Ryder's mom is. Again I itch to ask more questions, but I need to focus right now on the immediate plans. Frederick will never let me leave by myself tonight, but I want to go. And it's no longer because I need the locals to give me information.

It's because ... well, I like them. A lot. I like who I am with them.

Myself.

I *don't* like that I'm lying to them, but hopefully they'll understand why when I'm allowed to reveal all. Hopefully I can keep things vague enough that they know what I did share with them was the truest version of myself I was allowed to be. But it requires figuring out a way for Frederick to accompany me.

Then an idea strikes. "You said the Loveland brothers will be loading crates tonight?"

"Yes. Why?"

Here's hoping Frederick doesn't kill me for this suggestion. "Do you think they need another pair of hands?"

I love Kentonia, don't get me wrong. It's beautiful with its mountain ranges, its thriving fishing industry, its beautiful harbor.

It's where my family is. Where my people are. And it's home.

But I didn't choose it.

And if I wasn't a royal, wasn't obligated to return so I could see what marriage prospects my parents would throw my way next ... I'm not sure I would.

Then again, maybe if I wasn't royal, I would want to.

Either way, sitting here on the back deck of the Lovelands' home, staring out over the rows of grapes that lead to rolling green hills in the distance, I know one thing: I am blessed to be here, and I wouldn't want to be anywhere else in this moment.

"Anyone want a top off?" From her place on the white wicker loveseat, Kelsey holds up a bottle of her family's wine, with its bright yellow label.

"Hit me up!" Lucy rocks forward in one of the Adirondack chairs in our little circle, where Elisse, Marilee, and I are sharing a couch with tasteful blue cushions that matches the shorter love seat.

Kelsey pours a ribbon of dark red liquid, finishing off the cabernet, some of which is currently in my glass. "Anyone else?"

The rest of us are still working on our first glasses, so we refuse a refill, and chatter resumes as the women gossip about the latest goings on in town. A fire pit table sits in the middle of our circle, flicking heat our way in an attempt to combat the cool evening breeze. I tug my sweater closed as I lean forward and take up my plate filled with wonderful goodies from the charcuterie board in the kitchen: a selection of fancy meats, cheeses, and crackers, as well as olives and grapes. And, not that I need the calories after the cake testing today, but I've also grabbed a white chocolate cookie that Marilee made.

I pick that up first and sit back against the cushion. In the distance, the sun has begun to set behind the hills, but it's not so dim that I can't clearly see a group of guys loading up three pickup trucks. The group includes four of the six Loveland brothers—who are all well-built and handsome—and Frederick, who actually seemed happy to come tonight. Perhaps he needed to do some manual labor. After all, he's been hindered from completing his normal workout routine, which has to be quite rigorous to create the bulging muscles I currently see on display under his tight T-shirt as he lifts crate after crate of wine into the truck.

When he wipes his brow with the back of his forearm, my insides swoop at the sight of his triceps on full display.

"Enjoying the view, are we?" Elisse pokes me in the side, and I nearly drop my cookie.

All the women giggle.

"It's quite lovely." I know she's teasing me about watching the guys, but I pretend to be oblivious as I point to the sweeping landscape. Besides the open land extending from the end of the vineyard to the hills, there's this main house—two stories and completely lovely, a mix of modern and classic—as well as another building Frederick and I passed on our way in. And on one side sits the underground cellar cut out of the side of a hill where the Lovelands store their wine. "How long has this winery been in your family?"

"Our grandparents bought the land for our parents when they got married," Elisse says as she steals a cracker off my plate. I love that she feels comfortable enough to do that. Then again, maybe she simply has no sense of shame. "Our parents basically built it from the ground up. It was always Dad's dream to do that, so Mom went along with it." She stuffs the cracker in her mouth.

Marilee frowns into her glass. "That's hard, when one spouse calls all the shots."

Sounds as if she's speaking from experience, and if the scowl on Lucy's face is any indication, there's definitely a story there.

But I shift the focus back to the Lovelands, turning to Kelsey, who is cute and put together tonight in an adorable green baggy jumpsuit over a white tank, her brown hair in relaxed curls that fall to her shoulders. (And PS, I need to find out where she got her clothes—along with her long, boho fringe necklace—but I digress.) "And what did your mom want to do?"

"She always dreamed of putting up cabins along the

perimeter of the vineyard, running it like a resort, holding events, that sort of thing."

"Ah, like you do at The Purple Seashell."

She pinches her chin between her thumb and the middle knuckle of her pointer finger. "Well, I don't own The Purple Seashell, but Janine's talked about retiring soon. So it's possible I'll get promoted to the main manager someday. I have a lot of ideas for how she could improve—"

"Boring!" Elisse tosses a cracker—not the one from her mouth, but a new one she takes from her own plate—at her sister. "We all know you have your brilliant business mind, Kels, but what we really need to talk about now is Chloe and this wedding."

Kelsey laughs good-naturedly, but I can't help but wonder if her sister's big personality might be hard for her. I wait for her to look at me, and then flash her a sympathetic smile.

She smiles back. "Yes, I'd love to hear all about your plans so far. Any luck with a venue yet?"

"No, but thanks to Marilee, we finally have a lead." I explain about the Graber house.

"Ooo, come and find me tomorrow at The Green Robin's booth and I'll take you over to meet Greta and my aunt and uncle," Lucy says. "Uncle Burt's heard all about you and said any friend of Shelby's is a friend of his. He wants to meet you guys."

"I forgot you said he knew Shelby." So why didn't we meet him when we were here to finalize details of Shelby's wedding?

"Yes," Lucy nods so enthusiastically that her wine nearly spills over the rim of her glass. "And he was so sad he and Bea were out of town when she came by to see him last week. He's actually the very first one to meet Shelby and Eric—who was not yet her fiancé—when their car broke down on the way to somewhere else."

Ah yes, I've heard the story. Back when Shelby and Eric were just best friends. How Hallmark Beach was where they first admitted their love for each other.

"Guess there's just something about this place that calls to all the lovers out there." Marilee gives me a wink. "So once you get a venue, you'll have everything sorted?"

"Maybe. It depends on whether the venue offers food packages or if I need to hunt down a catering option."

Lucy groans. "I know for a fact Greta usually recommends the Robin for any events at her place, but Tiny's got a big catering order next weekend already."

Drat. I frown. "Well, if you ladies can think of anywhere else that caters ..."

Marilee chews on her thumbnail. "How formal does it need to be?"

"At this point, I'd take any recommendations."

"Don't even think about suggesting it." Lucy points at her best friend and scowls. "He wouldn't come back anyway. He made his choice."

"I wouldn't be asking him to come back permanently," Marilee says. "Just for the wedding."

"That's a long way to come." Folding her arms across her chest, Lucy fixes Marilee with a stare.

I'm really and truly lost. "Who are we talking about?"

Marilee flinches at the very un-Lucy-like glare on Lucy's face and moves her attention to me. "My brother, Blake."

"Or Flake, as we like to call him."

"*You* like to call him," Elisse says. She turns to me and mouths quite obviously, *She's obsessed with him.*

Now Lucy's pools of rage that used to be eyes are directed at the sofa. "You take that back, Elisse Loveland."

"What? It's true. We all know you had a major crush on him in high school."

"I most certainly did *not*." Lucy throws her hands into the air, apparently forgetting her wine glass. Wine splashes all over the fire pit, sending a wave of hissing flames into the air. "Why would I like a jerk like him?" Yikes. I've never seen Lucy so worked up. Didn't even know it was possible, but apparently her best friend's brother can bring it out in her.

Marilee sinks down into her seat, but then turns away from Lucy back toward me. "Anyway, he has a food truck down in Los Angeles. I can see if he's free if you're interested."

"Oh, that would be great. Thanks so much."

"Of course. I'm just so impressed that you have gotten as much done as you have in such a short time."

"What can I say? I'm good at planning parties." I finally take a bite of the cookie in my hand. Ooo. It's divine. The creamy white chocolate is satisfying, but leaves me wanting more.

"Maybe you should take over for Rhonda then," Elisse says as she snatches up another bottle of wine sitting on the edge of the fire pit.

"What do you mean, take over for Rhonda?" Marilee's eyebrows go up.

"Yeah, what are you talking about?" Lucy demands.

Elisse stops working the cork. "Don't tell me you guys didn't hear?" A quiet pause brings the cicadas calling, answering her question. "Rhonda and Huck eloped. She's putting the shop up for sale and moving to L.A. with him."

"What?" The women break out into chaos, asking questions over each other, Elisse attempting to answer them.

"I don't know much more than that." The breeze ruffles the edges of her long hair as she holds up her hands. "Only that she asked if I wanted to buy it and I said no way."

"I thought you loved working there." Marilee fidgets with her glasses.

"Eh, it was fine, but I quickly got tired of brides complaining about the most trivial things when there are real problems happening in the world." She turns to me. "But you would be perfect. People like you, and you've clearly got a brain for planning. Want to move to America and leave your job—" Then Elisse squints at me. "Wait, what is it you do now? And where do you live?" A pause. "Why don't I know much about you yet?"

The cookie sours in my stomach.

Marilee laughs. "That's so funny. I don't know hardly anything about you either, Chloe, but I feel like I've known you forever. How is that possible?"

I chuckle, praying they can't hear the pounding of my heart. "Guess I don't like talking about myself. I'm more interested in you all." And I'm realizing something—I'm a terrible liar. Because I'm about to spill all the tea right now with nary a nudge of my teacup.

The thing is, it's been easy in many ways to fake it with Frederick, because I have real feelings for him. And I've been able to be vague enough so far about the wedding and who we are. But if these ladies persist in asking me specific questions, and I have to make something up ... ugh. No. I can't do it.

I won't.

The good thing is, I trust them—every single one, even Elisse, who likely rubs some people the wrong way.

Oh boy. This is going to require some stamina, so I down the rest of my wine and polish off Marilee's delicious cookie. Then I open my mouth to tell everyone the truth and—

Headlights swing around the bend, coming toward our grouping of vehicles beside the house. We all turn our heads around to see who's headed down the unpaved road. Gravel pops beneath the tires of a hot pink Volkswagen Bug.

"Aw, you invited Steph," Lucy says.

I freeze. Steph? As in ... Stephanie?

But no, surely there is more than one Steph, even in a small town. It's a common enough name.

"Yeah," Kelsey replies. "I was in today buying a new outfit and we hadn't chatted in a while. She mentioned how much she was looking forward to stopping by and getting some of our wine at the festival so—"

"So you invited her here." Elisse rolls her eyes. "Well, ladies. Hope you've said all you're going to say, because no one else will get a chance to talk the rest of the night."

"Be nice to my cousin," Lucy warns.

Wait, Stephanie is Lucy's cousin? Oh no. What if she reveals the truth to her about me before I get a chance? This is so not ideal.

Sure enough, the boutique shop employee I met just yesterday—i.e., the only one in town with the knowledge of my true identity—steps from the car, along with a woman with shoulder-length red hair wearing jeans and a baggy T-shirt. The sound of the shutting car doors might as well be the slamming of my heart against my chest.

Maybe even the slamming of the door to some true friendships made in Hallmark Beach.

"Hey, ladies!" Dressed in a black harem jumpsuit paired with a long red waistcoat (what others might call a *vest*) that nearly reaches her ankles, along with chunky yellow wedges that I am tempted to steal right off her feet, Stephanie is carrying a platter of brownies as she comes up the steps to the wooden deck. This woman doesn't let her petite stature dictate her personality, and she is loud and in charge.

I would take the time to admire her if her very presence didn't scare me.

"Look what the cat dragged in." She hooks a thumb at the redhead, who offers a bright smile and a wave. There's definitely a family resemblance between them. Something in their eyes and noses.

"April!" Lucy exclaims as she rushes the new woman and pulls her into a hug. "I didn't know you were coming into town! Is Scarlet with you?"

"It was a last-minute thing." April laughs and pats Lucy's back before pulling away. "And yeah, she's at the house regaling her nana and papa with tales of first-grade girl drama." Her eyes scan the group before she quirks an eyebrow at me. "Hi. I don't think we've met. I'm April Reynolds, Lucy's cousin and Stephanie's sister."

"Chloe. Nice to meet you."

And that's when Stephanie must first see me, because her jaw drops. "Chloe, hi."

"Oh, you guys have met?" Lucy asks.

Stephanie's eyes dart between me and Lucy, then to the fire. She laughs, but it comes out all staccato and raspy. "Uh, yeah, she ..." Her eyes find mine and they widen—as if she's asking me what's okay to say and not say. Then she holds the brownies out to Elisse, who takes them.

"What, did you help her commit murder or something?" Elisse sets the brownies down along the table portion of the fire pit. "Not often we see you at a loss for words."

"No, ha, that's funny, Elisse." Stephanie puts her large yellow bag down on the empty Adirondack chair. "She ... um ..."

Oh, for goodness's sake. "I came in yesterday to find a dress for the wedding."

Stephanie's shoulders slump with relief. "Yes, that. She did that." The woman sounds like a broken record about to jam up and never work again.

"Why are you acting so weird?" Lucy wrinkles her nose at Stephanie as she sinks back into her own chair.

"Um, I'm not ..." Stephanie bites her lip, sits, then stands again. "Chloe, would you mind ... can we talk for a minute? In private?"

Yeah, that's not suspicious at all. But how can I say no now? "Of course."

Just please don't blow my cover.

FREDERICK

This is exactly what I needed today.

Grunting, I squat and use my quads to lift yet another wine crate. My legs burn with the effort, but it's a good burn. It's the burn of muscles that need to be worked, if for no other reason than that they've become a conduit for pent-up emotion. And I will lift crate after crate after crate until my arms and legs fall off if that's what it takes to dispel what's raging inside of me.

Because I nearly kissed Chloe today.

I don't know what I was thinking—honestly, I wasn't. When my eyes narrowed in on that icing left on her lips by the chocolate cake, it was all I could do not to lean in and lick it off.

Sure, I was able to play it off as part of our fake engagement ruse. But on the inside, my heart warred with my head until my brain eventually won—and I retreated like a soldier being chased on the battlefield to the hallway to get my heart on straight.

"Holy heck, dude." Nathaniel, the youngest of the Loveland brothers—and also the tallest—slaps me on the back as I push in my last crate. "You're a freaking beast."

"Yeah, you sure you don't want to stick around and come

work here?" Malcolm, one of the middle brothers, leans back against the cab of the truck. He barely lifted a finger tonight, though he's got the muscles to show he could've if he'd wanted to. "A workhorse like you would make a fantastic cellar rat."

"Stop trying to give away your job." His oldest brother, Oliver, walks up to Malcolm—who's wearing nice jeans, a button-up black shirt, and boots—and sticks a crate into his gut. "And work a little, why don't you." Scowling, he storms off toward the underground cellar.

Malcolm rolls his eyes. "I'm leaving for a date soon!" he yells at Oliver's retreating back. "Getting my best shirt all dirty," he mutters under his breath as he walks to the back end of the truck and slides the crate in with ease. Then he winks at me again. "Seriously, though. You ever want to give up police work to come do menial labor with few benefits and long hours, you just give us a ring." Then he finger guns me and stalks off toward the house.

I allow my gaze to wander back to Chloe, who's sitting and laughing with the women across the yard. I'm not surprised they've taken her into their fold.

"Aw, don't mind him." Nathaniel walks over and hops onto the lowered tailgate. "He's just grouchy because he hates being stuck in this dinky town. His words, not mine. I love it here."

"I see." I run a hand through my hair and tug on my shirt to create some airflow. Thankfully, the night air is cool and soon begins to dissipate the sweat on my brow. "Why doesn't he just leave then?"

"Oh, he tried. Not sure why he came back, but apparently he couldn't hack it. Not like Flynn and Adam. Though now that I think about it, nobody knows exactly where Flynn is. Good guy, but he's one of those drifter types." Apparently Nathaniel doesn't have a filter. But he's genuine, and I like him. Not only that, but his chatter keeps my brain busy so that I don't dwell on how gorgeous Chloe looks in her leggings and oversized shirt with a high-waisted belt that she's somehow made look extremely sexy.

Then again, I'm pretty sure she'd look sexy in a potato sack. So there's that.

"Shew, man, you've got it baaaaad." Nathaniel pokes me with his booted foot just as his brothers—Oliver and Dallas, who's still muscular but on the leaner side with a blond man bun and a clear affinity for music with his Beatles T-shirt—lug the final two crates of wine out into the open.

Once they load them in, Oliver smacks Nathaniel lightly upside the head until he jumps down and snaps the tailgate shut. Then Oliver turns to me, hand outstretched. "Thanks for your help, man. You're welcome anytime."

"Thanks for the work out. Other than walking everywhere so we can plan the wedding, I've had no exercise."

Oliver's eyebrows lift, and it looks like he's going to say something when car headlights flood the deck leading from the house. He squints through the darkness until the lights click off, then mutters, "What's *she* doing here?" and turns on his heel, hauling rear back to the cellar.

"Who's *she*?" I try to make out the figure as two women climb the steps, one wearing a bright red and black outfit. That one looks vaguely familiar, but the waning light hasn't done me any favors in being able to recognize her from this distance.

"Oh, nobody," Dallas says. "Just Oliver's old girlfriend. Stephanie Reynolds."

The hairs on the back of my neck stand on end. Stephanie. Not her again. Is she stalking Chloe? "I need to g—"

"Here." Oliver's back and he's handing out a round of cold water bottles. "Drink up. It's not that hot, but you can still get dehydrated out here." The man clearly takes his job as vineyard manager very seriously.

"Thanks." I uncap the water and take a guzzle, the plastic creaking under my fingers as I do. Then I glance over at Chloe again.

But she's gone.

Both her ... and Stephanie.

I've been distracted and now she might be in trouble. "Sorry," I say. "Where's the loo?"

"Just through the deck doors, past the kitchen, and on the right," Nathaniel says after chugging his entire bottle of water. He wipes his mouth with the inside collar of his white shirt.

"Thanks." I take off at a clipped pace toward the house, but instead of heading for the four women still sitting on the deck, I go north along the house's perimeter, keeping an ear cocked for Chloe's voice. In this moment, I know it's likely an overreaction, but I wish I could reach for my firearm that I'm allowed to wear at home and on official visits to the States, but don't have the clearance to wield on this particular trip.

Finally, I hear voices coming from around the side of the house, so I slow my pace and inch toward the corner of the structure, peeking around the edge when I arrive. Thanks to large floodlights fastened to the sides of the house, I can see both women standing beside a lovely home garden with an abundance of flowers planted in old wine barrels. Thankfully, Chloe looks at ease where she leans back against a full-sized barrel that hasn't yet been transformed into a planter, arms casually folded across her chest. "It's fine, Stephanie. Truly."

The other woman paces, though how she doesn't trip in those platform shoes is beyond me. "I just didn't expect to see you, so I was flustered."

"It happens." Chloe's voice is soothing as she smiles.

"I haven't told anyone who you really are, I promise."

"And we appreciate that so much."

Stephanie frowns, and cocks her head. She plays with one

of her orange dangling earrings. "Okay, so don't kill me, but after you left, I looked you up." A pause. "Well, not you, but Frederick."

My toes tingle inside my trainers.

Chloe bites her lip, but doesn't say a word. Like any pro on trading secrets, she's waiting to see what information Stephanie already has.

The other woman starts pacing again. "You mentioned he was a bodyguard, and I realized that's how I recognized him. Did you know there's a ton of podcasts out there about his—"

"I'm aware." Chloe's tone has gone slightly icy.

"Oh, I didn't mean any disrespect." Stephanie's eyes go wide, and she tries to curtsy again. The result is just as disastrous, if not more because Stephanie stumbles a bit in her shoes before righting herself. "It's just that, he's kind of the last guy in the world your family would ever let you marry."

I grimace at the bald-faced truth, out there for Chloe's ears.

As for Chloe, the only visible sign of distress is her fingers digging into her side.

Stephanie continues rambling. "Um, and I know this is probably a huuuuuge stretch, but I've read the rumors about how soon-to-be Princess Lauren isn't happy with all the arrangements for the royal wedding." She pauses and studies Chloe, who could be winning at hiding her emotions if this was a poker game. "Well, it got me thinking ... like, what if you were actually planning a second wedding for Topher and you and Frederick are just pretending to be engaged?"

Oh no. There it is. Stephanie's got it figured out, and there's literally nothing I can do to stop her from spreading the truth. We're done here. We have to be. If she tells the world what's happening, paparazzi will show up—and then it will be impossible to keep Chloe safe. Impossible for there to be a wedding.

We never had much chance that this would completely work out, but there was always a chance.

Now, though? We're sunk.

And, given the emotion finally seeping into Chloe's features—a trembling lip, one hand massaging the opposite upper arm—she knows it too.

"What do you mean are she and Frederick pretending?" Lucy comes around the corner of the house opposite me, eyeing Stephanie with a disbelieving tilt of her chin.

Chloe freezes and blinks, her whole body stiffening. I know she hates this lying. And now, she's been caught in it.

I need to get her out of here. Just go in there and lead her away, straight to the inn to pack our bags and then to the airport to fly home. But I see how much she's come to care for the women here, and it feels almost cruel to end it so abruptly.

Maybe there's a way to salvage this. *Think, man, think.*

Stephanie's face has gone a bit red and she's sputtering. "Well, I just ..." She glances at Chloe, who is staring at the ground now.

"Chloe? Everything okay?" Lucy marches over to Chloe and slips an arm around the princess, squeezing her shoulders before letting her go and advancing on Stephanie. "Shame on you for your accusations. I know you like reading tabloids and sensational stories, Steph, but not everything is a conspiracy theory."

"I don't think that!" Stephanie scoffs. "There are just a few ... discrepancies I saw in the few minutes I spent with Chloe and Frederick." At least she's not completely outing us, but still. "And I just—"

"Okay, you've spent a few minutes with them, but I've spent a few days, and it only actually takes a few seconds to see that they're head-over-heels in love." She shakes her finger at Stephanie. "You should have seen that man rip Ricky Jenkins off of Chloe last night at the bar. I thought he was going to commit actual murder. He's so in love with her I'd find it disgusting if it wasn't so adorable and awe-inspiring."

Now Chloe looks like she's going to cry. She's about to crack.

And suddenly, I know what I have to do. This moment perhaps can be saved. I just have to put aside every doubt I have, stuff them down deep, deep, deep.

Shoulders back, I saunter around the side of the house. "Hey there, ladies."

All three shoot their gazes at me, but Chloe's is the only one I care about. It looks like a mix between relief and regret. "Hey," she says weakly. "You guys all done?"

"Yeah. Did you miss me?" I wink as I draw closer to her.

"Mmm-hmm." She's trying for a smile, but it's not all the way there.

And I can feel Lucy's and Stephanie's eyes on me. I've got my audience primed and ready to watch.

To be convinced.

Stepping in front of Chloe, I loop my arms around her waist. It feels so small beneath my palms, so delicate—but strong too. "Sorry if I smell."

Her smile softens into something real, and she moves her hands up around my neck, where her fingers brush at the bottom of my hairline. Her subtle vanilla perfume wafts under my nose, drowning out the array of floral scents surrounding us. "I'm used to it."

My fingers tighten around her and shift up her back as I take another step nearer. Her eyes blink at me, curiosity rimming her irises—but there's also trust there.

She trusts me, and I pray what I'm about to do doesn't break that trust. I pray that it enhances it.

Leaning in so close I can feel her tremble beneath me, I set my lips against the outer shell of her ear. "Hi." Then I press a light kiss there.

She inhales sharply at the contact.

And saints, the subtlest taste of her skin is not enough. I breathe in a tiny kick of air, force the stampeding horses inside of me to stay steady, stay slow.

"Hi-i," she chokes out in surprise, her grip pulling me forward, an indication that she's okay with this.

Whatever it takes to sell our love story, right?

Just do it, man.

I straighten and tuck a loose strand of hair behind her ear before finally doing the thing I've longed to do for nearly twelve years.

I kiss Chloe Huntington.

When our lips meet, soft and hesitant and hovering at first, we both draw deep breaths. I hope I'm not making her nervous or uncomfortable, so I pull back slightly and remain still, letting her come back to me if she wants to.

And she does. This time, our mouths are more sure, and as one of her hands slides down my chest, she grips my shirt and tugs as if she's as lost in this moment as I am. One hand still pressed against her back, my other supports her head as she cranes her neck upward. My thumb strokes along the bottom of her jaw and I slant my mouth against hers, plunging deeper into the abyss as I savor every angle of her kiss.

She tastes like wine and sunshine, like every flower petal opening and every chocolate morsel melting into pure sweetness against my tongue.

This sampling will never be enough.

But it's all I'll ever have. And I plan to make it count.

"What did I tell you?" comes a voice behind us.

I freeze. Chloe's eyes blink away the haze, and I have a feeling mine are doing the same. Her lips are slightly swollen, and that does things to my brain I can't even comprehend. I want nothing more than to swoop back in, to see if I can drive her as wild as she's driving me.

I never want to stop kissing this woman.

Wait, why *did* we stop kissing? We should always be kissing. Kissing is good.

"Do you believe they're really in love now, Stephanie?" a voice taunts.

Oh. Right. We have an audience.

Pressing a final kiss against Chloe's forehead, I turn to face Lucy and Stephanie, slipping an arm around Chloe's shoulders. "You didn't believe I loved this woman?" I say in the most incredulous manner I can manage. (Rubbish actor over here, remember?)

Stephanie fists her long waistcoat thing in her hand. "I just ..." She pouts. "Well, clearly I was wrong."

Yes, Stephanie. Clearly you were.

fifteen

CHLOE

I've been complete rubbish today at anything having to do with wedding planning.

All I can think about is that kiss. The way Frederick took charge, but also gave me a choice. The way he held me like I was the most precious gem in the world, but also handled me like he wanted to break me open. A whole day later, I still shiver thinking about it.

"You need to wipe that lovesick grin off your face, chickadee." Lucy tuts at me as we walk along Main Street, where a plethora of different colored awnings and tented canopies dot the closed-off road. Pedestrians mill about, collecting wine samples, cake samples, coffee samples, you name it. It's a beautiful afternoon, bright and clear with a bit of extra warmth that feels like a hug.

"I don't know what you're talking about." But of course, I do. I peek back at Frederick, who's walking along at a good distance behind us with Jordan and Ryder. He's laughing at something Ryder's saying, but I know he's always got one eye on me, making sure I'm safe. He's such a good man, and last night, I allowed myself to get lost in the fantasy. I know that, despite what Lucy said last night, Frederick's just playing a role —he confirmed as much on our drive home from the winery.

"I hope I didn't take things too far," he said.

Too far? Not far enough was more like it. "No," I managed. "It was all right." I nearly kicked myself at the gross understatement because that was like saying breathing is "kind of" important to sustaining life.

That kiss ... it was pure euphoria and the barest whisper of a dream—one I only got to live for a few suspended moments in time.

Because it was over far too quickly.

"Good." He glanced over at me as he turned onto Main Street. "It's just that I thought Stephanie needed convincing of our feelings for each other. Our fake feelings, I mean."

Fake feelings. Right. The good thing is that she was most definitely convinced. The bad thing? I nearly was too. Because I'm not sure someone can manufacture a great kiss like that. But even if Frederick feels a little bit of attraction for me, he's clearly committed to the crown. I wish I knew why he's given up on his dreams of traveling to work this job. Maybe someday, he'll tell me.

I sigh.

Lucy's elbow finds my side with a playful jab. "Oy, girl, we need to get you married off." She fans her face as we dodge around an elderly couple holding hands and toddling along like there's nothing more important in that moment than experiencing the world together. "I can feel the heat between the two of you coming from a mile away."

I force a smile. I should be glad that we've been so convincing, but I only feel sad that I can't tell her the truth. Not only could I use someone to talk to, but I don't want to lie anymore. Not to any of the ladies, really, but especially to Lucy, who started this whole thing with me.

We leave the food section, where I picked up Lucy from The Green Robin's booth that's serving a limited menu of sliders, chicken tenders, and chips (or french fries, as my American friends call them), and enter the section where vendors have art on display. Photos, paintings, jewelry, hand-painted ornaments … it's all quite lovely. After talking with Greta Graber, I may need to come back here and do some shopping.

"Thanks for coming with me to meet Greta." Marilee was right and all of my calls have gone straight to voicemail. "Here's hoping she has some good news for me, because otherwise the wedding might have to happen at the tiny public park at the top of the hill," I joke.

"Well, would that be so bad? There's always the beach too. Why don't you guys want to do it there?"

I can't very well tell her that it's too public—she wouldn't understand.

Ugh. I just can't do this anymore. I'm not someone who is built to lie, and even if it's for a good reason, it's just not sitting well with me. I glance back at Frederick again. His distance means he can't hear exactly what I'm saying right now, and he's talking with Jordan anyhow.

Shaking out my hands, I prepare to tell Lucy the truth. "Lu—"

"Here we are." She points to a very plain booth—just a folding table and chairs with no covering and a tacked on, hand-written sign that says *Burt's Auto*. Three people in their late fifties, maybe early sixties, sit there. The two women drink glasses of white wine, while the man—a gray-haired, stooped chap with glasses and leathery skin wearing mechanic's dungarees—tosses back a beer. "Hey, guys."

At Lucy's greeting, they all look up. The women both say "Hello, dear" and the man jumps up, rounds the table, and picks her off the ground in a giant squeeze.

She pats his shoulder, laughing. "It's only been three hours since I saw you at home, Uncle Burt."

"I know, darlin', but I gotta hug you like this in public, so everyone knows you're my favorite niece." His accent is much stronger than Lucy's, but just as peppy.

"I'm your only niece," she deadpans.

"Not true. I've got that one on Bea's side who lives in Io-Way."

Haven't heard of that place. I scrunch my nose.

"And by that he means Iowa," she says to me. "Uncle Burt, this is my friend Chloe."

"Burt Reynolds—not the actor—at your service." He bows to me, then grabs me up into the same kind of embrace he held Lucy in. "Lucy's told us all about you."

Oh, he's brilliant. "Pleased to meet—"

"Chloe?" Frederick's by my side in an instant. "Everything okay?"

"It's fine," I say as Burt releases me. "Frederick, this is Burt."

The man turns to Frederick and assesses him, then breaks into a big grin and snags his hand lightning quick, pumping it up and down. Given his furrowed brow, Frederick's still trying to process whether this man is a threat. I poke him in the side and give a tiny shake of my head along with a grin when he looks my way.

"Do you have any candy, Auntie Bea?" Ryder darts around us all and straight to the table where the women are sitting. He addresses the woman who had been closest to Burt. She's got gray hair that falls to a pair of wide shoulders.

"Well, shoogs, I most likely do." She tugs a giant bag from the ground at her feet onto the table and palms through it with her large hands, pulling out a wilted flower pen, a handkerchief, a bottle of Butt Paste that looks like it's been around for a while, and a pack of earplugs before finally locating a zippered bag of gummy bears. "Is it all right if he has some?" she asks Jordan.

"Sure," Jordan gives a thin smile. His eyes look tired today. "He's already had a couple donuts but what's a little more sugar?"

"There you go, my sweet." Bea hands him the candy and he skips back to Jordan. "Now, who are you lovely newcomers? I didn't hear your introductions because Greta here was gabbing my ear off."

It was definitely Bea herself doing the talking, but nobody corrects her.

"Aunt Bea, these are my friends Frederick and Chloe, the couple that's getting married next weekend. Guys, this is Aunt Bea. She and Uncle Burt are Stephanie and April's parents. They've also got my oldest cousin Jeff, who lives out of state. He's married with four kiddos."

"Pleasure," Frederick says as he takes her hand and covers both of their hands with his other.

Bea lifts her brows and giggles. "Well, ain't you a charmer. Don't you think, Greta? Oh, y'all, this is Greta Graber, my best friend since grade school."

Greta's much more petite than Bea, and if we're going off appearances alone, I can sense she's more demure, more refined, with her nice trousers and pressed blouse, compared to Bea's thick jeans and cotton-blend shirt. Greta's hair is more silver than gray, and the cut is smooth and trendy. She nods our way. "Nice to meet you."

I step forward, my stomach in knots. "So nice to meet you both as well."

"What purty accents, don't ya think, Bea?" Burt bounces back behind the "booth" and takes a seat. "Now, what can we do ya for? Do ya need a tune-up on your vehicle?" He tilts his head, narrows his eyes, strokes his chin that's peppered with gray and black stubble. "You look like a Jeep man yourself. Do y'all even have Jeeps wherever you're from?"

Frederick laughs. "I've just got a rental at the moment, but at home we have all the vehicles. And"—he leans in as if intimating a great secret—"we even drive on the right proper side of the road."

His shoulders loosen as he slips a hand into mine. I nearly sigh at the contact—it's the first we've had since we left the winery yesterday.

"I thought you'se people in England all drove on the left." Burt scratches behind his ear.

"They're from Kentonia, Uncle Burt, not England," Lucy says.

Frederick squeezes my hand, an assurance—it's okay. We can trust these people. I turn to him, surprised. But his eyes remain on the others.

Maybe he won't care if I decide to tell Lucy. Maybe Marilee too. Heck, all of the ladies I've come to know and—quickly—love here in Hallmark Beach. It's my secret, after all. And Frederick's on my side.

Then again, that would mean that all of his efforts last night might be wasted. Well, I suppose not. Stephanie still thinks we are an item, which will throw her off the ridiculous —and very true—notion that it's Topher's wedding I'm planning.

"Ms. Greta, Chloe and Fred here have a favor to ask of you." Lucy folds her hands together under her chin in a pleading motion. I shoot her a look of thanks, and she winks back at me. "I've gotta get back to the Robin's booth, but just know that I vouch completely for them."

Without waiting for a response, Lucy flits off down the street. I'll have to tell her the truth later, though I'm not sure when. She said she'll be working the festival all weekend, opening to close. The woman never rests.

Greta drums her fingers on the table. "What can I do for you two?"

I glance at Frederick and he finally looks back at me. Nods for me to go on. "We've heard wonderful things about your home as a potential wedding venue—"

"I've never held weddings there. Only a few corporate events."

"Right. Well, we're kind of in a bind right now. The wedding is supposed to be next weekend, but we don't have a venue yet."

"Oh, my." Bea's hand flutters against her chest and she begins stuffing things back into her purse.

Greta narrows her eyes at us a bit. "Why didn't you secure something before this?"

"Um, well ..." I don't like it when people look at me so suspiciously. It's not something I'm used to.

"It's last minute because I couldn't go another day without making this woman my wife." Frederick lifts my hand, kisses it. All my nerves explode, and his gaze melts into me. Times like this, it's so easy to forget this is all fake.

They make me wonder ... what if?

Bea sighs and jabs Burt in the side. "Ain't that sweet, Burt?"

"Course it is."

"Then why ain't you sighing too?"

"Come off it, woman." Burt says this in a syrupy tone. He might as well be saying *I adore you* or *you're beautiful*. "Just let me observe their love story. They remind me of us when we were young, don't they?"

"He looks at her the way you look at me, darn tootin'."

They nuzzle noses.

Meanwhile, Greta's still inspecting us, and the woman is a

vault, locked up, her feelings hidden. "My house isn't cheap." She names her price—steep, for sure, but not terribly extreme, especially given the last-minute nature.

"That price works fine for us," I say, hopefully not too enthusiastically. The woman seems to be a bit of a shark, but one that can sniff out joy instead of blood. "Do you know if it's available?"

"I need to check my schedule." She makes no move to do so.

"Greta, come on now," Bea says. "Surely you can see they're a nice couple. Just like you and Charlie were."

Oh no, she said that in the past tense. Perhaps our joy makes her sad for what she used to have and has no longer. "I'm sorry for your loss," I whisper.

Her head jerks up and she studies me. Then she nods, as if she's decided something. "All right, you can have the place next Sunday."

"Really?" And before she can say another word, I drop Frederick's hand, lean forward, and catch her in a hug.

She's a bit fragile, her bones thin, but she squeezes back before tapping my upper arm. "Don't get all mushy, girl. It's just a house. You can come by and tour it Tuesday around four if you'd like. I'm leaving town tomorrow and Monday."

"Thank you. We'll be there."

But Greta is wrong. It's not just a house.

It's the final puzzle piece in the wedding planning. Most everything else is done. I just need to find a caterer—Marilee's still asking her brother about that—and a photographer, confirm that everything else is going all right on Shelby's end.

No, it's not just a house.

It's hope that my crazy idea just might work out after all.

I'm fairly certain I made a grave error in kissing Chloe on Friday evening.

Once again, I'm lying here on my makeshift bed staring up at the hotel room ceiling in the middle of the night, because sleep won't come. It's only been thirty hours since we kissed, but I cannot stop thinking about it.

About doing it again, this time in private when nobody is watching, and we can take all the time in the world ...

That can't happen, though, even in the context of this all being fake. Because something became abundantly clear to me in the aftermath of the kiss. If I'm reading her correctly, there's interest there. I'm not sure why I didn't notice it before. Perhaps because I told myself this was all a ruse, but when I really think about it, Chloe wears her heart on her sleeve. She's not really capable of pretending—not *that* well, anyhow.

And the way she looked at me after that kiss ...

Of course, that changes nothing in the long run. Even if she finds me mildly attractive, there's no future for us, which means I have to be even more careful to not take advantage of her.

I stretch my calves and pray for even the tiniest hint of a

yawn to tickle the back of my throat. Not even my little counting trick has worked this time around, and it doesn't help that my head is hurting too. Not terribly, but that familiar dull ache that migraine sufferers are used to living with. The pain is compounded because I'm lying here, just feeling it. And thinking of her.

I just might be doomed to pull an all-nighter, and the reason has nothing to do with studying, drinking, or carousing in any manner.

It's all because of *her*.

At least one of us is sleeping peacefully. As soon as we got back to the room after a long afternoon and evening spent browsing the wine and art booths, and hanging out with Marilee and Jordan—who invited us on a hike tomorrow— Chloe changed into her PJs and flopped into bed, humming to herself. Securing a venue seemed to put an extra big pep into her step tonight, and I'm grateful for it.

Rolling over onto my side, I place my pillow over my head. *Come on, sleep. Take me. I surrender.*

But it's no use.

I first sit up, then stand, and pad into the restroom, which I navigate in the dark because I don't want the light to disturb Chloe or make my headache worse. After using the facilities and washing my hands, I pull open the door, stretch, massage my neck muscles, and head back for my pile of blankets on the floor.

But before I make it there, I hear a noise.

Chloe's moaning.

My eyes have adjusted to the darkness, so I can see her thrashing around in the very middle of the bed. "No. No. Nooooo." She's not exactly screaming, but her voice sounds frantic. "Stop! Go away!"

It's clearly just a nightmare, and she's not in any real

danger, but I can't stand to hear Chloe upset. I take the few steps toward the bed and sit on the very edge. "Chloe." Reaching out my hand, I touch her shoulder.

Chloe whimpers, and now there are actual tears streaming down her cheeks. What in the world is she dreaming about?

She rolls farther away.

In order to reach her, I have to climb fully onto the bed and lean over her, this time giving her shoulder a firm but gentle shake. "Shh, Princess. It's all right. Wake up, now."

Her voice quiets, and her body becomes less agitated, but she still doesn't open her eyes.

Instead, she rolls again—this time, right toward me.

I don't expect the move and, in an attempt to scramble backward and off the bed, I end up flat on my back.

And she ends up in my arms.

Her head settles just under the spot where my right arm meets my shoulder, her right hand flat on my stomach, her nose pressed against the side of my chest. Then, she sighs deeply as she curls her whole body against me, her knees bent so that her top leg rests slightly on mine, her toes teasing the top of my right foot.

I didn't think things could get any worse for me, but clearly, I was wrong.

She's fully at peace once more. I, on the other hand, will never get a wink of sleep again if I don't put a stop to this immediately. Of course, that's not what I *want*. I can't imagine anything more blissful than turning my head and burying my nose in her honey-vanilla hair that smells like heaven. Than wrapping her up against me all night long. Than being the one to chase away her nightmares.

But what I want and what's best for Chloe are two different things.

So the bliss has to end.

I run my fingertips lightly down her arm. "Princess," I whisper. "Chloe. Wake up, love."

It takes a few moments of saying her name before her eyes flutter open. In those seconds before she's fully conscious, Chloe smiles and her hand flexes against my abs. A rush of heat follows. She's branded me with her touch.

Then, finally, her eyebrows pull together, and she glances up. "Freddy?" Her voice, so vulnerable, so questioning.

"Sorry, Princess," I say as gently as possible. "You had a bad dream and I tried to wake you, but ..."

"Somehow you ended up in bed with me?" The corner of her mouth twitches, and oh, how I long to dip in and kiss her there.

"Something like that." I should move away, but she's not trying to escape my hold either—then again, she's still waking up. It's on me.

So I start to sit, but her hand that's resting on me slides all the way to the other side, holding my body in place. "Don't go. Not yet," she murmurs. "You make an excellent pillow."

"Guess you're not the only one," I tease. Has it really been four days since I lay my head in her lap, and she gave me the world's best head massage? How nice would it be to feel her fingers on my head again? My muscles relax just thinking about it.

"Hmm." She burrows into my hold even further, and I'm forced to stay.

So much for relaxing.

All right, I probably could move if I wanted to—but I don't. And I'm too tired to fight my desires any longer. "Princess?" I whisper into the dark.

"Yes?" Her voice sounds more alert now.

"Do you remember what gave you the nightmare?"

"No." There's a pause, a fluttering against my side as her

fingers tap out a rhythm I can't hear. "But I wouldn't be surprised if it's the one I always have."

Dare I ask? The air vibrates above us, all around us, with that three-a.m. magic that somehow impairs judgment, that encourages people who are normally perfectly rational to spill their secrets and lie next to the one person they shouldn't. "And which one is that?"

It takes her a moment to answer. "The paparazzi ... they're chasing me. Their cameras are humongous and I'm running, and I trip. And every time they take a photo, somehow a new scratch appears somewhere on my body." She's trembling and I turn slightly toward her, lending her my warmth, my strength. "By the end of the dream, I'm dripping blood and weak and they're gaining on me. Just before I wake up, I fall down a cliff, and all I can see are those cameras, snapping away. The people themselves are safely hidden behind them, and they don't care what happens to me, so long as they get their photos."

How awful. "Aw, Princess." I tuck her head against my chest. "You're safe."

"I know. For now."

"For always. I'll make sure of it."

Her fingers play with the bottom of my shirt, skimming the skin just underneath. "You can keep me safe physically, Muscles. You're very good at that. But there are some scars that go deeper than flesh."

Are we still talking about the press ... or a person? I lean back so I can look in her face, and before I know what I'm doing, I place my hand against her cheek. "Who hurt you, Princess?" The intensity of my words should scare me, but I feel a strange calm as I say them. "Because I swear I'll rip him limb from limb if you just tell me his name."

She leans into my touch and smiles. "I believe you would. But it isn't just one person—oh, sure, one of my rubbish ex-boyfriends once sold a story to the media outlets feeding them some garbage about what a bad kisser I am."

"Just give me a name," I rumble. "But also, what an absolute idiot. I can vouch for that rumor being completely untrue."

Sakes. I should *not* have said that.

Thankfully, Chloe chuckles. "You aren't so bad yourself there, Muscles." The sound of her laughter hits me in the chest, a warmth I can't explain growing, expanding. But then she sighs and frowns, and right alongside her, I fall down that cliffside from her nightmare. "And no, I'm not giving you his name, because he truly is inconsequential to me. Of course, there was also Troy."

Oh, yes. Troy Benson, that blighter Chloe dated in her early twenties, the one with the trust fund and political connections up the Thames. It was a good thing Topher and I were away at university for most of their relationship, because every time that pretty boy put his hands on the princess, I nearly broke my own jaw with how hard I ground my teeth. I'd love an excuse to check up on good old Troy now and teach him a thing or two about respecting women. "What did he do?" I can't help the way I'm positively growling.

"Freddy." She sounds embarrassed—or perhaps delighted? —with my much too passionate response. "He didn't do anything. Not like that." A pause. A frown. "He just … well, he abandoned me. The media decided to portray me negatively, he couldn't take what my life entailed, and he dumped me for an American supermodel."

"What a pathetic excuse for a man."

"I don't think about him much, anymore. I'm over him. But still … people who claim to love you shouldn't leave."

She says she's over him, but her words are tinged with so much sadness.

"I'm sorry, Princess. He should have treasured what he had

in you." I shouldn't say more—I can't. Not without laying my feelings completely bare before her. So I shift the focus back to the reason I'm here beside her in the first place. "So, the nightmare. If it's not about Troy ..."

"Then what is it about? Thankfully, I don't think I need to read any books on dream interpretation as I think this one is quite clear."

My hand drops so I can see her face. Not knowing where else to place it, I let it fall to her hip. Probably a mistake, but blinking, I refocus on what she's saying. "You hate being in the limelight?"

"It's less about that and feeling like"—she bites her lip— "like I'm just a joke to my entire country. My whole life, they've been watching and finding me wanting."

"Then they're idiots. They don't know you like I do."

"You're entirely too sweet to me." She pauses. "I could go on and on, but I should let you go back to sleep. I'm sorry I woke you up with my thrashing."

"I was already awake." I won't tell her why. "And if you need to go on and on, I'll listen." Because truthfully, I want to know what lies she's believing so I can soothe them away with the truth. Or, if she doesn't need answers from me, I love being allowed to hold her, to give her some measure of peace.

Even if it's just for tonight.

It's a little while before she speaks again, her voice hushed in remembrance. "When I was young, I didn't really pay attention to the cameras. They just were a part of my life. I even started to love the attention they brought me. I felt pretty and special, and what little girl doesn't want to feel like that?"

I want to tell her she has every right to feel those things, but I'm silent. My thumb circles the smooth silk of her PJs, saying things my voice can't.

"Then"—she continues—"one day I realized the only reason they were watching me was because I was royal. They didn't see me, Chloe Marie Huntington. They saw the princess of Kentonia. Any other girl could have been born in my place, and they would have treated her the same way."

It's not true, because she has the kind of beauty that radiates out of a person no matter what they look like on the outside. But it's not time for me to speak yet. So I draw her back against my chest, inhaling a whiff of her honey-tinged skin, settling in for her story. I will listen for as long as she will share.

"Do you remember the time I was twelve or thirteen, and I had to give an inspiring speech to a bunch of graduating kids from grade five?" She doesn't wait for me to answer before plowing ahead. "Well, that day will be burned in my memory forever. For some reason, the teleprompter was acting wonky, and I was nervous because giving speeches was something Topher did really well, not me. And I fumbled all over my words, not making a lick of sense. I even told the kids to 'arm high and dreach for their reams' instead of 'aim high and reach for their dreams.'" Chloe snorts. "Obviously, ridiculous of me, but again, I was nervous. It shouldn't have been a big deal, but then ..."

"Then?"

"Then, the media was all abuzz about the Illiterate Princess who was better off sticking to shopping and fashion instead of anything that requires use of a brain."

"That's terrible," I say. "But for what it's worth, I don't remember that at all."

"But I do. And that kind of thing ... it just hits hard, especially when you're a teenage girl."

"Of course. I didn't mean to imply it shouldn't hurt. Just that I don't believe anybody thinks of you that way now. Definitely not anyone who matters."

"Thanks, Freddy." She squeezes me. "I think that was the start of really caring too much what other people think about me. I just ... I didn't want to be the butt of any more jokes, you know? I tried to prove myself, to be smart, to be funny, charming, winsome, all of the things a good princess should be. And then, all of that went down the toilet when I was twenty-one and accidentally flashed the media when getting out of a vehicle. What made matters worse was that I was so flustered that I tripped. In one moment, there went all of the careful crafting I'd done of my image. Now I became the princess who partied so hard she got drunk right before an important gala for cancer patients."

I do remember that one. "They were much too harsh. And a pack of liars." I'd been with both Topher and Chloe that whole night and hadn't seen Chloe have a single sip of anything but water.

But after that, she'd changed. It had broken my heart to see it. And I'd never put two and two together until now—never realized how everything had affected her on the inside, because on the outside, she'd acted completely unaffected by everyone's opinion of her.

I don't want to assume, though. "Is that why ...?"

"Yes." She sighs. "I decided that if they were going to think the worst of me, I'd at least give them a reason to. If they were going to brand me as the Partying Princess, I'd embrace that label full tilt. So I started staying out late. Dating men I shouldn't. Drinking too much. Escaping my protective detail. And for a while, the release felt wonderful. I let go of everyone's expectations and was just myself. At least, I thought I was being myself. Until ..."

Now she's the one to pull back, nestling herself against the pillows behind us instead of my chest. Our feet remain connected, but she folds her palms against each other and places them under her cheek.

My fingers itch to haul her back to me, to play with the curls cascading over her shoulder, spilling onto the mattress between us. Instead, I turn on my side to face her. "Until what?"

"Until you found me one night in the garden. Do you remember?"

How could I forget? I'd been off duty, out for an evening run, when I'd stumbled across her. As always, she'd looked striking in a teal party dress that only reached mid-thigh and her blonde hair loose and shimmering in the moonlight. But she'd wobbled on her tall heels, and her makeup had been smeared and her eyes had just looked ... haunted. Lost. "I remember," I say, my voice quiet. "Do you?" I had sworn that she'd been too wasted to recall any of it, so I'd never mentioned it again.

"Every detail," she says with conviction. "You held my hair while I got sick in the bushes. You walked me back to my room and made sure I was safe. You never told a soul." Chloe swallows hard. "And do you remember what you said to me?"

Not really, not exactly. I just remember aching for her, wanting her to know that she was special, that whatever she was trying to prove ... well, that she didn't have to. "No."

"I told you I was so sorry that you had to see me like that. And you told me you knew that this wasn't who I was. That I could be whoever *I* wanted to be, and I didn't have to let the media or anyone else define what that was. That I didn't have to let anyone else determine my worth." Starlight pours in through the window behind me, alighting on her face. She's a pure angel, and she's focused on me. "I was so tired of trying to be whatever everyone else wanted me to be, and you gave me permission to be myself. Truly, Freddy, you changed my life with those words."

"I had no idea." My voice is gruff, and the back of my eyes burn. "But I'm glad that you got something out of my bumbling."

"It's not the words or the way you said it. It was your heart. You saw me, and I can't ever thank you enough for that." She smiles, and I feel it down to my toes. "Now, I still struggle with knowing my place in the world, but at least I feel more sure about myself and who I am. If only I could figure out what to *do* with that."

"You will." And I allow myself this, to reach out and stroke her elbow. "And if I know you, you have some ideas."

"Ridiculous ones, maybe."

"For example?"

Pursing her lips, she's quiet. Then, "The ladies said something at the winery the other night ... about how Rhonda is selling Something Blue. The wedding shop." Another pause. "About how I should move here and buy it."

Oh. My stomach twists. "Wow."

"I know. Like I said, ridiculous. I have duties at home. My father wants to marry me off, for one."

Another twist.

"And for two, that's just the sort of thing everyone would expect me to do, right? The partying princess, turned pauper and party planner." She says this with self-deprecation, sticking out her tongue. "I think I'm just getting lost in the fantasy here, you know? We're far away from the royal life. Nobody knows who I am. And they treat me normal. But if I moved here, it wouldn't be the same, I'm sure. Then again, maybe it would."

She hasn't mentioned the part of the fantasy that's got me the most enthralled—the two of us together. So maybe that means I've misjudged her feelings. I hope I have, honestly. I'd much rather carry this burden alone. It would be that much harder knowing that she might be hurt when we inevitably can't be together.

Pushing thoughts of that aside, I prepare to do what a friend would—gently challenge her. "Princess, I think it's a fine idea. You'd be brilliant if that's what you wanted to do, and I know you'd find a way to do it."

"Thanks, Freddy." She studies me. "I sense a *but*."

"You always do." I chuckle. "Here goes. You say that you feel more sure of yourself, and that's wonderful. But the fact that you're even talking about what others might think of your preferred career choice is an indication that perhaps you still need to let go of that worry a bit."

"I can see that. I think part of the problem is that, deep down, I wonder if the things I'm good at are not what are most valuable in this world. And I do long to contribute. I am royal, after all, and I want the blessing of my birth to mean something. I want to bless the world, the people in it, with my talents. But ... I'm just not really sure my talents are worth much."

Oh, Chloe. "I don't know if you know this about me, but I like to read travel memoirs and things like that in my free time."

Her eyebrows lift. "That sounds fascinating. And right in line with what I know about your love of travel."

I nod. "Well, in one memoir, the author quoted this famous theologian who had inspired him to journey around the world. And the quote really stood out to me." I pause. "I think it might help you too."

"What is it?"

I call up the exact memory. "It says, 'Don't ask yourself what the world needs. Ask yourself what makes you come alive, and go do that, because what the world needs is people who have come alive.'" I reach my hand forward and touch a piece of Chloe's hair, rubbing it gently between my thumb and fore-finger. It's spun silk, just like her—soft and giving. "If planning parties is what makes you come alive, Princess, then that's what you should do. Because you make the world a better place just by being you."

"Freddy ..." She reaches for my hand. "You are, without a doubt, the best man I know."

She cannot say that, especially not here when I'm mere centimeters, mere seconds from reaching for her and pulling her into yet another kiss. I need to move, need to break this spell she has over me. "You should get to know more men, then, Princess."

Laughing, she swats at me, then shifts so she's lying on her back, staring up at the ceiling. "I meant what I said, Muscles."

Her words harken back to what I said to her in the dress shop. I laugh and move to my back, shifting a hand behind my head. "You're incorrigible."

"I do try." A yawn slips out from her, inspiring my own. Finally. We lie quiet and still as a cloud obscures the moonlight outside.

Blessed sleep is almost here.

Then she asks one final question of me. "So I've been an open book." Another yawn. "What about you? What makes Frederick Shaw come alive? Travel? Work? Or ... something else?"

You.

It's on the tip of my tongue and it's all I can do to shove it back into my throat. "Ah, well ..."

"Well?"

"It's different for me," I say. "Whenever I get what I want, someone gets hurt." First Matthew, and Mum and Dad as a result. Then Topher. And I'll be darned if Chloe joins the ranks. "But I have a good life. After all, I'm here with you, aren't I?"

Then, before she asks me any more questions, I slip from the dream back to reality, and return to my bed on the ground. "Good night, Princess."

She must be asleep, because she doesn't reply.

And that's just as well, anyhow.

seventeen

CHLOE

I'm beginning to think that perhaps I was wrong.

And riding in Jordan's Jeep with Marilee, Ryder, Jordan's dog, and Frederick toward the destination for our Sunday hike is giving me lots of opportunity to replay last night—or early this morning, whatever you want to call it—in my mind.

To consider that maybe Lucy was right after all.

Okay, maybe Frederick doesn't *love* me, but my gut tells me he feels a heck of a lot more than mere attraction. The man keeps such a tight lid on his emotions, but as we huddled together in my bed not eight hours ago, I got a peek behind the curtain. When he held me, every nerve ending in my body was on fire, but not in the way that burned. More in the way that sugar caramelizes under a blowtorch or a marshmallow cooks from the inside out at the end of a roasting spit.

But it wasn't until I looked in his eyes, until he told me *"You make the world a better place just by being you"* that my heart melted too. He said it like he believed it, with conviction —but it was different than the way he encouraged me after that night in the garden. That was all brotherly affection, firm encouragement coming from someone who knew me.

But this ... it was imbued with something else.

And I need to figure out what that something else is.

Because maybe he's right. Maybe I *do* need to go after something I want. It might be taking things too far to ask my father to allow me to live a non-royal life right here in Hallmark Beach. But would it really be so off base to ask him to put aside whatever he feels or thinks about Frederick's father and allow us to be together, *if* that's what we both want?

I've held off on telling him how I feel all these years because I didn't think he'd ever want me or the life that came with me—and maybe he doesn't. But I now know he doesn't want to be a bodyguard, not really. I still don't fully understand why Frederick stays, but if I can only get him to admit that he has true feelings for me, then we could actually figure this thing out.

Together.

The thought is equally thrilling and terrifying.

"You all right?" Frederick's voice bursts into my thoughts and his hand finds mine from his spot beside me. We're crammed into the back seat of the vehicle, with Ryder in his booster in the middle row so Jordan's golden retriever Chase can lie down under his feet. The little boy chatters on and on to Marilee and Jordan up front. Marilee's turned halfway so she can look at Ryder and reply to his questions with patience and a smile.

I stare at Freddy's hand set over my own, at the strength in each of those fingers. Enough to snap a man from "limb to limb" as he threatened last night—I warm at the memory—but also to take my burdens and make them lighter with a sweet stroke. "I'm fine."

"You sure you want to do this hike?" He squints out the window as the Jeep turns off the highway, following the signage for the trail. "The weather's looking rather ominous."

Is it? Yes, the sky is a bit dark on the horizon, but the clouds seem far enough away. I shrug. "I'm not afraid of a little rain. Are you?"

He presses his lips together. "Just want you to be safe, Princess."

I roll my eyes. "Jordan said it's a fairly simple hike. And he wouldn't take his son out if it was dangerous. Besides, you know this is what he does for a living, right?" I tease. Besides teaching surfing lessons during the main tourist season, our new friend leads adventure tours of all kinds with the company he founded when he came back to Hallmark Beach after college.

"I know." Frederick's brows stay knit together, but I don't have a chance to ask what's bothering him because the Jeep comes to a stop in the trailhead car park.

We pile out and grab our backpacks filled with water and snacks. Jordan clips a leash on Chase and turns to us. "Ready?"

When we nod, we set off as a group toward the start of the trail, which begins as a flat boardwalk over some seasonal wetlands. The tall grass sways and bends, and Ryder runs ahead, his fingers swooping against the reeds as he laughs. Jordan and Chase hustle to keep up with him.

Marilee loops an arm through mine. "So glad you guys could take a break from the wedding planning and join us."

"Thanks for the invite," I say as we set a leisurely pace, Frederick somewhere behind us. "It's nice to get away from town for a bit. And we couldn't do much planning today anyway. Everything's closed up for the festival, plus the fact it's Sunday. I'm surprised you could get away, though. Seems you've been pretty busy lately."

"Marla got back into town yesterday, so my workload is now cut in half."

"More time for you to invest in making cakes, then, eh?"

"Oh, no, not really." She waves away the suggestion. "But

I've got a little more time to help Jordan watch Ryder. His mom's got MS, so some days it's hard for her to keep up with her grandson."

"That's a shame."

"She does all right, but her flare-ups can get pretty bad."

Maybe now's the perfect time to gauge the situation between Jordan and Marilee. I know they've said they're just friends, but I sense more there, at least on his end. Then again, I still don't know anything about Ryder's mom. "So you help out. Is Ryder's mom not in the picture?"

Our steps echo on the walkway, which turns and bends past a gorgeous view of the ocean and beach. It's a secluded spot, protected by rocks on either side of an inlet. On the way over, Jordan said this is one of his favorite hikes, because it's got a little of everything—beginning with the beach but straying through the forest and ending in the hills.

Jordan lets the dog off the leash, and Chase bounds into the water, startling some geese and seagulls. Ryder claps his hand and giggles hysterically.

We stop and Frederick joins us as we watch from afar.

Marilee sighs. "Georgia actually died a month ago. Cancer. It happened quickly, and ... it's been hard."

"Oh, wow. Jordan and Ryder must be devastated." If Frederick died, I wouldn't be able to function, but I haven't sensed that level of depression in Jordan.

Frederick crosses his arms over his chest, taking in this information along with me.

"Ryder still doesn't understand. He keeps asking ..." Marilee stops, presses her lips together as she composes herself. "He keeps asking when Mommy's coming back from her trip. That's the most devastating part for Jordan. He's having to navigate parenting alone for the first time. I try to help, but I've never been a mom. Was never able to ..." She shakes her head.

"Anyway, he and Georgia might never have been a real couple, but they were great co-parents. Even friends. And so, this is just all ... yeah. Really hard."

I lean my head on her shoulder and squeeze her arm against my body. "Sounds like you all need today, then."

"Yeah."

We stand like that for a time, watching Jordan run around with Ryder, swinging him onto his shoulders after tickling him like crazy. When I peek at Frederick, he's wearing an expression I've never seen. Almost like ... longing.

He may act like he's all right with never having a family, never being a dad, but that look right there tells me differently.

I turn my attention back to Marilee. "Why don't you go join them?"

"Oh no, it's father-son time."

"Please." I roll my eyes and hip check her. "You're Jordan's best friend, his biggest supporter, right? Go out there and have some fun."

"What about you? Come join us."

And break up that family moment? No. I drop my hold on her arm and step toward Fredrick. "We'll keep going on the trail. We have some things to talk about anyway. You guys catch up whenever."

She nibbles her thumbnail for a moment before nodding. "All right. See you up there." Then she steps off the boardwalk and sinks into the sand, kicking off her shoes and running toward them. Ryder turns and calls her name from his perch on Jordan's shoulders, and the dog runs straight for her.

I smile. Someday, I hope Jordan and Marilee figure out they're meant to be together.

"What do we have to talk about, Princess?" Frederick says in a low, teasing voice.

He has no idea what's coming. And really, neither do I.

"You'll see," I tease right back as I hold out my hand for him to take. "Let's go."

I wait until we're a good distance from Jordan and Marilee to talk again.

Instead, we stroll along the trail, which does just what Jordan said, climbing until the wooden boardwalk gives way to a dirt path that winds through the trees as they gradually grow thicker. Birds call a merry song in the canopies above our heads, and we pass only a few other hikers along the way. The whole world is full of color: a patch of large orange mushrooms, a green-and-red bush that Frederick tells me is poison oak, flowers beginning to bud at the base of the trees.

Thunder rolls in the distance, disturbing our peace.

"Are you positive you don't want to turn back? I don't love the idea of hiking in the rain."

"Oh, come now, Muscles. A little rain never hurt anyone."

He opens his mouth to speak when thunder cracks again. "Seriously, Chloe." His eyes look nearly panicked.

I stop walking and turn to him. "Hey." Taking both his hands in mine, I cock my head to one side. "What's going on?"

"Nothing." He studies the sky, or what little of it we can see through the trees. "Like I said, I just want you to be safe. It's my job."

There's that rote, mechanical answer again. Something lights inside of me, and this time, I'm refusing to accept it. "I think there's more to it than that."

He pulls away from my hold and starts trudging up the trail again.

Seriously? I bore my entire soul to him last night and this is how it's going to be? No way, buddy. He's going to tell me what's going on or meet a very different Chloe than the one he's used to. Earlier this week, he called me determined.

He has no idea how determined I can be. Especially when something means this much.

As I hurry to catch up with him, the landscape opens up again, this time into a vista viewpoint. It's breathtaking with its wide angle of the valley below, of trees and ocean and other coastal bluffs in the distance. Frederick's got both hands on the top of his head and he's breathing hard as if he just ran a marathon. He's discarded his bag near a tree, so I do the same with mine.

Then I march right up to that ledge in front of Frederick, stand on the rock, and twirl to face him.

His hands immediately drop. "Chloe, come away from that ledge. Please."

From here, I can see that the dark clouds have rolled in. They're about to unleash their displeasure on us. Well, get in line, Mother Nature. My hands find my hips. "Not until you tell me something real, Freddy."

"What are you talking about?"

Where to even begin? But my brain lands on the last thing he said last night before I fell asleep. "What did you mean last night when you said someone always gets hurt when you get what you want?"

He huffs. "Chloe, really? Can we just talk about that later?"

"No, I want to talk about it now." Because later, I know he'll find some other excuse not to let me in. "Please, Freddy. We're friends, right? And friends share. I told you my stuff last night. It's your turn." Then, because I don't know what else to do, I tilt my chin ever so slightly. Don't want him thinking I'm too much of a softie.

Frederick runs a hand through his short hair. Then he groans. "Fine, you win. Just come here, all right?"

"In a minute. Talk."

"Sakes, you're bossy."

That earns him a grin. "Why, thank you."

"It wasn't a compliment." He scowls at me, then rubs the edge of one of his temples. Hopefully he's not getting a migraine. Maybe we should go ...

No, Chloe. Don't chicken out now.

Ugh, my internal conscience is right. This is hard, knowing that he might not say what I'm hoping he'll say. Knowing that I might discover that Lucy was wrong, that Frederick *does* only think of me as a sister.

But it's worth the risk. Because if she's right ... that changes everything.

I tilt my chin further and spear him with the most royal look I can manage. "I'm waiting."

"I just ... it's just something I've observed, all right? Everyone is better off when I just go with the flow and don't ask for anything special."

"When did you observe this?" What would possess a man as good and loyal as Frederick to believe he'd hurt anyone by getting what he wanted? "Give me an example."

"I don't know, Chloe."

But the way he trails off tells me he does. So I just wait.

He huffs again and starts to pace. Three steps one way, turn, three paces back, turn. "When my father got accused of treason, and Topher was at university, he put his life basically on hold to prove that my father was innocent."

I know this. "Yes. And?"

"And then he got reamed by the media, saying he had poor judgment. That he was destined to be a terrible king someday.

That he had no sense of family loyalty—that he was more loyal to a mere bodyguard than to his own kin."

"All ridiculous lies." I wave my hand as if swatting away a fly. "What does this have to do with anything?"

"Because I asked him to do it."

Oh. That *is* news.

"Things weren't looking good. My mum was trying but she couldn't even get a barrister to take his case. Nobody believed he was innocent. The evidence was too damning. But still, I begged my best mate in the world to do whatever he could." He stops pacing, looks at me. "And he did. To his own detriment and near ruin. He's only just gotten his reputation back intact, and that's largely due to Lauren. Everyone loves her."

This is true—all of it. Except for one thing. "Frederick, Topher would have done what he did whether you asked him or not. I'm sure of it. That's just who he is. He's logical and something about the facts didn't add up, so he followed them until he figured out the discrepancy."

A plop of rain hits the dirt beneath his feet. "Perhaps."

"There's no *perhaps* about it." Then I realize something else. "This ... this is why you're determined to remain a body-guard even though you hate it."

"Hate's a strong word."

More drops fall around me, but I'll be darned if we don't get to the bottom of this right here, right now. "You feel beholden to him."

His eyes flash at me. "Of course I do!" His hands fling into the air. "He saved my father's life. And my father can no longer serve, so I'm serving in his stead."

"There are other ways to serve your country than being stuck in a life you don't want."

"I told you—I'm content."

"Are you, though?" I finally step off the ledge and head straight toward him as rain begins to fall more steadily. If this was a paranormal book, I'd be the girl who could control the weather because right now, it's reflecting the storm inside of me as my heart beats wildly. "All of your excuses are melting away, Frederick. When are you going to admit that you don't want this life? That you don't want to be lonely, stuck inside the palace walls instead of being free to have whatever it is you *do* want?"

Now my breath is coming quickly. I stand in front of him, rain dripping down my face as I take hold of his shirt. The water pelts the copse of trees behind Frederick, and the path is quickly becoming mud beneath our feet.

"Come on," he urges. "Let's take some cover."

But I stand my ground. "Not until you answer me."

"Chloe." He closes his eyes for a moment, then opens them to me again. "It would do absolutely no good to admit what I want, because it would only hurt the people I love most."

"I thought we already determined that you weren't the one who hurt Topher." A shiver wracks my body, but I ignore the chill. "You told me last night that the world needed me to do what made me come alive, that it would be better for it. Isn't that true of you too? How would the world be different if you did what you truly wanted?"

His gaze flashes to my lips, and my legs turn to jelly at the heat in his eyes. I take a step closer, so my hands are both flat on his hard stomach, and I lift my head upward. We're making progress—I can feel it. But I'm not kissing him first, not until he admits that it's *me* he wants.

Water rivulets run down the tracks of his face—his nose, the corner of his lips, his jaw, his chin—and I want to trace every single one. But I hold still. "What do you want, Frederick?"

"Sakes, Chloe." He sets his forehead against mine. "Isn't it obvious? Hasn't it been obvious for the last twelve years?"

Twelve years? My mind does the math.

My eighteenth birthday party. Could what he told the group at the bar that night be real? *"I just knew. She was it for me."*

"Say it." I move my hands up his shirt, which is plastered to his well-formed chest, until they hitch high enough to feel his heart thundering against his ribcage.

Lightning flashes somewhere overhead, and the wind blows against us, but we are anchored here in the mud, in the details, in the most pivotal moment that's ever existed.

"I can't." His own voice is raised, because the rain has become sheets around us. Water coats my lashes, making it difficult to see him, but I blink furiously because I don't want to miss a moment.

"Why?" And I swear I won't cry, but frustration makes my voice as battered as a raging sea tossed against the hull of a boat.

"Because I don't want you to get hurt too." There. It's almost as good as admitting it.

I slide one hand up to his face, feel his strong jaw beneath my fingers. "The only way I get hurt is if we never admit what's happening. If we continue to go on, doing this dance around each other, pretending like ..."

"Like we aren't mad for each other?" His tone is questioning. Does he doubt that I'm mad for him too?

Well, I'm not going to leave him in suspense any longer. There are no prying eyes here, no reason to kiss him other than the fact that this—that *he*—is what I want.

"Like we aren't mad for each other," I confirm before lifting on my tiptoes and pressing my mouth hard against his. I wind my hands up and around his neck, not giving him any choice in the matter.

Thankfully, it doesn't seem he wishes to back down. At last, his arms press around me, and he kisses me in return with so much force, I'm afraid I'll sink in this mud. Frederick must realize we're on slippery ground, because he reaches under me and lifts me like I do indeed weigh as much as a feather.

I wrap my legs around his torso and, still kissing me, he walks us back to the grove of trees, where the leaves overhead form a pocket of protection from the elements. Some rain still filters through, but even in the heat of the moment, he's keeping me safe.

He's also lighting me up from the inside out.

My skin warms in all the places he's touching me as he sets me on my feet in front of a particularly wide tree. Planting a hand on either side of my head, he stops kissing me for a moment and leans over me. Water drips down his nose. "Are you sure this is what you want, Chloe?"

I frame his face with my fingers. "This is *all* I want."

And apparently that's all he needs to hear, because he swoops in and kisses me again, as if he's afraid I'll change my mind. His mouth fuses with mine, becomes a part of me as we lean together and pour out all the desire that's built for years, in all the moments of wanting and looking and not having.

That desire spills out and down as his kiss finds my neck. I gasp when his lips graze along my skin, chasing away the goose-flesh with the heat from his tongue. One of his hands moves to grip my waist, pulling our bodies flush against each other as that beautiful mouth of his explores the planes of my collar-bones. Tilting my head back against the tree's trunk, I coil my fingers through the belt loops of his shorts, holding on for dear life as Frederick takes me to a heady somewhere I've never been.

Sure, I've been kissed before, but even with Troy, it always felt like I had to do so with one eye open. I never fully trusted that the man kissing me would treat me with the kind of dignity I deserved, so I never allowed myself to fully let go. But Frederick has always treated me like a princess—not the kind I am, with royal blood flowing through my veins, but the kind any woman is—and I just know I'm safe with him.

I close my eyes and let loose the hum vibrating inside of me with a deep sigh of pleasure, contentment. Joy.

Frederick pulls back, and my eyes flit open.

"What's wrong?" I ask.

"Nothing." He takes a clump of my wet tangled hair, running his fingers along it with a look of pure awe on his face. "You're just so beautiful. So regal. You belong up on some pedestal. I ... I don't want you to have to step down into the mud to be with me."

"A pedestal's a lonely place to be," I whisper while the rain patters the leaves over our heads. "And that's not the life I want."

"But you deserve more than me. More than the stain my family name will surely bring you."

"I don't care about all that. I know your father is innocent. Topher does too."

"But what about your father?"

"We'll deal with that later. Right now, more kissing, please."

He laughs, but there's pain rimming his eyes. "There's more."

"Then tell me."

He studies me, his eyes following the contours of my face, down my cheeks to my lips and back to my eyes. "Chloe, I'm the reason my brother is dead. And I just ... I don't want you to get hurt too."

His eyes widen, like he can't believe he just told me that. Frederick takes a step away from me. He's expecting me to be shocked, I think, but I'm not—mostly because I know it can't be true. Though I'm sure *he* believes that's the case.

I tug him over to a tree stump nearby. "Sit."

He's stoic, and I can see in his eyes that he's already erecting the wall back between our hearts. Nope. Not happening. I simply won't allow it.

So I lower myself onto his lap.

He groans. "Princess—"

"I'll brook no argument from you, peasant."

That draws a chuckle from him, and he finally puts his arms around my waist, leaning in to set his mouth against my bare shoulder. I probably should have worn a jacket with my camisole, but I regret nothing in this moment.

"Yes, Your Royal Highness," he whispers into my skin.

"That's better." I somehow manage to say this without a waver in my voice, because the sensations his nearness are generating make me want to twirl and forget this need to talk. Bravo to me. "Now." I place my hands on top of his and lean back against his chest. "Tell me."

He sighs, but doesn't need any more direction to understand what I mean. "Matthew died because ..." A pause. The rain's calmer now, a soft and steady trilling against the ground. "Matthew was everything he was supposed to be. Intelligent. Charismatic. A born leader, the natural heir to take over my father's duties as advisor someday."

I snuggle against him, remind him I'm there.

"He was seven years older than me, but he was my best friend. He always had time for me, even with his studies. He knew how much I dreamed of traveling, which is why he offered to take me anywhere I wanted to go for my twelfth birthday." His hold around me tightens. "I chose Machu Picchu. Peru."

"Oh, Freddy." Tears well in my eyes for the little boy inside of him. The one who blames himself for what was surely an accident.

He inhales a sharp breath. "It was just the two of us, brothers off to see the world and have an adventure. And that's all it would have been ... if not for the rain."

The rain.

I gasp and turn. "I didn't know."

"I know you didn't." He swallows. "The rain made the trail slick, but Matthew was an expert hiker. Me, on the other hand ... I was so excited to get to the top of the big mountain. And I took a turn too quickly, slipped ..."

I already know where this is going. "And he saved you?"

A nod, almost imperceptible. "Pushed me out of the way. I banged my head on a big rock." He points to his eyebrow, where that scar I love sits—a visible ghostly reminder of everything he lost. "I came to in the hospital with a concussion and stitches. My parents had both flown down, and there was no Matthew in sight. By the looks on their faces, I just knew what had happened." He looks away. "And I knew it was my fault."

"But it wasn't." How can he honestly believe that? "You were a child, Freddy."

"I know that logically speaking. But I can't help feeling like I'm cursed somehow. That my family is cursed." A kiss, pressed against the place where my neck meets my shoulder. "And I don't want to drag you down with me."

I turn more fully so my legs are slung across his lap and my left arm is around his neck—his right arm supporting my back. "Just like I am not what the media says I am, you are not the sum of the things that happened to you. You had no choice in any of it, Freddy." Then I reach up with my right hand and trace the scar over his eyebrow with the pad of my thumb. "The thing you *have* chosen is to honor Matthew's life, to honor your father despite the downfall of his reputation, by becoming a man of honor yourself. You are the bravest, most loyal man I have the privilege of knowing. I believe that."

He takes my hand in his, turns it, and kisses my palm.

"But if you don't believe it too, then you'll never be able to move on. You'll never be able to find happiness."

"I've found happiness, Princess." He leans in and kisses me, slow and deep. "It's sitting on my lap right now."

"Freddy," I breathe.

"I don't know what will happen, Chloe. I can't promise anything. I'm still your bodyguard. Topher's still your brother, and my best mate. My family is still not favored in the kingdom. The obstacles are stacked against us." He kisses my nose. "And it's very hard to think with you this close."

He's right. There's more to this than rainbows and fairy dust. Things aren't magically going to be completely fine. But I believe that love truly can conquer all. For now, though, I simply want to bask in the glow of this moment, when we only have to answer to each other.

"Then don't think." Both of my arms circle his neck.

His lips quirk at the corner, like they do only for me. "Is that an order, Princess?"

Tilting my head, I pretend to consider. "No. It's a request." Because though we like to be playful about it, I'm no better than him simply because of my last name. "Do with it what you want."

"What I want"—he leans in tight until his mouth hovers over mine, and his voice is low and dangerous—"is to kiss you senseless."

Oh, goodness. Somehow I manage to play it cool. "I'm amenable to that. So long as you actually do it," I tease. "I want zero sense left in my brain when you're finished. Do you promise?"

He holds up his hand, a teasing glint in his eyes. "This I do solemnly vow."

Then he takes his time, proving that he's quite thorough and committed to his promise. Yes, sir. Frederick Shaw is most certainly a man of his word.

FREDERICK

I've never been that fond of the circus.

Oh, I admire the talents and abilities of the performers. The lion tamers, who stare down a fearsome beast and yawn in the face of its roar. The trapeze artists, flying through the air—sometimes without a net below to catch them.

And then there are the tightrope walkers, whose lives depend on their ability to balance.

Despite all of the wonder a circus brings, as a child I was too nervous to watch the performers properly, always afraid that someone would get eaten, would break a leg, would fall.

But here I am, two days after finally admitting to Chloe Huntington that I'm mad for her, and I believe I've never related to anyone more than I do a circus performer.

The last forty-eight hours have been pure heaven. Yes, we've accomplished more on the wedding to-do list—booking a photographer, securing Marilee's brother Blake as the caterer, and confirming details with Shelby and Topher about everyone's arrival in three days' time—but we've also snuggled, laughed, and talked about everything under the sun.

We've also kissed, probably more than we should.

But how can I stop? My favorite person in the world feels the same way as I do, and I couldn't be happier.

And yet, I'm constantly ignoring the roar of my doubts, flying, and then falling as I try to conquer this new thing, walking a wire that could snap at any moment and end whatever is pulsing and growing between us. But as I walk hand in hand with Chloe toward our rental car in The Purple Seashell car park, I remind myself that she's worth more than any doubts.

I try to meditate on the words she's been repeating to me: *we'll figure this out.*

"In that head of yours again, Muscles?" she says as she peeks up at me from behind her large white sunglasses.

"Why do you ask?"

We reach the car and I hit the key fob to unlock it. But instead of climbing inside, I lean back against the passenger door and keep hold of her hand.

She steps between my legs and presses a fingertip against the side of my mouth. "You get these little grooves right here."

The clouds from two days ago have long cleared away, leaving a bright shine in their wake. The sun warms my hands as I rest them on her hips. "Hmm. Guess I'm rather predictable then."

Tossing her head back, she laughs and loops her arms around my neck. "I just know you and all your little tells."

"And I know yours."

"Such as?" Eyes bright, she nibbles her bottom lip.

"That." I point to her mouth. "That's the one that tells me you're nervous or thinking really hard about something. That's the one"—I tug her in—"that always drives me wild."

Then I kiss away whatever nerves she's feeling. I can't promise her forever, not yet, but I can make her feel happy and secure in what we have right now, in my feelings for her. They pulse hot and strong as we rev up the kiss, which I finally end by tugging at her bottom lip with a gentle nip of my teeth. "We'd better get going or we're going to miss our appointment with Mrs. Graber."

"Do we have to?" she whines.

I love the power I have whenever I kiss her—not power over her, but because of her. She makes me feel powerful, like I can conquer anything because she believes I can.

It's the Chloe Effect in action.

"Yes, we have to." Because I'm trying desperately to stay respectful of her, to take things slowly, but I'm just a mere mortal constantly staring down the temptation from my personal Siren. I've already established a no-kissing rule inside the hotel, which we've somehow managed to enforce (though Chloe likes to edge riiiiiight up to the boundaries of that particular rule).

I open the car door and put on my sternest voice. "Get in the car, please, Princess."

"You're no fun." She drops into the passenger seat, but not before giving me a quick peck. Cheeky bird.

Laughing, I stroll around the front of the car and climb in, starting the engine and backing out. The drive won't take long, but it's up the hill and we're due to arrive soon.

Chloe grabs my hand across the console. "So ..."

"Yeah, love?" Have I mentioned I adore getting to call her that?

The vehicle's air vent kicks on, cycling in the smell of the sea from outside.

"Have you talked to my brother yet?"

I groan internally. "No. I know I need to." I really do. "I will."

"Why are you avoiding it?" She doesn't sound petulant as some women might. Just curious. And perhaps a bit concerned.

At first, we considered telling Topher together, in person. But we don't want to take away from the wedding festivities, and it might be difficult to find time to be alone with him. It might also ruin the party if he decides to gut punch me for getting with his little sister when I was supposed to be merely protecting her.

At least telling him over the phone will give him time to process things.

Squeezing her hand as I take Hillside Drive up and around the bend, I search for a suitable answer. "Part of me wants to keep it to ourselves just a tad bit longer. It's more fun that way, don't you think?" I try for a tease, but it falls flat.

"I get that." She looks out the window at the town below us. "But I just wonder if you're not telling him because you're still doubting whether it's something you want."

"Chloe, that's not it. I do want this." We arrive at the Graber mansion, and I input the code Greta gave Chloe at the box. The iron fence slides open. "But I've been honest about the fact that I don't know exactly how this will all work. There's still a lot to figure out."

"True, but the first step is talking to Topher."

She's right. And I'll man up soon. Today. Probably.

We pull to a stop at the end of the long parking lot. The house looms over us, over the whole neighborhood where it sits on an oceanside promontory. It's classic, perhaps a hundred years old, with updated paint, and three gables. What little I can see of the backyard from here is grass, flowered bushes, and sunshine.

It's the perfect place for a wedding.

I unclip my belt and twist in my seat. "I'll tell him. I promise." Then I lean in and kiss her blues away. When I pull back, she's smiling again. "For now, let's go see where we're getting fake married."

We get out and head down the path where a staircase brings us up to the gigantic front door, which would be intimidating if it wasn't so awe-inspiring with its wood and stained-glass finish and see-through windows flanking it on both sides. The door even has an honest-to-goodness wooden knocker in the shape of a sunburst.

When Chloe uses it, the knock reverberates through the cavernous foyer that's visible through the windows.

It takes several long moments, but then Greta is there in her sweater and pressed trousers. And she does not look happy to see us. "What are you doing here?"

Chloe looks at me, frowns. "I'm Chloe Marie and this—"

"I know who you are. But why are you here?"

"Did I get the time for our meeting wrong?" Pulling her phone from her purse, Chloe begins flipping through her calendar. But no, Greta said Tuesday at four. Even I remember that.

Greta sighs, leaning against the door frame that completely dwarfs her short stature. "Didn't you get my voicemail?"

"N-no."

"Hmm. That's odd. I know I left one." Greta waves her hand through the air, dismissing the notion. "Regardless, I told you I had to cancel our appointment because termites were discovered here. I thought you were the exterminators coming to tent the place."

"Wait. What?" Chloe tugs at a piece of her hair. "O-okay. Well, when can we come back?"

"Do you have cotton for brains, girl? You can't have the wedding here. The tenting and fumigation process takes time, and the house won't be ready for this weekend." Then she has the decency to look chagrined. "I am sorry. It all happened so suddenly. But you can't let termites go on. Once you discover them, you need to act quickly. I have to protect my home."

"Of course." Chloe's chin trembles but somehow she

manages a smile. "Well, thank you for your consideration and t-time."

I've got to get her out of here before she breaks down. "Thank you, Mrs. Graber."

"Yes, well."

We turn to go, but Greta calls back to us. "For what it's worth, I think you're a nice couple. I hope you find somewhere to tie the knot."

I offer a small smile and a wave, then place a hand around Chloe's waist and help her back to the car, where she turns into me and starts to cry.

"Shh, love." I tuck her head under my chin, run my hands up and down her back. "It's all right."

"It's not all right, Frederick. Don't you know what this means?" Her makeup is already smudged under her eyes—and on my white shirt. Not that I care. "We don't have a place for Topher and Lauren to get married."

"Then we'll find one."

"There isn't one! Remember? We were lucky to find the Graber house. And now ..." She stomps her foot and lets out a frustrated, muted squeal. "Everything's ruined. I ... I failed. I failed them, Freddy."

And I can't take the breaking in her voice. I hold her by the shoulders and wait until she's looking at me. "You have not failed yet. And you're not going to fail. And do you know why?"

"No."

"Because you're Chloe Huntington."

"That means nothing here."

"It means *everything*." I emphasize the last word. "You might not have an answer, and I certainly don't, but what did you do before when you needed to find a venue?"

She shrugs. "I asked the locals for help."

"Exactly. And that's what you're going to do again."

"I can't." And Chloe's shaking her head. "I already decided that the next time I saw Lucy and the others, I would tell them the truth. I don't want to lie anymore."

"Is that why you've avoided them the last few days?" I arch an eyebrow. "And here I thought you wanted me all to yourself."

"Well, that was part of it." She pokes me in the side, and that's how I know she's rounded the bend, leaving despair behind, and rallying toward hope. "But you're right. I need to ask them again." Chloe pauses. "I only hope that when I tell them the truth, they'll still be willing to help."

"The good thing is, the Chloe Effect doesn't just work on me."

"I'm sorry, the what?"

"The Chloe Effect."

"And what, may I ask, is that?"

I take her face between my palms and wipe the black makeup from under one eye with my thumb. Then the other. "*That* is the phenomenon whereby you make someone feel so special they are willing to go to the ends of the earth for you."

"That's not a thing."

I huff out a laugh. "I assure you, it is."

nineteen

CHLOE

The moment of truth has arrived, and my stomach won't let me forget it.

I might be sick in the lovely bushes outside Burt and Bea Reynolds' house, where Lucy has lived since she moved in at the age of sixteen. She hasn't told me exactly what happened to her parents, but I gather it's not good. So she moved here from Texas and has lived with her aunt and uncle ever since.

Ah, drat. *Just knock already, Chloe.*

But the last time I knocked on a door—thirty minutes ago—everything fell apart.

I glance back at Frederick, who is standing beside the car and gives me the thumbs-up. He wanted to come inside, but this is my secret to tell. Sure, he's been part of this lie, but I'm the one who originally started it. Or, who went along with Lucy's assumptions, anyhow.

The good thing is, Frederick feels comfortable enough with Lucy that he's okay with me going inside alone. He'll just stay stationed out here, offering me protection—and emotional support. Goodness, I lucked out with that man.

Blowing out a breath, I finally knock on the door. The brick home is simple, modest, a far cry from the grandeur of Greta's house, but not in a bad way. The shutters on the front windows are painted a cheery blue and the small grass yard has been well maintained. A huge tree provides shade for the home. I think that a home like this would make me quite happy someday.

So long as a certain someone is sharing it with me.

Before I get taken away by my fantasies, the door opens, and Lucy pops her head out. Her hair is piled on her head in a ridiculously high ponytail-braid thing, and her face ... well, her face looks like a makeup kit threw up on it. Bright green eyeshadow encompasses not just her eyelid but the entire section of skin between her lashes and eyebrows. Blush that should be discontinued for its extreme gaudiness has been caked on her cheeks, and her lips are a purple color that is definitely made for people with a darker skin tone than hers.

"Hi," she says brightly and pulls back the door with a sweeping gesture. "Come on in."

I follow her into the house, which is just as warm and inviting as I'd imagined it. "Um, I don't mean to be rude, but what happened to you?"

She glances behind her and then leans in toward me. "Scarlett happened to me." Then Lucy pulls me into a hug. "I've missed you! Sorry I couldn't meet you somewhere else, but I'm babysitting this afternoon while April has a job interview over at Bluestocking Books. I guess they decided to move here from San Francisco, which is super exciting but also very spontaneous. Anyway, Scarlett wanted to do makeovers." She frames her face with her hands, makes a duck face, and strikes a pose.

"You look fabulous, darling." I laugh at her antics. "And no worries. I know it was last minute, but I had something come up and needed your help."

"Always. I pulled up a show on Scarlett's tablet and she's

tucked away in her room for a bit so we can talk." Lucy moves into the living room, which is small, but cozy, with homemade quilts thrown over the back of the worn blue couch and a beige recliner that I can picture Burt using to watch the huge television mounted across the room. There's also a chipped oak coffee table, side tables that don't match, lamps with striped shades, and family portraits on the wall.

It's the complete and total opposite of my home in Kentonia. And while my mother has tried to make that a home, there's no real way to tone down the opulence when you live in a palace.

Lucy keeps talking. "You want anything to drink?"

"Sure," I say, wondering if my stomach will rebel if I try to put something into it. "Water would be lovely. Thanks."

Lucy heads into the kitchen, which is adjacent to the living room, talking over her shoulder. "Just move the stuff on the couch out of the way."

I pluck a makeup kit from the center of the couch and place it on the coffee table before sitting down. Something feels like it's tap dancing on my stomach—in heels. As Lucy bangs around in the kitchen, I spy a folded-up quilt and pillow on the floor beside the side table, along with a suitcase. How odd. I would have thought April was staying in one of the bedrooms.

Lucy strides back into the living room carrying two glasses filled with ice and water. She hands me one and places hers on a coaster on the coffee table. "Here you go."

"Thank you." Holding the iced beverage in one hand, I point to the stuff in the corner. "Is April sleeping in here right now?"

"No, that would be me." Lucy makes a face. "Burt and Bea only have three bedrooms here."

"So why don't April and Scarlett share?" I decide to brave the water in my glass. Maybe it'll calm down what's going on inside me. I take a sip and the cool liquid does at least refresh my throat.

No relief from the evil tap dancers in heels, though. Likely that will only happen after I confess my lies to Lucy.

"They did share at first, but I could tell April just needed a break, you know? And Scarlett's the kind of girl who needs a safe place to retreat to. Besides, April's an author—she's not published, but she needs the time and space to pursue her dreams."

"And they can't live with Stephanie?"

"No, she's in an apartment with a roommate. No space there."

"What about your Aunt Janine, then?"

"She lives on the property at The Purple Seashell. Only has a small bedroom tucked away on the main floor next to the manager's office. Besides, she's great but having a child underfoot would probably be hard for business. And Scarlett is just as feisty as her mama." She points to her face. "Case in point. I asked for a 'subtle makeover.' I swear the child's lips curved into a Grinch-like grin before she did this to me."

I snort. "Oh, my."

Lucy pulls the rubber band out of her hair, which falls around her shoulders. "It's all good. She's got a sweet heart. Things have just been rough for them. April's awesome, but being a single mom has to be hard." She finger combs through her blonde locks.

"I can't even imagine." I set my water beside Lucy's on the table. "But that's no fun you had to give up your room."

"To tell the truth, it's been time for me to move out for a while. I only stayed because I was able to help Bea out around the house. She's not exactly old yet, but has some arthritis starting in her hands. She's a quilt maker, so I want her to conserve her energy for that, you know? But now that April's here, I guess I'm not needed anymore." Lucy fidgets a bit in her seat, frowning at the floor. Then her eyes lift, and she seems to shrug off whatever cloud's hanging over her. "Anyway, I probably need to find a new place to stay. Whenever I have time to look, which hasn't been easy with my crazy work schedule."

"I'll bet." I press my quivering lips together. Lucy's one of the friendliest, most bubbly people I've ever met. How will she react to what I'm about to tell her?

I can't do this.

But I know I have to. Even though I will only be in Hallmark Beach for five more days, she's quickly become one of my best friends. The only other person besides Lauren I've connected with so well is Kennedy back in San Diego, but now that she's got a serious boyfriend and is helping to nanny his nieces, I'm not sure how much time she will really have to talk and text—especially once I return to Kentonia.

I guess the point is, when you find something as rare as a real friendship, even if things are complicated, you do what you can to nurture it.

And that means coming clean.

"Sorry, I've been blabbing on." Lucy turns to me, tucking her feet up beside her on the couch. "What did you need help with?"

Where to begin? I suppose with the easy part—the impetus for being here right now. "Greta Graber had to cancel the venue."

"What? Why?"

I tell her about the termites. By the time I'm done, she's got tears in her eyes for me. "Oh, Chloe, I'm so sorry. I know you had your heart set on that."

"I did. It was perfect too, Luce." I sigh. "Do you have any other ideas? Any at all?"

"Okay, hmm. We can figure out ... something." She cocks

her head as she pulls her hair back up, this time into a low ponytail that's much more signature Lucy. "You sure the beach won't work?"

"Positive."

"Can I ask why?"

And there it is. My opening. The opportunity I've been waiting for—and dreading. "Um." I stare up at the ceiling and blink.

She scoots closer to me and places a hand on my knee. "Hey, it's okay. Don't be upset. We'll figure out a new venue."

I lower my gaze and find hers. "That's not why I'm upset. Well, it is, obviously. I've got less than five days to find a place for the wedding. But ... there's more." Now I put my hand on top of hers. "Lucy, I've been lying to you." The tap dancers on my stomach increase their pace and intensity, jab, jab, jabbing me.

Her eyes flicker and she sits back ever so slightly. "About what?"

"The wedding ... it isn't for me and Frederick."

She wrinkles her nose. "Well, that's ridiculous. I mean, who else would it be for? And why would you lie about *that*?"

Here goes. "The wedding's actually for my brother, Topher, and his fiancée, Lauren."

"That literally makes no sense, Chlo." She pretends to knock a fist against my skull. "Did you fall and hit your head on that hike with Marilee and Jordan on Sunday?"

"I know it sounds crazy. And it probably was. But my brother is ... someone important. And this is actually kind of a surprise wedding. Like, the 'real wedding' is happening in April, but it was getting out of hand, and I wanted to give them this fantastic memory of a day that's truly all about them."

Lucy takes her glass in hand and takes a sip, her eyes squinting at me. "So, is he like, a celebrity or something?"

"Or something." I gnaw the inside of my cheek. "He's actually a prince."

She spews water at me, and her eyes widen. "Sorry!" Jumping up, she races into the kitchen and returns with a towel, which she hands to me before plopping back down. "But wait, are you serious? A prince? But wouldn't that make you ..."

"A princess. Yes."

"Like ... a real one?"

"No, a fake one, Luce," I tease as I wipe the droplets of water from my face and toss the towel back at her. Then I sober. "And there's more. Frederick is my bodyguard. I hadn't thought of trying to put any sort of cover story on the wedding, but when he arrived, and you made assumptions about it being my wedding and him being my fiancé, well ... we sort of went with it."

Lucy's just staring at me, and for once, I can't read her.

I tuck my head down. "I'm so sorry for lying to you. I've felt terrible about it ever since, but at the time it made sense because the paparazzi have been all over the coverage of the wedding back in Kentonia. And then, you and the rest of the gang here became true friends, and I wanted to tell you the truth but ... I was so afraid of losing you." I race on, afraid she'll shut me down before I've fully shared my heart. "In my world, it's so hard to find real friends, people who don't care about the power and prestige that come with my position. You have no idea how nice it was to just be ... normal. But I have no excuse for lying, and I understand if you don't want to help me anymore. If you want me to leave. But either way, I had to tell you the truth."

Lucy is silent for a good while, brushing her purple lips together. Finally, she speaks. "So let me get this straight. You're a princess."

"Yes."

"And your brother is a prince who's getting secretly married ahead of schedule."

"Yes."

"And you're planning the wedding."

"Yes."

"And you traveled all the way here, to random Hallmark Beach, to do that."

"Yes, though to be fair, my future sister-in-law is from San Diego, and I've been there for a few months. And because Shelby is getting married here, I got a chance to visit a few weeks ago with her. I fell in love with the town in a matter of days. So it wasn't random." I inhale. "I believe it was fate."

"Hmm." She rubs at her hot pink cheeks. "I won't pretend that it doesn't hurt to be lied to, but I understand why you did it. I was just a stranger at first. One with a big mouth. You didn't know if you could trust me with a secret."

I reach for her hand again. "But I know I can now."

She studies me. "So you want to keep it a secret still?"

"From most people, yes. But I'm going to tell Marilee, Jordan, the Lovelands. You can tell April, if you want. Stephanie already knows."

"She does?"

"That I'm royalty, at least."

Then she nods. "Of course she does. She's always reading those celebrity gossip sites online. I'm surprised she hasn't blabbed."

"I asked her not to. And I think we convinced her it's not Topher's wedding. She was suspicious until Freddy ..." I trail off.

"So wait. He's just your bodyguard? You and Frederick aren't together?" Lucy folds her arms over her chest. "I call bull-honky on that one."

Oh, Lucy. I love this girl so much. "Well, that *was* the case up until two days ago."

Lucy squeals. "Ooo, I need details!"

That brings tears to my eyes. "You do?"

"Of course. Hello! My own love life isn't exactly thriving. I need to live vicariously through my friends."

"So, we're still ... friends?"

"Of course we are." She tilts her head. "Friends confess when they've done something wrong. And friends forgive those friends for their mistakes. So, see? We're friends."

I tackle her with a hug, holding her tight. "Thank you, Luce."

She pulls back, and the white of her smile glows against her dark lips. "Thanks for being honest with me. And don't worry. I'll send out an SOS text to the ladies to put on their thinking caps. We'll get together if we have to and hunt down information. We'll find you a perfect venue. I'm assuming the beach isn't private enough, right?"

I nod. She understands perfectly.

"All right, then. We'll get this sorted. But first"—she looks me dead in the eye with as serious a look as Lucy ever has—"I need to know alllll the details about how Bodyguard Frederick came to be Lover Boy Frederick. And don't leave anything out."

Watching the woman I love in her element is a new favorite hobby of mine.

A gaggle of women flit around Something Blue, tearing the place practically apart as they search for clues. All right, they're not destroying anything, but they've got stuff spread out all over the sitting area in back. It's a bit of a mess, but despite the challenge of finding a new venue, Chloe looks happier than I've seen her in a while.

She's got Lucy on one side of her, Marilee on the other, and they're flipping through a huge album of photos, presumably of past weddings organized by Something Blue. April's stretched out on her stomach on the floor, feet in the air behind her as she pages through some old documents from a file folder that came from the office. Elisse is in the big armchair, her legs flung over the side as she leans back on a pillow, a binder open.

All of Chloe's new friends except for Kelsey—who had something come up at the last minute—are here. She called them one by one last night after her chat with Lucy. Told them the truth. Asked them to forgive her, and then, if they were willing, to help her.

Obviously, they did. And they were. Because here they are.

Chloe must feel me watching her, because she glances up at me. "You sure you don't want to help us, Muscles?"

"I like my spot right here, thanks." I'm standing in the corner, which gives me the perfect vantage point to observe everyone in the room and also the front door. At this point, I don't expect any threats to crop up, but with this many people knowing Chloe's identity, I'm not taking any chances.

Elisse narrows her eyes at me, as if she's trying to puzzle something out. "I knew there was something off about you. You watched Chloe like a hawk every time you were together."

"That's because he loves her," Lucy says from across the room.

Is it possible to feel your face redden? I mean, I do love Chloe, but I haven't told her that yet. And I won't feel comfortable telling her that until I speak to Topher. Until I know how things will work out between us. Ignoring Lucy's comment, I subtly check my watch, which connects with my phone. Still no return text from Topher. I messaged him this morning asking him to call when he had time for a "casual chat."

No, it's anything but casual, but by phrasing it that way, I knew he wouldn't rush to call me.

Am I a coward? Maybe. But I haven't wanted anything to ruin the time I've had with Chloe in near-perfect bliss here in Hallmark Beach. Topher knowing about us brings another element into things.

It makes it real—and while I'm ready to be real with Chloe, I'm not sure I'm ready for reality back home.

"Aw, look, he's blushing." April's watching me from over her shoulder. "That's freaking adorable."

"There's nothing *adorable* about me," I say with as much dignity as I can muster. Women and their adjectives.

"I can think of a few things," Chloe whispers, and the group breaks into giggles.

My phone vibrates in my pocket. Yes! A distraction. But when my watch tells me it's Topher calling, my heart sinks. I pull my mobile from my trousers and stare at the screen. "Sorry, ladies, I need to take this." Turning toward the front door, where I can station myself just outside for privacy's sake and still stay between Chloe and any potential intruders, I start walking as the hot potato keeps buzzing in my hand.

"Is it Topher?" Chloe calls from behind me.

"Yes."

"Tell him I say h—" The jangling bell over the door drowns out the rest of Chloe's words as I step outside onto Main Street. It's not as crowded this week as last, a welcome relief that means we were able to secure enough rooms at The Purple Seashell for the coming weekend.

Finally, just as the phone hits the last vibration before rolling over to voicemail, I answer. "Hello, mate."

"Sorry it took me so long to call, old chap," Topher says. The wheels of his office chair squeak out a hello. "Been in back-to-back meetings all day long. This future king stuff is for the birds."

"Ever wish we could go back to the good old armed forces days?" I know I do. Back then, we were just friends, didn't have the extra complication of his father employing me. And even though we were mostly stationed in and around Kentonia, at least we were largely on duty outside.

Topher chuckles. "I much preferred the uni days, myself."

Ah, the endless studying, the classes, the books. "You would."

"So." Another squeak. "How are things going there?"

I lean against the front window of Something Blue, where there's a wedding dress hanging from a display. Despite what little I know about fashion, it seems the sort of dress Chloe might like. Strapless, shimmery, with flowing material that would hit her curves in all the right spots.

Am I really going there? Imagining her in a gown? Dare I picture myself as the groom waiting for her at the end of the aisle?

It seems too good to be true.

I clear my throat. "Yeah, no, it's good. Plans are well underway for the wedding. A few obstacles, but nothing your sister can't handle." Can he hear the blamed adoration in my voice? Best tone it down. "How are you feeling?"

Topher sighs, and I can picture him rubbing his forehead. "Tired, mate. Just ... tired. But looking forward to seeing every-one." He pauses. "To marrying Lauren. Finally."

"It has seemed a rather long time coming, hasn't it?"

"Endless." A pen rat-a-tats in the background, likely against his desk. "Look, you know Chloe almost better than anyone."

Where's he going with this? Does he suspect what's been going on between us? "I do."

"Do you think *she's* ready for ... marriage?"

My gaze scoots past the wedding dress in the window, finds her inside with her friends. And it strikes me—what if marriage isn't what she wants? What if going back to Kentonia isn't even what she wants? She said something the other night about buying this wedding shop, about loving how normal she felt here. I know it's what she is planning to do, but what if she's really meant to stay here?

There's so much we haven't talked about, because ... well, even though it's also felt like a long time coming, this thing between us is still new. Shouldn't I know what *she* wants before I talk to Topher and bring a whole other host of complications into the newness of this relationship?

"I think she's mature enough to get married, for sure," I say cautiously. "But whether that's what she wants, I don't know. Why?"

"Father has someone he wants her to meet. A local dignitary's son. He's wealthy, intelligent, and from what I can tell, a true gent. He's got a solid reputation, the people love him, and he'd bring great connections with a few other countries nearby, as he has family in high positions there as well."

I slump against the wedding shop's window. It's cold against my arm. "Wow. He sounds ..." Perfect. He sounds perfect for her. His reputation wouldn't mar hers. Sounds like it would bolster it. Unlike—

Shaking off the jealousy Topher's revelation has wrought, I straighten. No. I'm not going to give in to the doubts again. Chloe's chosen me, and so far, there's no actual evidence that my family's reputation might harm her.

Besides, whoever Chloe's with, I want *her* to decide, not her family. This is her life, and I want her to feel complete freedom to choose it.

Still, maybe it's not the worst idea to give her time—to present her with all of her options—before we go announcing our relationship to the world.

Or to her brother.

"I don't know, mate," I say, evening my tone. "An arranged marriage? Really?"

"No, not really. It'd just be an introduction. She wouldn't be forced into anything." He pauses. "This guy just seems really perfect for her, if she'll only give him a chance."

Bile rises in my throat.

"Anyhow, I was just curious about your thoughts. What was it you wanted to chat about?"

"Nothing." For now. "Nothing at all. Just wanted to check in."

"Oh. All right. Well, if there isn't anything else, then I'll head out. Supposed to chat with Lauren in five."

"Have fun, mate. Enjoy that almost wedded bliss. She still doesn't know the wedding got moved up, does she?"

He laughs. "Thanks. And no, she thinks they're going back to Hallmark Beach for a girls' weekend related to Shelby's wedding."

"Perfect."

We hang up and I set my head against the glass. Ugh. Perfect. Yeah, right. Chloe's going to murder me for not telling Topher. She thinks it has something to do with me doubting us, but that's not completely accurate. I know what I want, and I'm willing to fight for it—so long as it's what *she* wants. And maybe she needs time to make sure that's really coming back to Kentonia with me.

I'm about to head inside when my protective agent senses go haywire. I glance up to find someone running toward the wedding shop, but as she gets closer, I see that it's not a stranger. It's Kelsey Loveland.

When she gets here, she pitches forward, hands on her knees and breathing hard. "Where's Chloe?"

"Inside." I move to open the door and allow her through.

The women all glance up and throw hellos to Kelsey as we both move through the room toward the group.

Chloe looks at me with lifted brows, and she doesn't have to say it. She wants to know if I told Topher. I press my lips into a tight line and shake my head.

Her expression falls, but then her attention turns to Kelsey. "You all right, birdie?

"Yeah, Kels, you don't look so hot," Elisse says, sitting up as she studies her sister.

"Actually, you look *over*heated." Marilee pats the spot on her other side. "Come sit and cool off."

"I'm fine, guys. Chloe." She pauses and waves both hands at her red face. "I found you a venue."

"What? Where?"

Kelsey's gaze slides to Elisse, then back to the couch where Chloe, Lucy, and Marilee are all sitting on the edge of their seats—quite literally. "The vineyard."

Chloe's hand flies to her mouth. "That's ... perfect. But I thought you guys didn't do events?"

"Yeah, Kels." Elisse launches one eyebrow upward. "Dad hates outsiders on our property. Did you get his approval?"

"I got Mom's, and she convinced him."

"Seriously?" A long whistle from Elisse. "That's quite a feat, sis."

Kelsey sticks her hands into the back pockets of her trousers. "It's not that big of a deal."

"Are you kidding?" Chloe leaps to her feet, her hair falling around her shoulders in perfect waves. Sakes, that woman is beautiful. And with her eyes lit up like that? Pure enchantment. "You just saved my brother's wedding. I'm pretty sure that's a big deal."

"It's not saved just yet," Kelsey says. "Any event with more than thirty people requires a town permit."

"Really?" I butt into the conversation. "That didn't seem to be an issue with the Graber house."

"I guess Greta has a year-round permit. The winery doesn't." Kelsey blows out a breath.

"Okay, so we get a permit." Chloe shrugs. "How difficult can it be?"

Kelsey winces. "The only way to get one is via the town council."

The women all groan, as if they know something we don't.

Chloe turns to them, frowning. "What?"

"It's just that Alberta Jenkins is the head of the town council," Lucy pats Chloe's elbow, which is near her own face. "And she doesn't take kindly to outsiders."

"Oh." Chloe flops back onto the couch and puts her chin in her hands. Bites that bottom lip. "Well, we'll just have to convince her. Throw a little of the Chloe Effect her way." She glances up at me.

I laugh.

The others look confused.

"The what?" Marilee asks.

She winks at me. "I've been told it's a thing."

"Oh, it is, Princess," I say. "It is."

Turns out, Alberta Jenkins is the Al of Al's Grocery Store.

As in, the person I once imagined as being so anti-system that they refused to adhere to the town's standardized naming convention for their Main Street storefronts. The person I imagined having something in common with.

But I'm not sure I have a single thing in common with this woman. Taller than Frederick and twice as wide, with a head of bottle-red hair despite the wrinkles and liver spots dotting her skin, she's got a steely gaze that's scary as a snake about to strike a mouse.

And to be clear—she's the snake and I'm the mouse in this scenario.

"Come to order!" She bangs a wooden gavel against the high-top table where she's sitting inside Rainbow Ice, apparently the only building in town that can accommodate this many people on short notice since there's no official town hall. Bathed in fluorescent light, the place is a hodgepodge of colors with a huge rainbow painted behind the counter where a chalkboard menu of ice cream flavors hangs. Scattered throughout the room are a mix of high-top tables and booths, which are filled with people. There's standing room only left, and in fact, the crowd spills out of the place.

At Alberta's announcement, someone shouts to the group on the back deck that overlooks the beach. "Be quiet, you lot!"

I'm standing not far from Alberta between Frederick and Lucy, both of whom are holding my hands. After Kelsey broke the news to us about the vineyard being available just a few hours ago, the women have gone to bat for me, calling up Alberta and the other four town council members. Two of them are out of town at the moment, but Burt is one—and he's firmly in my corner, thank goodness—while Simone Zalenski, the owner of Red Sauce Pizza, is the other. She's a complete wild card, though the women have assured me she's pretty fair.

I only need two of them to approve the permit. Majority rules.

They truly have no reason to deny me. Except for Alberta's glare, telling me she's already against me. Simone will have to be my saving grace, then.

"I said, order!" Alberta bangs the gavel again. The woman's clearly power hungry as her eyes roam the crowd. I recognize a lot of townsfolk I've met over the last week since I arrived. Bea, Stephanie, Jordan, Landon, and a few of the Loveland brothers. Even Greta's squeezed onto a stool in the corner, eating a bowl of what looks to be vanilla ice cream. That would be very Greta of her if so.

Each person whose gaze I catch nods at me. They've got my back.

This town is literally the best. It breaks my heart to think about leaving in four days. But once the wedding is over, I'll have no reason to stay.

At least I have a brilliant life waiting for me back home, with Frederick.

"We're meeting tonight—at a most inconvenient hour, I

must say"—Alberta glares at me—"to discuss the matter of whether a last-minute event permit can be issued to Loveland Winery for a wedding"—she spits the word—"between Chloe Marie and Frederick Shaw."

"Is this really necessary?" someone yells from the crowd. "I just wanted some ice cream, but now I can't make it to the counter."

"Shut up, Earl," Alberta yells back. "Your feedback was not requested."

An older gentleman grumbles and flicks his fingers across his white mustache.

Alberta continues, reading off of a piece of paper in her hands. The woman has no need for a microphone. Her voice booms through the small restaurant. "Hallmark Beach by-laws state that a town council meeting is required to issue permits for events over thirty people unless an establishment already has a year-round permit for events."

Frederick leans close, and the scent of his masculine aftershave tickles my nose. "It's going to work out, love."

Love. I can't get over hearing him call me that—even if I'm still a bit mystified over why he didn't tell Topher about us on their phone call. But that's a question for another time. I squeeze his hand in response.

Alberta drones on about official policy, finally reaching the part of the meeting where we get to say our bit. "I believe a representative of the Loveland Winery is here?"

Kelsey squeaks as Elisse and their oldest brother Oliver push her forward. She looks completely darling in a ruffled purple blouse that makes her brown eyes pop behind her glasses, which I notice she sometimes wears later in the day. "Y-yes." She clears her throat. "Yes. Here."

"Well, go on then." Alberta waves her gavel in the air again. Her muscular forearms sink into the table. "Your parents are really okay with this? I thought Dan felt the same way I do about outsiders." She turns her glare on me again.

Lucy pats my hand in solidarity. I lean my head on her shoulder as thanks.

"He and my mom both agree that Chloe and Frederick are no longer outsiders." Kelsey glances at us both, smiles. "They're friends, and we want this wedding to be everything it should be."

Burt shoots us a thumbs-up and exaggerated wink. Simone smiles at us. Both good signs.

"Hmm." Alberta rolls the gavel between her fingers. "And can anyone show just cause for why this wedding should not be allowed to take place at Loveland?"

I hold my breath. It's like those few seconds at a wedding ceremony when the preacher asks a very similar question about why two people shouldn't marry.

Someone coughs in the background. But nobody says a word.

"All right, then I suppose it's time to take a formal vote. All those in favor of granting the permit so Chloe Marie and Frederick Shaw can marry this Sunday at Loveland Winery, say aye."

Burt lifts both his hands high above his head. "Aye!" His voice rings loud and clear.

Alberta rolls her eyes at him.

Simone presses her lips together and smooths a stray blonde hair back into her bob. "Aye," she says.

Alberta doesn't say a word, just frowns, because even though she's clearly opposed, there's nothing she can do to stop this from happening. "Fine. By the power vested in me—"

"You're not a freaking priest, Al!"

"I said shut up, Earl," she snarls, then composes herself and lifts her gavel again. "By the power vested in me—"

"Wait! Stop."

My blood goes cold because I recognize that voice. I turn and look over my shoulder at the giant of a man staggering through Rainbow Ice's front door, pushing people out of the way despite their protests.

It's Ricky, of Black Hole drunken fame.

"What's that blighter doing here?" It's Frederick's turn to snarl.

"Easy, Muscles," I say, though I'd like to know the same thing.

Alberta sighs. "You're supposed to be minding the store, Ricky. What do you want?"

"I've got some information, Ma."

I nudge Lucy in the side. "Ma?"

"Oh, yeah, did I forget to mention that?" She grimaces. "Don't worry. Alberta despises him almost as much as the rest of us do. She doesn't take anything he says seriously."

"And he doesn't know anything," I say. How could he? Nobody here would tell him my secrets.

I relax my shoulders. For all I know, Ricky's *information* is that we hooked up after he hit on me at the bar. Obviously, the man is delusional if he thinks he knows anything that will change the minds of people here.

Ricky finally makes his way to the front. He stands hand and foot over everyone else. "This wedding"—he slurs—"is a sh ... a sh ..."

"Spit it out, son. You're wasting our time."

"A sham!" He nods happily. "That's it. This wedding's a sham."

Alberta places her head in her hands, clearly embarrassed by her son. I almost feel bad for the guy—though what he says next makes me feel less so.

"It's not for the two of them." Turning, Ricky points at us. "It's for her brother."

My mouth drops open. How—?

But Ricky isn't finished. "She's some foreign princess and this guy's just her bodyguard. They've been faking it this whole time." He grins at me, his teeth more fang-like than I remember. "I knew you didn't have a fiancé. You were coming on to me too hard. Putting out all the signals."

Frederick starts to move toward him, ready to pounce, but I keep hold of his hand and draw him back to my side. "He's not worth it."

"I won't have him slandering you like that." He's positively seething.

"I'm fine." But it's quite possible I'm not. At least, that our permit's not.

A murmur has gone up through the crowd, and people are all looking at me and Frederick. Burt's sitting back in his chair, stroking at his non-existent beard, while Simone's studying us with a thoughtful gaze.

The snake-like gleam in Alberta's eyes has returned, and it's delighted in the confident way a predator gets when it knows it has its prey in its sights. "And where did you get this information, Ricky?" She leans forward in her seat.

His gaze travels the crowd before landing on Stephanie, whose eyes widen at his appraisal. She drops her gaze to her phone and slurps on her soda.

"Stephanie!" April, who's sitting beside her sister, smacks Stephanie in the arm. "How could you?"

"I'm sorry," Stephanie wails. "I didn't mean to tell him." Her eyes flick briefly to Oliver Loveland of all people, then back to her soda. "He caught me in a weak moment at the bar."

We're sunk. Absolutely sunk. Nobody is going to trust us now. I don't realize I'm biting my lip until Frederick leans close, his lips skimming my ear. "Time for the Chloe Effect, love." Then he spins us around to face the crowd.

I open my mouth ... and freeze. Turning my face into his shoulder, I breathe through my nose. All the memories of the last time I spoke publicly race through my mind. I'm fine one on one, but this? I'm liable to jumble my words again. I don't even have a teleprompter this time. There's just ... no way. And the stakes, they're so much higher this time.

"I can't," I whisper.

He takes his finger and gently crooks it under my chin, lifting it until I'm looking into his eyes—so sure of me. So sure of this. "Yes, you can. You are strong, Princess, and you are not the same girl who gave that speech years ago. Go on now. Speak from the heart, and I know you won't fail."

Gah. How does he believe in me *this* much?

I take another deep breath, nod. "For Topher and Lauren."

"Good lass." Then he takes my hand and waits.

My insides trembling, I turn back to the crowd, which has gone mostly silent, a buzz of anticipation spinning and gathering. I rack my brain for the right words, but then, I remember —*from the heart*, he said.

Okay. I can do this.

"What Ricky says is true," I begin, and there's more murmuring. A few people shift in their seats, but all eyes remain on me. "I'm from a small country in Europe called Kentonia, and there, I'm a princess. All that means is that, just like you, I was born into a particular family. Only, being born into my family comes with certain privileges. But also, certain obligations."

I pause, licking my lips. People are still with me, so I go on. "Before I came to America a few months ago to be with my future sister-in-law in San Diego, I felt ... lost. Just like many of you might have felt at some point in your life, I didn't know what I was meant to do, or who I was meant to be. I mean, yes, I'm Princess Chloe of Kentonia, but that's not *who* I am."

My eyes scan the crowd and land on Lucy, whose hands are folded in front of her mouth. She shakes them at me, urging me on. Then I find Marilee, whose eyes are filled with tears as she snuggles a sleeping Ryder against her chest and leans against Jordan, who nods at me.

"A few weeks ago, I visited your town with my sister-in-law and her friend, who is getting married here in the summer. I saw then what a special place Hallmark Beach really is. You are some of the warmest"—I seek out Kelsey, April, yes, even Elisse —"friendliest"—there's Janine, smiling at me like a proud aunt —"and most interesting people"—I grin at Burt in the chair beside me—"I've ever met. And I've never felt more myself than I have right here."

Several people nudge each other and smile, clear pride in their town showing through. And they should be proud. I mean every word.

"So when I decided to throw my brother and sister-in-law a secret wedding—because when you are a royal and get married, nothing you do is private or your own, not even a wedding—I knew exactly where to come. Hallmark Beach."

Frederick keeps an even pressure on my hand, grounding me in this moment. I glance at him. "And it's true. I lied to you all, and I can't say I'm sorry enough for that." My eyes find Stephanie next. Her hand stills, hovering over her drink. Then, slowly, she nods, mouths *I'm sorry too.* I smile at her, letting her know it's okay. I forgive her for going back on her word. "The thing is, my past experience taught me to be afraid of strangers. Strangers have always wanted something from me, whether it's power or prestige or simply photographs they could spin however they pleased. But you've all taught me that I don't have to be afraid anymore. So thank you. Whether you decide to grant this permit or not, thank you for just being you. And for allowing me to be me."

My shoulders collapse, and Frederick sneaks his arm around my waist as I lean against him. "You did it," he says, low and soft.

The crowd's whispers grow louder as people inevitably discuss what I've just said.

"I did," I reply to him. And I couldn't have done it without Freddy, without his encouragement. "Let's hope it was enough."

I turn to find Alberta staring at me, something ... different in her eyes. When she sees that I've caught her looking, she glances away and clears her throat. Bangs her gavel until the room quiets again. "Well, I suppose now that we have all of the facts, we can vote again for real this time. All those in favor of allowing use of Loveland Winery for the very secret wedding between the prince of Kentonia and his bride-to-be, say aye."

"Aye," Burt says.

"Aye," Simone follows.

Alberta purses her lips and looks at the ceiling. "Aye." Her voice rings through Rainbow Ice.

The crowd goes wild, whooping and hollering like someone just won a championship sports game.

Frederick takes me around the waist and somehow manages to spin me in the tight space before setting me on my feet and kissing me breathless. I laugh with abandon, and then I'm being tackled with hugs by Lucy, Marilee, all of my new friends.

The cheering is brokered by a new wave of gavel banging. All of our attention swings back to Alberta, who is now standing, towering over us from behind the high-top table. Her eyes swing menacingly over the crowd. "I expect all of you to keep your mouths shut about this event until after it's over. No one will be going to the press or putting this on Facebook on my watch."

Well, that, I did not expect. But I toss her a grateful smile all the same.

"I guess the Chloe Effect really is a thing," Lucy says with awe. "I've never seen anyone win Alberta Jenkins over."

"That's my girl." Frederick slings his arm around my shoulders and kisses my temple.

And I'm fairly certain that nothing can top this moment. The only thing that would be better is if I was planning my own wedding to the man at my side.

Yes, we just started dating. But when you know, you know.

Do I hate the idea of declaring to the world we are dating and getting bombarded with the inevitable bad press that will come because of Frederick's last name? Or letting Felicia Flutterbum ruin my wedding with all of her terrible ideas? Or struggling to explain to my brother, my father, my entire country that what I feel for him is a once-in-a-lifetime kind of love?

Do I wish instead that I could marry him quietly here? To make a life away from the noise and the cameras?

Yes. Of course. To all of it. But Frederick Shaw is it for me —and I will take him any way I can get him.

I only hope he feels as strongly as I do. And that his unwillingness to tell Topher about us earlier today doesn't mean otherwise.

twenty-two

FREDERICK

Apparently everyone in town is too afraid of Alberta Jenkins to defy a direct order, because twenty-four hours after the impromptu town council meeting, I still see absolutely no evidence online that anyone has gone to the media about Topher and Lauren's secret wedding.

I'm not sure how it's possible that an entire town can keep a secret like that, but when I say as much to Jordan as we clear piles of wood and old tools from the patch of land at the edge of the vineyard where the wedding will be held, he just shrugs. "We protect our own here."

And clearly, Chloe has warmed her way into their hearts in the same way the town has into hers, because there are dozens of people here, helping. A few of the Loveland brothers— Oliver and Nathaniel, mostly, since Malcolm's off flirting with some women—are directing traffic, giving anyone who wants to do manual labor instructions on where to help out and where to store the various odds and ends that have taken up this space over the years.

Not only do we need to clear the space, but then there'll be the yard work needed to get it into tip-top shape for Sunday.

We have today and most of tomorrow to get that done, since Topher, Lauren, and their mates arrive sometime tomorrow afternoon before we whisk them off for their bachelor and bachelorette parties.

Saturday will be spent decorating and setting up here, followed by the rehearsal.

Then, the wedding on Sunday.

Grunting, I move with a wheelbarrow filled with stray rocks toward a building that's being used for storage. Jordan's on my tail with a stack of boards. Once we deposit our items at the feet of the guys who will bring some semblance of organization to what's being stored and how, I head back out with the wheelbarrow for more. My back aches from hours of labor, and there's a slight pain at the base of my skull where a constant headache almost always sits, but my muscles also sing with the exertion. I breathe in the loamy scent of the earth, refreshed last night by a spring shower. Thankfully, the forecast for the rest of the week and weekend ahead is clear.

When I can't take the burn in my arms and legs any longer, I head for the area where some of the ladies have set up a table filled with food and drinks. Tugging off my gloves, I stick them in the back pocket of my shorts, wash my hands and run them through my hair, over my grimy face. Then I snag a water bottle from one of the cool boxes and take a seat on a makeshift barrel chair.

"That was some fine hauling you were doing, man." Oliver Loveland claps me on the shoulder and grabs himself a drink as well. He takes a long swig as he surveys the field, where we've made loads of progress. "You sure you don't want to come work for us?"

I allow the cool water from my bottle to wet my parched throat. "Nah, mate. I've got a job."

"Right. Bodyguard, I hear?"

"Yep." Although I haven't been much of one today. Chloe requested that I only watch over her from afar, insisted that she needed my help with the manual labor more than she needed me hovering around her in bodyguard mode.

Said she trusted the people here, and that should be good enough for me.

"Well"—Oliver shrugs—"if you ever change your mind and want a job that allows you to work outside, with your hands, give me a call. It's not for the faint of heart, but the intense hours during harvest season mean you get a lot of time off other times of year. You could travel or just hang out and enjoy time with your family and friends." He drains the rest of his water, crushes the plastic bottle, and tosses it into the rubbish bin. "Think about it." Then he strides away.

What he's proposing sounds ... amazing.

But I could never leave Kentonia, could I? Abandon Topher? Certainly not my parents. I just got a text from Mum this morning after I sent a message checking in. She said, *Dad's not doing so well. A new bout of depression rearing its ugly head. But no fear—got him on new meds. Will keep you posted. Just keep making us proud. That keeps Dad going more than anything.*

Of course, Mum couldn't know that that was the last possible thing I needed to hear. After all, bodyguards can't marry. So at this point, I'm not even sure that I could continue in that line of work and be with Chloe too.

But after hearing her speech this afternoon, I'm not sure that returning to Kentonia is even what she's meant to do.

I hear a laugh, one I know well, and turn my head toward the deck attached to the Loveland family home. Lights are strung overhead, and there stands Chloe beside an easel and whiteboard, leading a discussion about something to a group of women. She's using a marker to point to markings on the board.

Our country doesn't know what it has in this princess. No one appreciates her, or her talents, like they should. But the people of Hallmark Beach ... they seem to.

Which makes my gut twist again with the same thought that I've been trying to ignore since yesterday: what if Chloe is supposed to stay here?

"Oh, wow, that cake looks amaze-balls, doesn't it?" Jordan approaches in his sleeveless gym shirt. He shucks off his own gloves and shoves them into the elastic waistband of his athletic shorts before cutting a huge slice of chocolate cake. He forks a bite and eats it with a single swallow, then groans. "Dude, you have to try this."

"Nah, gotta keep my girlish figure." I pat my stomach and laugh. "Just joking." Joining him at the table, I cut myself a more modest piece and take a bite and sakes, it's like a candy bar exploded on my tongue. "That's delicious, mate. Did Marilee make this?"

"Yeah." Jordan takes another bite. His eyes wander to the deck, finding the woman in question.

Ah, yeah, he's got it bad. "So, what's the story between you two anyhow?"

"What?" he coughs out, choking on his cake.

I lift the creaking lid from the cool box and snag him a water, which I toss, and he catches.

"Thanks," he says, twisting off the lid with one hand and downing half the bottle in a single swig. "And there's no story. We're just friends."

"How well I remember saying the same thing before Chloe and I got together." I waggle my eyebrows and laugh at the expression on his face. Poor chump. "But if you say so."

Jordan frowns around his fork. We both finish our cake in silence, then dump our plates and utensils into the rubbish bin and walk back toward the field together. The long grass tickles my calves and I take in the sight of the sun hovering just over the hills that surround the vineyard. We only have a half hour, maybe a bit longer, before we need to bust out the floodlights.

"I overheard Oliver offering you a job." Jordan's presence beside me isn't like Topher's. He's more light-hearted, more jovial too. But he's still been a good mate to me in the last week since we first met. "You thinking about taking it?"

"Much as I wish I could, I can't." Retracing my steps to the wheelbarrow, I lean down to grab a rock to place inside.

Jordan joins me. "Why not? From what I can tell, you're an outdoors kind of guy like me. Can't really picture you cooped up standing against a wall, just ... invisible." He shudders under the weight of a boulder.

"It's not my first choice of employment." I place my hands under the other side of the rock, and we carry it to the wheel-barrow together. "But I owe my friend—the prince—a lot."

"Seems to me if he's really your friend, he'd want you to do something you love. Imagine if the roles were reversed."

The man's got a point. But there's more to the story. There are my parents to consider too. I don't want to take away the only point of pride my father has left—me serving the crown when he can't. Which is why I need to speak with Topher. If I'm going to remain a bodyguard, if Chloe and I are really going to try this thing, he's going to have get rid of that rubbish law about bodyguards not being allowed to marry.

Chloe reminded me of my promise again last night as we snuggled before bed. I assured her of my affection in the only way I knew how—a rule-breaking kiss that left us both aching for more. But even after she fell asleep in my arms, I stayed awake long after, wondering if she was slipping away from me little by little. If she would honestly be happy going back to Kentonia after experiencing true freedom here.

Wondering if I'd have to do the hardest thing in the world

and let go of her so she could find her forever happiness. Because I know one thing, and that's that my place is in Kentonia.

I say as much to Jordan.

"That's too bad," he replies. He points at Chloe, who is positively glowing under the string of lights that burn brighter as the world around them falls dim. Just like her. "Because it sure seems like she belongs here."

He's right. And it's time I fully admit it to myself.

Holding back a groan, I squat and lift a boulder that's probably much too heavy for me. The burn is real as I turn and take a few steps before letting it crash into the wheelbarrow with a resounding thud.

twenty-three

CHLOE

Last night, I had a terrifying dream. It was worse than the one I always have about the paparazzi.

I lost Frederick.

No, I didn't just lose him—he left. Just like Troy. We were at the beach, flirting, kissing, enjoying the waves, when he suddenly turned and walked away. Mist started to cover him, and I called for him to come back.

But he never did.

And no matter how fast I ran after him, my feet kept sinking into the sand. He got farther and farther away, until he finally disappeared on the horizon.

I jolted awake and nearly cried with relief when I found myself curled up beside him. After that day we went hiking, he tried to go back to his bed on the floor, but I refused to let him. So he implemented a silly rule about not kissing in the hotel room.

Okay, fine, it wasn't silly. It was sweet. *Really* sweet, considering what other men would have tried.

But then, two nights ago, he broke his own rule in response to me asking why he hadn't told Topher about us yet. And,

241

ridiculous as it may sound, there seemed a bit of a goodbye in that kiss. I only wish I knew why, but I'm terrified to ask. Terrified for him to confirm that he's pulling away from me.

Because even though he was holding me last night, I think I was holding back tighter.

So all day today, as we've finished getting the vineyard ready for the wedding on Sunday, I've told myself we are fine. That the reason he hasn't kissed me except on the cheek this morning is because we've been busy. Because we're tired. Because Topher and Lauren will be here any moment and we've had to bust our rears to get everything done that needs to be done.

But it *is* done. Ready for the decorating day tomorrow.

I stand on the edge of the Lovelands' home deck and look at what all the town's hard work has wrought. What was once a field full of odds and ends and rocks and rusty tools is now a gorgeous plot of grass that's been mowed and given new life with an array of plants potted in old wine barrels. Earlier today, the men installed wrought-iron poles all around the area, and thousands of outdoor string lights bound from pole to pole.

A simple but elegant wedding arch, which is carved to look like it has ivy curling down the sides, sits at the top of the space where the poles begin, and I can picture how it will look tomorrow when we get the rows of white chairs set up in front of it.

The wooden dance floor will be delivered tomorrow as well, along with the reception tables and benches. The inside of the Loveland home currently looks like a bridal bouquet exploded, but the centerpieces that a dozen ladies from the Hallmark Beach Craft Society started on yesterday are going to look incredible on the rustic-chic picnic tables I ordered for the reception.

Pressing a hand against my chest, I feel this community's

love. It's visible here, alive in a way I've never felt. These strangers have chosen to make me an honorary member of their society, and my heart beats right back for them.

If only …

But no. My life is back in Kentonia, with Frederick.

If he would ever consider leaving there, then maybe I would consider staying here. But my life would not be complete without him. And when flashes of that terrible dream —that nightmare—from last night assail me, I remind myself of that.

Tires crunch on the gravel behind me and I do a quick spin to find two large black SUVs approaching. "They're here, people!" I half shout, half squeal.

It's not like there are a lot of people still here anymore, most of the helpers having left an hour ago, eager to return and help set up for a prince's wedding in the morning. I know Lucy wishes she could be here for the big reveal, but she's over at The Green Robin getting things ready for our bachelorette party dinner. The Loveland twins, Marilee, and April are off somewhere, as are Loveland brothers, Jordan, and Landon, but I think they're giving us our privacy.

Now it's just me and Frederick, who joins me on the deck. He slips in beside me and puts his hands in his pockets.

I shouldn't read into that, right? He wouldn't take my hand in front of Lauren and Topher. Not until he's talked to Topher, which he plans to do tonight. At least, that's what he said on Wednesday when I asked. I guess he changed his mind about telling him the news in person.

"Hi," I whisper with a smile.

"Hi," he says back, no inflection in his tone as he keeps his eyes on the road.

My heart nosedives into my stomach, but I have no time to feel anything, because in minutes it's pure chaos as Topher and his security team climb from the SUVs—including Tia, my previous bodyguard who abandoned me for a family emergency. Guess all is well, though I'm surprised she still has a job. Good for Topher.

Speaking of the prince, he strides across the lawn and climbs the stairs, and my strong, handsome brother wastes no time kissing both of my cheeks and pulling me into a hug. "Chloe."

"Hi, Toph." I pull back. Despite the fact he just traveled for nearly fifteen hours, not a hair on his head is out of place, and his beard is neatly trimmed. He's got on his jeans with a non-wrinkled, red, button-up shirt that makes his green eyes pop. "What do you think?" Then I sweep my hand behind me and turn.

He whistles, shakes his hand, and scrubs a hand down his jaw. "It's incredible, Chloe. You've outdone yourself." Then he nudges Frederick and puts his hand out for a shake. "And you! Thank you for keeping my sister safe." They do one of those bro hugs, clasping hands first and then pulling each other in for a love tap on the back.

"Of course." Frederick doesn't look at me. Is he afraid to give everything away? Why? Why not just tell Topher now? But then again, Lauren will be here any moment and we don't want this moment to be about us.

"He did more than that," I say. "He helped clear the field, plan the wedding. He was a fabulous assistant."

That draws a tiny smirk from Frederick, and Topher barks out a laugh. "I'd have paid good money to see that."

"No, Your Royal Highness. You would have been wasting that money." Finally, Frederick looks my way, and his eyes shine with something like pride. "Your sister did all the work. And she got the whole town involved. We never would have gotten all this done otherwise."

That sharpens Topher's gaze. "The whole town knows about this?" He groans. "Chloe, I thought we talked about that."

But before I can defend myself, Frederick's doing it for me. "Calm down, mate. She did what she had to do to rally the troops and get everyone to keep your secret. She was brilliant, I tell you."

Topher gives a start and studies Frederick for a moment. He opens his mouth to say something else when another two cars pull up the drive. One's a red Prius and one's a silver minivan.

The ladies have arrived.

"Go hide," I hiss to Topher.

"Right." He signals his people, and they all move quickly into the house. Hopefully Lauren hasn't caught sight of them yet and won't think anything of the SUVs.

In mere moments, there's a crush of women piling out of the vehicles, and I rush down the steps to say hello. First I find Lauren, a tall thin brunette with classic beauty despite the very little makeup she wears, and when she sees me, she squeals and pulls me into a hug. "Chloe! It's so good to see you. We've missed you at the house."

"I've missed being there."

Shelby climbs out next, her short blonde hair freshly cut. She's wearing an adorable yellow skirt and white top with cap sleeves that screams kindergarten teacher. She also hugs me, lifting on her tiptoes because of her short frame. "I told her how you were spending extra time in Hallmark Beach helping me with some wedding stuff." She winks.

Before I can reply, I'm tackled by Kennedy, who is brighter and happier than the last time I saw her. "Hmm, love looks good on you," I tease.

She blushes, then looks at me, back up the stairs to where I know Frederick is staying. Then she leans in, whispers, "Looks good on you too."

I shove her with a smile, and she giggles while the others—Kayla and Evie, both with their newborns, and Kennedy's sister, Alexis, who's rocking orange hair—get out of the car.

Lauren stretches her arms over her head. "When Shelbs mentioned you needed a girls' weekend, none of us could say no."

"I didn't know babies were allowed at girls' weekends," I tease Kayla and Evie.

Kayla adjusts her sleeping daughter in the baby sling wrapped around her. "I was told you'd secured a babysitter. Sorry, Baby Rey, but girls' weekend isn't girls' weekend with a baby strapped to your boobs the whole time."

We all laugh. "Yes," I say. "I have a pair of aunties just itching to get ahold of those cherubs." When I asked Bea and Janine if they'd be okay helping out with the babies this weekend, they both gave a resounding yes.

Evie claps. "Oh, that sounds like heaven."

Lauren grabs my hand. "So, is this where we're staying? I thought the only place in town to stay is The Seashell."

The other women exchange excited looks, but they leave the explaining to me, which is exactly how I want it—to get to be the one to tell Lauren what's happening. My chest expands. "Here, come with me," I say, tugging on her hand.

She gives me a puzzled look but follows me up the steps. When her eyes see the vineyard, there's a sharp intake of air. "It's so beautiful! What a lovely place for a girls' weekend."

This is it. The moment of truth. I feel the women's eyes on me, Frederick's too. "Lauren," I say.

She turns her big brown eyes on me. "Chloe," she mimics with a smile.

"We aren't here for a girls' weekend."

Lauren blinks hard and her mouth twists at the corners. "What are you talking about?"

"We are here"—I sweep my hand out in front of me—"for your wedding."

"My ..." Her mouth drops open. "My wedding isn't for another month."

"That will be your public wedding." I take her hand in both of mine, turn to face her. Behind her, some of her friends are tearing up, some rocking on the balls of their feet. Then I see Topher sneaking out of the house and coming our way. "We know that being in the public eye isn't easy for you, and that you're giving up a lot to marry into our family. So we wanted you to have a special day, just for you. Something that's all about you and Topher, not the media or Flutterbum or anyone else."

I can see I've shocked her, because she's standing still—something Lauren never does—and blinking at me as if I'm speaking a foreign language. Then, at last, she speaks. "We?"

My brother slips his hands around her waist from behind. "We, love."

Lauren *eeks*, spins, throws her arms around Topher, and starts crying—all in seemingly simultaneous fashion. "I can't believe you're here." Then she's kissing him with such abandon and passion that I feel like I maybe should turn away to give them some privacy. But then she pulls back and smacks his shoulder, and points a finger at all her friends, at me. "And I can't believe all of you, lying to me like that! You ... you ... beautiful people, you!"

We all rush her with hugs, and before we know it, another truck has pulled up with the rest of the groomsmen—Evie and Kayla's husbands Connor and Josh, Shelby's fiancé Eric, and Kennedy and Alexis's boyfriends Ryan and Dax—and it's pure madness on that deck.

I take a step back and observe it all with a smile, warmth in my heart.

And yet, even though I planned all of this, I can't help but feel a little on the outside of it. Yes, this is partly my family with Topher and Lauren at the center. And then there's Frederick, the man I love, who is slapping Topher on the back and shaking hands with the rest of the guys in greeting.

But he still won't look at me.

I sincerely hope I'm wrong, that I'm just knackered from all the late nights and stress of the last week and a half. But it feels as if I'm being edged out. I can see myself slipping further to the outside of the circle. I technically still belong inside of it, but maybe there's a concentric circle there too. One that connects, that's creating a new pocket of belonging for me.

If only I'm brave enough to step into it. But what would that even look like?

At that moment, my phone vibrates in my back pocket. I shouldn't answer it, not now, but it's actually kind of nice to have a reason to corral the thoughts and fears trying to overtake my brain at the moment.

I don't recognize the number as I step away from the group. "Hello?"

"Is this Chloe?"

"Yes. Who's this?"

"Rhonda Howard, from Something Blue."

Oh. Maybe she finally received the messages I left her when I first got to town. "Hi, Rhonda. I—"

"I hear you might be interested in buying my wedding shop."

Not where I thought she was going with that. "Um, well ... who told you that?"

"Lucy Reynolds."

Of course.

"Listen," she continues, "I'm going to be honest with you. My new husband is rather loaded, and I don't really need the money, but the town needs a solid event planner."

"I agree." If I hadn't had experience with event planning, then I'd have never been able to put together this wedding without Rhonda here. And there is so much more that could be done, so many packages that could be created. My brain explodes with the possibilities.

Rhonda goes on. "Hallmark Beach has the festivals that draw a crowd, but those only happen about six times a year. It needs more to recommend it, and creating a solid wedding economy is something I strived to do, but didn't achieve."

"I think you did a great job. Your shop is adorable, and when you met with my friend Shelby a few weeks ago, you were very professional and organized."

"Oh! I remember you now. You're Shelby's British blonde friend."

A breeze kicks up across the yard, and I shiver. "Something like that."

"The point is, I think you are the right woman for the job."

"What makes you say that?" Planner to planner, I truly want to know.

"I hear you've managed to get the Lovelands on board with renting their space, which is a huge boon, in my opinion. I tried to get them to do it for years. Always a no." She laughs. "So whatever you've done, then keep doing it. I think it's fate you turned up there just when I was leaving."

There's that word again. *Fate.* I'm not sure I like it, because it feels like it takes the control out of my hands. In the past, I've let other people make my fate. I've allowed them to tell me what I should be or what I should do. I've let them tell me that what I bring to the table isn't good enough. But now, *I* get to decide.

Still, there's so much to think about. Frederick, for one. We need to have a conversation before I commit to anything. "I'll have to see if I can gather the funds—"

"You don't understand," Rhonda says. "I want to *give* you the shop."

"What?"

"Yeah. Like I said, I don't need the money, but I still really care what happens to Hallmark Beach. It's yours. I inherited the building from my parents and everything, so there's just property taxes to pay on it, plus any business expenses, of course. But everything else is yours. If you want it."

I do. I do want it. I don't *want* to want it—but I can't help it.

Drat. What do I do now?

twenty-four

FREDERICK

It's a good thing Topher gave me the entire weekend off, because I can't focus.

Can't get out of bed either.

And yes, now that Tia's here to watch over Chloe, she's got the floor in her room, while I have my own room with my own bed.

It's not what I want, but I'm not sure I really get to decide what that is after all. There was a small sliver of hope, that perhaps, this time would be different. If Chloe truly wanted to come back to Kentonia, then we'd find a way to make it work.

But I don't think that's what she wants.

Haven't had a chance to ask her, though, between the decorating Chloe's done today plus the bachelorette and bachelor parties last night—the latter of which was a tasteful evening of steak dinner, bourbon, and cigars at a steakhouse one town over —I haven't seen much of her.

And now, after a few hours spent at the vineyard rehearsing the wedding itself, it's time for the rehearsal dinner at The Purple Seashell. We all took a break to get ready, but I just flopped on my bed and have been staring at the ceiling this whole time.

I never took myself for a coward, but this is the scariest thing I've ever faced. I mean, could I possibly be overreacting? Perhaps Chloe really doesn't want to stay in Hallmark Beach. Maybe I'm projecting. Maybe Jordan was wrong.

I'll only know once I talk to her.

A knock sounds on my door. "You coming, mate?" Topher asks from the hallway.

I stand and shuffle over, open the door to find him dressed in casual trousers and a plain shirt with a blazer over top. He takes one look at my rumpled self and arcs an eyebrow. "Did you fall asleep?"

"Not exactly. Just needed a rest."

"The dinner's starting soon."

"I'll be there in a jiffy."

"All right." Topher plays with the buttons at the end of his jacket's sleeves. "Hey, I know we didn't get a real chance to talk last night—or today—but I wanted to thank you again for taking such good care of Chloe while here."

I nearly choke on my reply. "Y-yeah, of course, mate." *It was my absolute pleasure*, I want to say. But I don't. I'm not talking to Topher about our relationship until I know what's going on with Chloe. "So, you excited to marry the love of your life?"

"More than I can say." Topher leans on the doorway and studies me in that way he has. The guy's too darn analytical, and it's making me sweat. "I hope you can find someone you love someday as much as I love Lauren. You deserve that happiness, mate."

I want to shake him, want to scream that I've already found it. But all I say is, "That would be a little difficult, considering that old law that says bodyguards can't marry."

But he just waves away my protest. "Nobody cares about that anymore. Don't you think I'd change that law in a minute if it meant my best mate was in love?"

My heart wrenches. It would have been so ... easy. If only Chloe wanted to come home too. "Never took you for such a softie, Your Royal Highness."

"I have my selfish reasons, of course." He grins. "Can't have you leaving me just because you meet a girl, now can I?" Topher cocks his head. "You really are invaluable, you know. I'm glad you took care of my sister, but I look forward to having you back at the palace."

I'm queasy at his words, but ignore that. Joking is the only way to make things lighter. "Is that your way of saying you missed me?"

"Of course." And there's serious Topher again. He straightens. "It will be nice to get things back to normal."

Is he the one joking now? "Except you'll be married. You'll have Lauren with you at all times to keep you company. You won't even miss me."

"Why, are you going somewhere?"

"No, of course not." My stomach drops.

"Good. Because I honestly couldn't do this without you, mate."

I roll my eyes and give him a punch in the shoulder. "Of course you could. But you don't have to. Now get out of here so I can get glammed up. Some of us don't have our princely charms to recommend us."

He laughs and shakes his head. "See you later then, mate."

Thirty minutes later, I've showered, dressed, and headed downstairs and out the back door onto a strip of private beach that Janine had cordoned off for our little gathering. Protective agents are posted along the outskirts, making sure that anyone who tries to walk that way knows the beach is closed for a private party.

Once again, Chloe's outdone herself. If the rehearsal dinner looks this good, I can't fathom how the actual wedding will be. There are twinkle lights everywhere, tables set up with white gauzy linens and centerpieces with some sort of vases, seashells, and flower petals arranged in a delicate way that my big hands could never manage. The sun is about to set, casting its final remnants of glow along the white sand.

The guests are gathered in small groups on the beach, many of them drinking cocktails, some eating hors d'oeuvres being offered by two servers with platters. Some sit, some stand, watching the water come and go. There's a mixture of bridal party and Chloe's new Hallmark Beach friends, who Lauren insisted attend thanks to all the help they've been to us. Lauren's younger sister Sam even made it out from New York today and has exclaimed more than once that Hallmark Beach is so adorable, and she wants to move here.

It's a fine group, and I feel blessed to call them my friends. But none of them are the one I need to see most.

"Hi, stranger."

Is it possible to stiffen and relax at the same time? Probably not physically, but emotionally that's what's going on inside when I hear Chloe's soft words behind me. I turn and suck in air at the sight of her in a blue dress that matches her eyes and hugs her hips before it flares out at the knees. Her curls are pulled up in some sort of large clips, cascading from them like a waterfall down her back.

"You look ..." I swallow. "Incredible."

There, a small smile. "You don't look so bad yourself, Muscles." Her hands go together in front of her, and she fidgets with her grandmother's ring.

I zero in on that ring. "You moved it back to your right hand."

"We're not fake engaged anymore, remember?" Her voice is soft, but also ... sad. What's making her sad? "I think we need to talk."

I want nothing more in this moment than to whisk her off somewhere and kiss away her sorrow—to kiss away the *need* for a talk.

But we don't always get what we want.

I certainly don't.

Then again, what she wants is more important. It always will be, and I don't think there's anything wrong with that. "All right," I say, and I take her hand.

She looks up at me in surprise. "Aren't you worried Topher will see?"

"Let him see."

Biting her lip, she nods, and we head around the tables and chairs toward an outcropping of rocks on the north side of the beach. Just on the other side sits the marina, but here we find a cozy crook to stand in, hidden from the others.

A place to talk.

Her fingers still looped between mine, I lean my back against the rocks. "What did you want to talk about?" Since I don't even know where to begin this conversation, I'll let her lead. Then I'll say my piece.

"Okay." She takes a step toward me, then seems to think better of it and steps backward again. "The last few days, things have just felt ... off. Between you and me. Am I imagining that?"

I blow out a breath. "No."

"Do you want to tell me why?"

"I'd like to hear what you have to say first."

"That's fair." She looks at our hands, strokes her thumb

against mine. Her chest heaves with a deep sigh. "Rhonda offered to give me Something Blue. Like, I don't even have to pay for it. I just have to accept it."

I should have seen this coming. And yet, a sudden cold expands throughout my core. "That's ... wow."

"Right?" Chloe's voice pitches higher, in competition with the echoes of the waves, which are much louder here because of the rocks. They beat out an impossibly sad melody. *Don't go.* "I won't deny that I've loved our time here. That I love the people, the way they've taken us in, the way we feel halfway normal here. And I think you've loved it too, yeah?"

"I won't deny that either. It's a great place."

"Right? See? And I was thinking—or hoping, rather—that we might give it a go. You and me. Here. Together." She pulls in close again, and runs her fingers down the lapels of my blazer. "We could build a life outside of the cameras, keep this going. Be free."

My heart breaks with every word. It's like watching a film of someone else, and you know what's coming and you scream at them to not go in that house because of course they're about to get slaughtered.

The worst part is that Chloe doesn't even know she's the one holding the knife.

Because she lifts up to kiss me, soft and sweet as ever—and I want to let her. Oh, how badly I want to say yes, to give into the fantasy. To ignore the fact that I'm about to die.

My hands slide to her hips and press firmly to stop her ascent. I turn my head into her hair so her lips can't touch mine. For a second, I just hold her against me.

She trembles. "Freddy?"

I pull back, look in her eyes. She deserves that much. "I think you taking over the shop is a brilliant idea."

"You do?" Her tone is tentative, suspicious, and who can blame her? Because my actions seem to be saying the opposite.

"I do." The breeze here is strong in this little alcove, and it whips pieces of her hair around. I smooth a strand down for her. "But I can't stay."

She licks her lips, then nods. "All right. That's fine. We'll stick to the original plan then. Go back to Kentonia in two days, talk with my fam—"

"No." It's the hardest word I've ever said.

"What do you mean, no?"

"I'm not going to let you sacrifice your dreams. You have to stay."

She scoffs. "I'm not staying if you're not staying. You're more important than any other dream."

"But I'm not. You long to be free, Chloe, and I can't give that to you. My loyalty lies at home, but you ... you have the chance to go. Your family would miss you, but ultimately they want you to be happy."

"*You* make me happy." Tears drip from those beautiful lashes of hers, and it absolutely guts me that I'm the cause.

"You'll get over me."

"You don't get to decide what makes me happy, Frederick Shaw." Now the tears are backed by flashes of anger. Good. Let her be angry. Let that anger fuel her into doing what I know she should.

What she knows she should too.

"Chloe, I only want what's best for you."

"You don't get to decide that either. Because I love you, you dumb idiot. I love you and I don't want to live life away from you. Ever."

Sakes, this is hard. My eyes sting and my vision starts to blur, but I remain as stoic as I can. "I won't keep you from doing the thing that makes you come alive, Chloe. The world would never forgive me." I lean in and kiss her impossibly soft hair. "You might never forgive me either."

"Of course I would."

She's clinging to my neck, and I'm clinging to her waist, both of us buried in each other.

Someone *has* to be logical about this. I pull back, drop my hands from her, and swipe at my eyes. I can't even remember the last time I cried. "Maybe you'd be fine with it at first. But what happens if we go home, and we stay together, and we get married? You'd have the exact same kind of public wedding that's made Topher and Lauren miserable. You'd have to face the naysayers who will inevitably speculate that you've betrayed your father by taking up with a Shaw. And what about any kids we'd have?"

She sniffs. "I don't even know if I want kids."

"But how much of that is because you don't want to bring them up in the same environment you were brought up in? In the limelight?"

"I ... I don't know." Her voice turns panicky. "But I don't care about all of that. I just ... can't we just figure out how to make this work? Love is worth it all, Frederick. Unless ... unless you don't feel the same way I do?"

Sakes. I pull a hand through my hair. I can't tell her I love her back. Won't say those words if I can't follow through on the rest. But I also can't let her think I don't care. How can I possibly bridge the gap between the two? "I ..."

There's no telling what emotions she can read across my face, but Chloe sees what she sees and straightens her shoulders. Shakes her head, lifts her chin. Goes regal on me. "Forget I said that. I won't beg, Frederick."

"You shouldn't have to beg for anything. Ever." And I mean it.

"And you shouldn't have to give up what you want to keep others happy. It isn't your job."

"If I don't do it, who will?"

"You're a good man, but in this, you're wrong." She pauses. "I'm going to walk away now, and if you don't stop me, you're going to regret it forever."

"That might be true." I allow myself to trace her face one more time with my knuckles. Her eyes flutter closed and all bravado seeps out of her onto the sand. I don't want to make her a weaker version of herself. I want her to be strong, resilient, like I know she truly is. And if she comes home with me, I'm afraid I will see her wilt one day at a time. "But I will regret it more if I have to watch you give up on your dreams. Don't ask me to do that, Chloe."

"Okay." She slips from my grasp, takes one step back, then another. "I won't."

Then she's gone, her footsteps in the sand, and it's just me and the moonlight and the mournful sea.

twenty-five

CHLOE

This should have been a gloriously happy day.

But at least it's a beautiful one.

The vineyard is swathed in light from the sun that's about to settle behind the hills. Everything is set for the ceremony and the reception. The guests and bridal party have taken their seats in white wooden chairs that stand just beyond the rows of growing grapes. Since there were so few guests aside from the bridal party, we decided to let Lauren and Topher stand up front alone, focused only on each other.

There's a hint of a breeze, just enough to make things chilly, but we've got wicker baskets with throw blankets and a chalkboard sign that says *Snuggle Up!* at the ends of each row. There's also a hot chocolate bar just waiting for us—and I've made a mental note to bring Lauren one later with extra whipped cream, just like she enjoys it.

I've discovered it's the little touches with weddings that make a difference. It's in the long, rustic-looking tables that will allow us all to be together in one place, to face one another, because I know that's what Lauren and Topher really want anyhow. The lights that will sparkle overhead along with the stars in the velvet sky that's coming. The dance floor where the groomsmen and Topher will perform a mashup—with both lip-syncing and a choreographed dance—of 'N Sync songs during the reception. It's even in the food truck that's parked on the grass, where Marilee's brother Blake will be serving up gourmet grilled cheese sandwiches, one of Topher's favorite foods from childhood.

It all comes together to make this *their* day.

Which means it's not about me and my heartbreak.

"I still can't believe you did all of this," Lauren whispers from her place beside me on the deck. It's just the two of us, waiting for Elisse to finish getting everyone to sit down. She looks amazing in the dress Shelby purchased for her, and I can see why it wouldn't have been "queenly" enough for Felicia Flutterbum. Though many would call it rather simple, with its A-line shape, flowy skirt, beaded waist, straps, and short sweep train, I call it perfect for Lauren.

"Of course I did all of this." I give her a hug, careful not to muss her hair, which is swept in a smashing updo, or her bouquet of calla lilies. "You're my sister now—well, in about fifteen minutes. But I love both of you very much."

"And we love you." She grabs my hand and looks me up and down. "You are the best sister ever, and you look freaking gorgeous to boot."

I admit, I feel rather beautiful in the dress I selected from Stephanie's boutique. Deeply bright pink in color, the backless halter gown harkens back to the one I wore on my eighteenth birthday. But I'm even braver today, because my favorite feature is the slit that travels just past the middle of my thigh. It's hidden in the folds of fabric until I walk and flash my bright green pumps beneath. "I don't hold a candle to the bride."

She blushes, but squeezes my hand. "That's not what a certain bodyguard thinks. He hasn't been able to take his eyes off of you since the moment the men saw the women and we started taking photos together."

"W-what?" I press my palms against my cheeks. "Who?" She can't possibly know ... can she?

"Please, Chloe." She rolls her eyes in that very Lauren way, and I find myself hoping that she never changes, no matter what the media or my countrymen throw at her. "I've known you two were in love since I first met you."

I blink and tears sting the back of my eyes. "Does Topher ..."

"He's completely oblivious about these things."

"Please, don't tell him. We aren't ..." I look away. "We aren't together."

"Oh." She touches my shoulder. "I'm sorry. I thought for sure this time alone would give you the clarity you both needed."

"It did." I peek at her. "Just not in the way I expected."

"Aw, sis." She starts to pull me in, but I hold up a hand and shake my head.

"Nope, you cannot do that, or I'll cry and then you'll cry and all of my hard work on your brilliant makeup will be down the toilet."

Her eyes crinkle around the edges. "I hope you guys can work things out."

"I tried. But he seems to think that if he's not a bodyguard in Kentonia, then he'll be letting everybody down." Ugh, there I go, saying too much. But Lauren is just far too easy to talk to.

"Who would he be letting down?" Lauren's nose wrinkles. "Surely not Topher."

"Topher, Frederick's parents. The country at large."

"Hmm." A pause. "And why couldn't he still be a bodyguard? I know there's that law, but you know Topher would abolish that in a heartbeat."

I shouldn't be having this conversation now. Still, if I know Lauren, she won't be able to focus on her day if she's worried about mine. But am I really ready to say it out loud? "I'm considering moving here. To Hallmark Beach."

"Really?"

"Really. I got an offer, one that would be hard to refuse."

"Have you talked with your parents or Topher about this?"

"Not yet."

She pats my shoulder. "Good. Don't. Make your decision first, then stand firm. You know your dad and brother are really just giant softies when it comes to you. And your mom ... I mean, she'll completely understand. They just want you to be doing what you love."

A breath whooshes out. All this time, I've fretted over whether my family will feel rejected or upset over my decision. But perhaps Lauren is right. "Even if it means I don't come home and marry some foreign dignitary or prince?"

She laughs. "It's true. You *were* the final hope for someone in the family to marry well."

"Stop it!" I poke her side. "Topher's made a brilliant choice, and now it's time to finally get you married off."

"First, just know ... I'm rooting for you and Freddy to work it out."

"Thanks. But that's up to him."

"Then I'll be praying he wises up before it's too late." Lauren bounces on her tiptoes, showing off the pink canvas Keds she's got on underneath her gown. Another Lauren-ism that makes me smile. "Now, is it time?"

"If you're ready."

"So ready."

"All right, then." I wave my hands at Elisse, and she flashes me the thumbs-up. Then she signals the string musicians, and they begin to play.

Lauren's head rears back. "Is that ...?"

"*God Must Have Spent a Little More Time on You?*" I smile. "Yep."

She squeals. "You are literally the best at this."

And she's right. I am. This right here, it's what I'm meant to do. Make brides happy. Let love win. And it strikes me then ... Frederick is right too, at least in part. If I gave up this opportunity to run the wedding shop in Hallmark Beach, I might always regret it. I might even come to resent him, or at least always wonder what life would have been if I'd followed my heart.

It's just awful that my heart is leading me down a path away from the man I love.

But he's the one choosing something else over me. Or maybe, instead, I simply need to think of it as him following his heart too. Just like he can't tell me what makes me happy, I can't decide for him either.

Though I still think that he's doing what he is for other people, perhaps that's just what makes him Frederick. Sacrifice. Loyalty. Generosity. All the things I love most about him are the things that are taking him away from me.

I squeeze Lauren's hands and we start our descent down the deck-side steps. I walk in front of her to slightly block the view of her from Topher. Of course, he saw her earlier when they took photos, but this walk ... it hits different. This is the last time she will ever walk toward him as something other than his wife.

And when I split off and grab a spot standing between Lucy and Marilee, I watch my brother as he catches sight of his bride.

The wonder, the awe, the joy that flashes across his face—it was worth all the heartache they faced, all the trials, to get here.

My gaze veers slightly to the right, to the front row where I feel a heated gaze. And it's Frederick, watching me. He's impossibly handsome in his tuxedo and bow tie, his short hair gelled to perfection, his shoulders as firm and strong as ever. My chest aches at the sight of him, at the emotions displayed in full force in his eyes.

Ragged heartache that matches mine.

Wanting, longing, untapped desire.

Anything but joy.

He didn't tell me he loved me back last night when I stupidly tried one last-ditch effort to get him to stay. When I reverted back to that girl who begged Troy not to leave me. But as soon as I realized I'd done it, I backed off. Remembered the words Frederick himself had spoken to me that night four years ago in the garden: *Don't let the fear of what others think hold you back. Surround yourself with people who know you, who are in your corner. Determine your own worth, Princess, and fight to keep it.*

So that's what I'm doing. As Lauren reaches Topher and hands her flowers to her sister in the front row, and the audience takes a seat, I take Lucy and Marilee's hands in my own. They both smile at me. Lucy winks.

And I know I'm home.

The wedding unfolds like a dream and despite my determination not to think about Frederick, everything reminds me of him.

The way Topher cries when he says his extensive vows to Lauren—which she teasingly calls a tome—reminds me of Freddy crying last night when we said goodbye.

When Lauren calls my brother SuperThor and he responds with a "You'd like that, wouldn't you, Tiger?"—I can't help but think of Muscles and Princess. The people we were before yesterday, when we became the people with broken hearts.

And when the sun is gone over the hills and the cheer goes

up from the crowd and Topher swoops in to kiss the woman he loves, I remember that first real kiss between me and Frederick. The all-consuming, never-going-to-top-this-but-we'll-try kiss in the rain that was the beginning of our real love story.

I hate this, that everything about this wedding that was supposed to be all about Topher and Lauren has made me think about something I will never have again with Frederick.

I also hate that I can't hate him. That I never really will, because I understand. He's not choosing something over me—I have too much worth to believe that. He's just doing what he thinks is best for him and his family.

And that's what I have to do too. Would I rather do it with him? Yes, of course. A thousand times yes.

But he hasn't made that an option.

So as Topher and Lauren are declared man and wife and a whoop goes up from the crowd, I pull my mobile from my purse and send Rhonda a text: *I'm in.*

FREDERICK

She looks so beautiful, it hurts.

And I was wrong, back when I thought there was nothing more torturous than lying close to Chloe and not being able to have her.

The more torturous thing is having her—knowing the taste and feel of her—and then giving her up. Because the real thing was far better than the imagined.

And now I'll know for the rest of my life what I'm missing.

Yet here I sit at the end of a long picnic table, all alone, nursing a glass of Scotch and unable to pull my gaze from her. She's dancing to some pop song with Lauren, Lucy, and Marilee, and they're singing along—yelling along, more like— tossing their hair and bouncing to the beat. Chloe is vibrant and alive and doing a much better job of faking happiness than I am in this moment.

And sakes, that dress ... talk about killing a man slowly.

I loosen my bow tie, let it hang around my neck as I slam back the last of my drink. It burns all the way down, only adding to the fire in the pit of my stomach. A headache floats around the edges of my skull, the base of my neck. Thank goodness I'm off duty tonight. I'd be complete rubbish at protecting anything, including my pride.

If it's not completely obvious that I'm in a sour mood, then someone isn't paying attention.

And then, as if my best mate can read my mind, he slides onto the bench beside me. I feel his eyes on me but just slink my elbows further down against the table. "Having fun?" he finally says.

"Best time of my life." I can't help the monotone in my voice. I've reached the *don't give a care* point of the evening. All day, I've held it together. Smiled and joked and frolicked and performed a rousing rendition of 'N Sync's *I Want You Back*—complete with choreography—with the other gents (much to the women's delight). But now?

I'm just done. I want nothing more than to pack it in, head home, and drown myself in work.

Not that work will give me that much mental stimulation. But maybe I can request an outdoor shift. Some time off to travel, perhaps? I did hear what Chloe said last night: *You shouldn't have to give up what you want to keep others happy.* And even though I can't figure out a way to not shirk my duties and responsibilities *and* have Chloe, at least I could go after other things that make me happy.

I could finally travel a bit, perhaps. Take a vacation. Surely my parents and Topher couldn't fault me for that.

Reaching for my glass again, I tip it back, remembering too late that it's already drained. I frown and start to stand so I can grab more from the bar.

"Do you love my sister?"

I freeze and plunk right back into my seat. Turn to stare at Topher. "What?"

"I said, do you love my sister?" Topher's frowning. He grabs a cloth napkin from an unused plate and flops it against the table. "Lauren seems to be under the impression that you do. But you would have told me that, yeah? Or I would have known? Am I that obtuse, or is she wrong?"

I pinch the bridge of my nose. "What does it matter, mate?"

"Why wouldn't it matter?"

Running my finger along the beveled edge of the glass in front of me, I stay silent.

Topher does too, for a time. Then, "Lauren also seems to think you're staying on as my bodyguard out of some sense of obligation. Tell me she's at least wrong about that."

Again, I don't say a word.

The music on the dance floor flips to a slow song. Chloe and Lucy dance together in an exaggerated manner, and Lauren peels off alone, scanning the crowd.

"Go dance with your bride, mate."

Topher sighs, tosses the napkin back onto the table. "She can wait."

"Making her wait is not a good way to start off your marriage."

"Don't be daft. She's the one who sent me over here."

Of course she was. "Look, I feel privileged to work for the crown."

"But you don't like it."

"I like it fine."

"But you don't love it." He pauses. "Tell me you aren't doing it because of me."

"Of course I'm doing it because of you. But that doesn't make it a bad thing."

He runs his fingers down his beard. "What I mean is, tell me you aren't doing it because you think I truly couldn't get along without you."

I scoff. "Isn't that what you literally just said yesterday?"

"I just meant ... I mean, yes, I rely on you, but even if you weren't my bodyguard, you'd be my friend. And that's all I need. My best mate." He narrows his eyes at me. "And if you were to someday add the title of brother to that, well ... I wouldn't mind."

That gets my attention. I sit up straighter. "You wouldn't?"

"Not if you love my sister. Not if you treat her right."

"What about my family's reputation?"

"That's rubbish and you know it."

My heart rate increases. To have Topher's blessing ... it's huge. I open my mouth to say so, but then my shoulders sink again. "That means a lot to me. Truly." I breathe. "I don't know if your sister has talked to you about this yet, but she might not be coming back to Kentonia."

"Lauren mentioned something along those lines as well."

"Wow, you have been rather busy talking about *other* people on your wedding day."

"When those people are some of the ones that I cherish most in this world—and one of them is being a cotton head— then yes. It tends to come up."

A cotton head? Really? "The point is, I can't serve the crown *and* be with Chloe. Not if she's here and I'm there."

"So? Go do something else with your life then. I release you from whatever obligation you seem to think I hold over you."

"I don't know what to say." But even without the obligation I felt toward Topher, there's still the matter of my parents. "My father still expects me to carry on the tradition of serving the crown. His depression has reared its ugly head again, and I'm afraid that if I ... well, they already lost Matthew. Father's already lost his dignity. Can I really ask him to lose the only thing that brings him pride?"

"Mate, *you* bring him pride."

Chloe said something similar. But I'm just not certain.

"Look, remember when my father was unsure about me

asking Lauren to marry me? And you said it didn't matter what my parents thought. That Lauren was worth it."

"That was different. My dad is sick."

"And he has your mum to care for him. He's got modern medicine. He's got his therapist. And he's got you for a son. What does it matter what job you have?"

A tiny shot of hope takes root in my heart. I've had these thoughts before, but Topher just lays them out so clearly, so logically, like he always does.

"Besides," Topher claps me on the shoulder. "The best way you can serve our country is to make the princess—my sister— happy. To take care of her. Cherish her. Keep her safe and support her. Can you do all of that?"

My throat burns, and it's not the Scotch. "I want to. You have no idea how much."

"Then do it. There's literally nothing stopping you, except your own fear." He cocks his head. "Don't tell me my best mate —the guy who will tackle any danger if it's coming after the people he's protecting—is actually a chicken."

With that, he stands and strides off toward Lauren, who's chatting up her friends. She laughs at something someone says, then turns in surprise when Topher grabs her into a dip, where he kisses her nice and solid.

Everyone cheers and knocks forks against glassware.

I remember now. Topher, he was worried once too. He had to learn to compromise. To communicate. To tell Lauren what he wanted, but also be sensitive to her needs. I know, because I was there for it all, on the outskirts, observing him fight for his happiness. It hasn't been easy, them getting here when they came from two very different worlds.

But it happened. They found love, and they held on. They were honest and true, and maybe that's all two people need to be.

That's how my parents are. Their marriage is the thing that first inspired me to believe in love, after all. Would they *really* tell me I should stay on as a bodyguard when my heart wants nothing more than to remain here with Chloe?

I thought so. I've run the scenarios so many times in my brain, but always get stuck at that point—what's expected of me, because Matthew isn't here. But maybe, just maybe, I was wrong.

I don't know for sure.

But I need to find out.

My breath increases as I whip out my mobile from the inside pocket of my tuxedo jacket. It's late here in California, which means it's wicked early in Kentonia, but it's possible my parents are awake since they like to rise at daybreak.

I find their number in my contacts and press it.

The phone rings. Once, twice, three times.

My stomach drops.

But then, "Frederick?" My mum's voice is tight with concern. "Are you okay?"

"I'm fine. Sorry if I woke you."

"You didn't. I was sitting here at the kitchen table drinking my tea and missing you. I thought I dreamed your call into being."

There's a smile in her tone now that it's relaxed. It's just like Mum, and suddenly, my insides ache with what I'm about to tell her. How will she feel about me moving so far away?

"You're sure you're all right? You never call this early."

"Yes, Mum." My eyes catch Chloe again, her hair spinning

out and afire as she dances under the lights. "More than fine, actually."

"Oh?" There's a muffled sound on the other line. "Hang on, your father's just shuffled into the kitchen. I'm putting you on speaker."

Talking to Mum is one thing. To my father? This conversation just reached epic proportions. But it has to happen, for all our sakes, and it might as well happen now. "Hey, Dad."

"Frederick?"

I can picture him, his bed-head hair slightly askew, more than grown out from his military and advisor days, as he lowers himself slowly into a wooden chair in their tiny kitchen.

"It's me."

He harrumphs in that way of his—the one where you never know if he's agreeing with you or disapproving.

"Where are you?" Mum asks. "I hear music and laughter."

"That's a funny story, actually. I'm at Topher and Lauren's wedding."

"I thought that wasn't until next month," Dad says.

"Chloe got this crazy idea to throw them a surprise non-official wedding in a small town in California, actually. She executed the whole thing and got the townspeople involved. It was brilliant to watch." I pause, swallow. "*She's* brilliant."

There's no response from my parents for a few long moments. Then, Mum says, "She's beautiful too, don't you think?"

"Mara!" my dad grunts. "She's the princess. That's inappropriate."

"Well, she is. Intelligent too. And kind. And Frederick has eyes. Plus, she's more of his best friend's sister than she is the princess as far as he's concerned."

I smile. My parents bicker in the most amusing way.

"That's not what her father would say if he heard you talking like that."

I wince at the truth in my father's words. But the king and his opinions are a problem I don't have the capacity to deal with right now. "Mum, Dad. Can I just ..." Oh, I can't sit here any longer, the pent-up energy roiling inside of me. So I stand and hurry off to the edge of the clearing. "I need to tell you something."

"What's happened?" My father's tone turns sharp, suspicious. Not of me, but of anything outside of his knowledge and control. Which, let's face it, has been everything as of late.

"Nothing." I pace. "And everything."

"We're listening, dear." Mum uses her soothing tone, the one reserved for Father when he's in one of his fits of frustration. She's got a pitch for every one of his moods, and knows him so well that I think it's just natural for her to bust them out without thinking. "Go on."

There's so much to tell them, but I start at the beginning. "I never wanted to be a bodyguard."

I wait for shock and outrage, but there's only silence. So I go on. "I only did it because Dad wanted it so badly. And because I knew that Matthew ..." My voice breaks, but I plow on. "That Matthew wasn't here to carry on the tradition of serving the crown. And of course, he would have been a brilliant advisor. He would have served proudly, so how could I do any less in his absence? If I'd had my way, I would have stayed in the armed forces or taken a year off to travel the globe or, I don't know, done something super bizarre and gotten a job in tourism. Something outdoors."

"You never said." That's Mum, and she sounds sad.

"Of course not. Because Matthew wasn't here."

"But ..." She trails off. "We never meant for you to carry the burden of any of this. His death. What his life would have been."

"I know you didn't. But I still did."

Mum sighs. Deeply. And I don't know how to move the conversation forward. Perhaps I've made a massive mistake in calling and stirring all of this up.

The music feels distant now. Chloe feels distant too—a wispy dream that's becoming a mere shadow sifting between my fingers.

"Matthew didn't want to be an advisor."

Dad's remark cuts through the silence. I blink, trying to grasp what he's saying. "What?"

"We fought. Before he left on that trip. Before he died." Dad's normal monotone gentles, and I can sense the pain rimming the edges. "He told me he wanted to move to America and pursue music, of all things. And I told him in no uncertain terms that he would be an embarrassment if he chose that path instead of serving on the king's advisory board. I'd already gotten the king to agree to allow him to shadow me. The cogs were in place. All that was left was for him to finish his schooling and his future would be set."

My pacing stops right there in the grass. I can't believe what I'm hearing. "I didn't know any of this."

"Of course not," Dad grunts. "I didn't want you to. Because then I'd have not just one son who despised me, but two."

"I could never despise you, Dad."

"I despised myself, Frederick. The last thing I told your brother was that unless he returned from Peru with a different attitude, I never wanted to see him again. And then ... he never came back at all." His voice is raw, and I fear he's spiraling right back into the pit. But something about it also sounds stronger. Despairing but not weak. Like he's finally letting go of something he's been holding onto for so long.

Coincidentally, I know just how he feels.

Dad continues. "For a long time, I thought that somehow I'd manifested his death with my terrible words."

"Dad." Wow. I had no idea. "But surely he knew how much you loved him. How you just wanted him to be happy."

"I told myself that's what I wanted, but what I really wanted was prestige for myself and my family. Our family status and reputation were everything to me. But then I lost it all anyway. It took a long time to be okay with that." He clears his throat. "I was raised not to talk about my feelings, but your mother has been instrumental in showing me a different way. I still struggle, but we are slowly moving forward one day at a time."

In my mind's eye, Mum is leaning her head on his shoulder, a gentle smile on her face.

The backs of my eyes burn. "I'm glad."

"But now, I discover that you have been unhappy, all because of me."

"Not all because of you, Dad. Because of me and my mistaken notions of what the boundaries of sacrifice really should be." I run a hand through my hair, gripping my neck. My fingers are cool against my skin. "I think that we've both been living enslaved to fear and guilt. Something Matthew would never have wanted."

"No, he wouldn't have." Mum again. "He would have wanted you both to live in freedom and happiness. And he never would have blamed either of you for his death. It was an accident, and it was terrible, but he would have wanted you to learn from it. To really live."

"She's right," Dad says. "And if that means not being a protective agent, then go do something else."

"Really?" My chest loosens. I take in a huge gust of air. I've been living my life at half tank, starving myself of oxygen for so long and didn't even realize it. "What if I wanted to do manual labor at a winery part of the year, and travel the other part? Would you be disappointed?"

"Of course not, so long as you're happy. Whatever you do," Mum says, "we know you'll give your whole heart and faithfulness to the effort." A pause. "Or perhaps, to the woman?"

How does she know? But maybe mums just always do. "You may regret telling me to follow this path."

"And why is that?" Her voice is fully alive with teasing and laughter now.

"Because"—and here's the crux of it—"it might mean that I move to America to be with that woman."

"Then that's what you have to do," she replies.

"Wait, is the woman in question actually the princess?"

Mum and I both laugh at Dad's confusion and disbelief. "It is," I say.

"Well, you can't get much better than her."

"I'm not in love with her because of her status, Dad."

"That's not what I mean. She's been precocious and lovely since the day she was born. And kind, to boot." He's quiet. Then, "I wish you every happiness, son."

"Me too." Mum's turned sappy now. "And who knows? If you really love America, maybe we'll start over there too. A change of scenery might be nice, eh, Martin?"

"Indeed."

Okay, this is much more than I expected. So much more. Just like that, all the pent-up everything I'm feeling releases.

"Thanks, guys. I love you."

"Love you too, dear. Now go get your woman."

"Yes, ma'am." I don't waste any time hanging up the mobile, stuffing it back into my pocket and rushing back toward the group.

Squinting against the lights, looking for pink against the greens and blues and purples.

Then I hear her laugh. It's golden and it's beautiful and it's everything I've ever wanted.

And I'm going after it with everything I've got.

twenty-seven

CHLOE

The wedding reception is still going strong, but my own reserves are dangerously low. I'm not sure how much longer I can last, dancing and laughing and pretending like my feet don't ache and my heart isn't completely shattered.

But at least my friends have me. I think something in them sensed my melancholy and knew what I really needed was some breathing space.

That, and a delicious grilled cheese sandwich, which Marilee is grabbing me from her brother's food truck while we wait several yards away.

"I still can't believe you're moving here." Beside me, Lucy does a little shimmy in her red dress. Her eye makeup, which I suspect she stole from her little cousin Scarlett, glitters under the starlight.

"It's magical." Kelsey squeezes my arm. Her brown hair is curled in ringlets around her shoulders. "But are you sure you want to give up on the love you and Frederick have?"

"Yeah," April chimes in. "Because if a man ever looked at me the way he looks at you ... hi." She shakes her hand like it's on fire.

"No way." Elisse shuts it down by grabbing April's hand. "No man should dictate what Chloe does or where she moves."

I sigh. "He didn't. He let me go."

"And isn't that the most romantic thing he could have done?" April glares at Elisse and yanks her hand from her grasp. Then she turns to me. "I still have hope that things will end well for you guys. Just have some hope."

"This isn't one of your romance novels, April," Elisse says. "There aren't always happy endings."

"Guys, be quiet. Can't you see she's upset?" Lucy gestures toward me.

Ugh, I don't want to be the downer, the one everyone is worried about. I force a smile. "I love each of you and your perspectives. I'm going to be okay no matter what happens with Frederick because I've got you all rooting for me."

"Aw, group hug!"

That would be Lucy, who crams us all together—some of us giggling, others groaning—until Marilee calls to us. "Hey, no fair! Don't leave me out."

I reach out an arm and pull her in, careful not to upend the plate of sandwiches she's holding. We all embrace for a few long moments before letting go. Marilee hands out the sandwiches but Lucy just looks at the one she's offered like it has two heads.

But I have no such aversion and suddenly find myself starving.

Looking out at the dance floor, I go to take a bite—and stop. Lower my sandwich.

Because from across the yard, I see him.

Frederick's scanning the crowd, clearly looking for something or someone. And when his eyes fix on me, my mouth goes dry, because he cuts through the dance floor and heads straight toward me.

The gaze he's wearing takes my breath. Completely steals it. It makes me a little bit angry that he still has such power over me. That he can melt my insides with one look.

And then he's there.

All of my friends' heads shoot up at his presence and they split around me to make room for him. I don't know whether to be grateful or call them all traitors.

"Sorry, ladies," he says. "I need to steal Chloe for a moment."

I open my mouth to protest, but he just takes the sandwich from my hands, tosses it into the grass, and tries to tug me away.

Hey! "What are you doing? Let go."

Frederick drops my hand, puts his hands across his chest, and drat it all if the posture emphasizes the muscles there. "Fine," he says. "Will you come with me, please?"

Oh, just like that? He expects me to stop what I'm doing because *now* he wants to talk, after a day of glowering at me and making me miserable? My own hands find my hips. "Why?"

"Princess."

"Frederick."

"Fine." He sighs. "Just remember that I tried saying please." People are staring at us, but he doesn't seem to notice. "And also that you left me no choice."

Then he advances toward me and hefts me up and over his shoulder. I feel myself falling, but then he's there, bracing me around my thighs as he walks with purpose across the grass.

"Frederick! Put me down!" Each of my words bobs in my throat as I'm whisked away. I try to push myself up, to get out of his hold, to beat against his back—and that's when I realize I've got no chance of escape and had better just enjoy the view.

And let me just say—the view is good from where I'm sitting. Er, hanging.

It's almost enough to extinguish my ire.

Almost.

But not even an amazing butt can excuse Frederick's horrifically embarrassing behavior.

The sounds of hoots and hollers follow us into the darkness of the Loveland house's side yard where Frederick first fake kissed me.

Finally, he sets me on an empty barrel.

I glare at him. "How dare you!"

"Is it weird that I find you attractive when you're mad like this?" He steps closer to me and wraps his arms around my waist.

I still. That, I did not expect.

"Princess," he says, his voice all throaty. Oh my. *Focus on your anger, Chloe. Do not give in to the handsome man who thinks it's all right to capture a woman against her will—even if it was a rather sexy display of his masculinity.* "If you truly don't want to hear what I have to say, then I will take you right back out there. I'm a gentleman like that."

I snort. "More like caveman."

"Only for you."

"I thought ..." I clear my throat. "I thought you didn't want me."

"You know that was never the problem."

"So, what's changed?" *Has* anything changed?

He dips toward me, our faces on level ground with each other. Then his hands hitch upward, grazing the bare skin of my back. My whole body wants to wave a white flag. I can't, though, right? He hurt me. Walked away from me. And yes, I realize that just a few hours ago, I'd come to terms with that, but unless he's ready to apologize and turn a full one-eighty, then I can't trust him again with my heart.

Can I?

"Everything's changed."

Oh goodness.

"W-what"—my voice trembles—"what happened?"

"I had a chat with Topher, and he helped me realize that you were right."

Did he now? For some reason, this makes me giggle. "He always was my favorite brother."

"You should do something really nice for him."

"Maybe I should throw him a huge party and invite all of his friends." I smile.

"No one could possibly be that generous," he teases. "I just meant you should get him a new book or something."

"He already has far too many of those."

"He really does, doesn't he?"

My shoulders relax because the banter between us is alive and well, and I'm so grateful to find that my anger's gone. It's drained away with the words of humility he's speaking. "So what specifically did he help you realize?" I finally get brave enough to ask.

"That what I want does matter. And do you know what I want more than anything in this life, Chloe Huntington?"

Oh, he just set himself up for this one. I set my nose against his, batting my eyes. "A fully stocked home gym? A thousand cheeseburgers? A trip around the world?"

That has him barking with laughter. "Yes, actually. How did you know?"

"Freddy!" I smack his chest, then settle back into something serious as my feet wrap ever so slightly around the backs of his legs. "What do you want more than anything?"

"To be with the woman I love."

I suck in a hard breath. Is this really happening? Did he really just say...? "She sounds like a lucky woman."

"That's true."

We laugh together, before Frederick sobers. "I do love you, Chloe, and I'm so sorry for putting you through all of this. I'll move wherever you move. If you'll forgive me, I'd like to spend a lifetime making it up to you."

"A lifetime, huh?" I pull back. "That sounds an awful lot like a marriage proposal, Frederick Shaw." Goodness, I'm being bold. But if he's really saying he'll move for me, if he really loves me, then his intentions are deep. But how deep?

"Well, perhaps not quite yet." Frederick grins, and his confidence melts my insides. "But let's just say you shouldn't get terribly comfortable in our status as a mere dating couple."

"Oh? Are we dating now?" How I love teasing this man.

"If you'll have me." He takes my hand and presses it against his chest. "This heart has only ever beat for you. Without you, it would cease. I've been walking around a dead man, but you woke me up. I want to spend every day trying to make you the happiest woman in the world. Chloe Marie Huntington, will you date me?"

"Aw, Muscles. I thought you'd never ask—for real, anyhow."

"It's real, all right."

His eyes blaze into mine as he takes my hand and rubs my grandmother's ring absently with his fingers. "So, is that a yes?"

"Yes, Frederick Shaw. I'll *date* you." I grab his face in my hands and kiss him slow. "Because I want to spend every day trying to make *you* the happiest man in the world."

"Oh, love." He drops a kiss against the corner of my mouth, my jaw, my earlobe. I gasp against his touch. "You already have." Then his Adam's apple bobs, and his eyebrows knit together. "I know I'm not the best at saying how I feel, but I want to say this. Happiness, I'm discovering, isn't in what we do. It's in who we are with. It's not in where we live, but where we belong." He pauses. "And the short of it is, I will always belong with you. I knew it twelve years ago and I know it now. You really are it for me."

Seriously, have sweeter words ever been spoken? "Freddy," I breathe. His name is an exhalation on my lips, an inhalation for my lungs, my heart, my everything. "You're it for me too. And I promise to show you every day just how much I love you." Then I lean in and kiss him and spend as much time as possible right there proving that he is not the only person in this relationship who can keep their word.

Is love like this for everyone? Just being with a person and knowing you fit? That you belong?

All I know is that I'm so grateful we found each other. That he loves me through it all—in the normal and abnormal, in the spotlight or in anonymity.

I'm so glad that we are Chloe and Freddy, now and always.

And that that's always going to be enough.

LUCY

And this is why I love Hallmark Beach.

It's been my home for twelve years now, and there's not a day that goes by that I don't love it a little bit more. I mean, where else could two foreigners who were already in love (and didn't know it) come and discover said feelings in such a magical way?

Needless to say, I'm thrilled for Chloe and Frederick. Even more thrilled that they're staying in Hallmark Beach.

It's nice when people stay—when they stick it out, even if things are rough. That's more than I can say for *some* people.

"You're doing that thing again, Lucy." Elisse tugs on my elbow and I jolt, moving my gaze to my long-time friend in her gorgeous gold dress. Next to me—who only managed to find a dress in the very back of my closet, quite possibly from the last high school dance I attended—she is like a runway model beside a little girl playing dress-up.

But no matter. We're having a great time at this wedding even if I had to get gussied up. Elisse's family vineyard looks as amazing as all get-out, so elegant and lovely and yet ... homey too. There's a dance floor filled with many of my favorite people (who Chloe was nice enough to invite to her brother's wedding), twirling in an array of colors that's creating a night-time rainbow under the bulb lights strung across what, two days ago, was just an open field filled with junk.

Music pumps through speakers and into the yard, and a cheer goes up from the crowd when the iconic YMCA song comes on. I take a sip of the champagne in my flute. Hold back a grimace. Give me a bottle of beer any time, but this is still tasty enough, and it will always remind me of this iridescent evening. There's always something good to find in every situation—even if you don't get exactly what you want.

I smile at Elisse. "What thing is that?"

Using her own flute, which she's had no problem draining, twice, she points to the food truck positioned at the edge of the revelry. It's not a fun bright color, like pink or lime green, or—heaven forbid—yellow.

No. This food truck is painted black and white, with red lettering that says The Urban Melt. It's as dull and grouchy as its owner—and like the man inside, it takes itself much too seriously. I mean, sure, this is a wedding, and the guests are all dressed up, but was it really necessary for him to wear a full-blown suit while he works a grill?

Even if that suit looks good on him, with the jacket discarded and the white shirt hugging his broad shoulders and trim waist, the sleeves rolled up to his elbows to reveal delicious forearms that are just wasted on such a jerk. And then there's the tie all loosened like he's just gotten off work and is ready to relax on the couch. How is it possible he looks even more hand-some now than he did six years ago—the last time he was in Hallmark Beach?

Oh, how I loathe him even for that.

Elisse continues. "That thing where you make crazy bedroom eyes at Blake Moffitt, that's what."

I fling a hand on my hip and squeak out a protest. "I am *not* doing that!"

"Are too."

"I was just ... reading the menu."

"You can't read the menu from way over here."

Elisse appraises me with those eyes that have always called me on my crud. Why do I keep hanging out with her again? She keeps my life interesting, though, and I love her dearly, just like all of my friends—new and otherwise. I mean, I've forgiven Marilee for having such an awful brother, so I suppose I can forgive Elisse for being able to discern things I never want to talk about, right?

"I can too." I wave my hand in that direction. "It's just a bunch of grilled cheese sandwiches. Guess some of us never grow up."

"Have you not had one yet? Because those sandwiches are completely divine. They're not like your regular grilled cheese. They're *gourmet*."

She says the last word with an eyebrow waggle, as if gourmet is the new sexy.

Like anything about Blake could be sexy. Objectively handsome? Maybe. But sexy? No. Sexy implies wanting, and there's no way in you know where that I would ever *want* Blake Moffitt. Not again, anyway. "I'm not hungry." My stomach chooses that unfortunate moment to gurgle. I've been betrayed by my own body.

"Girl, just go try a sandwich. You will be forever changed. They're that good."

And give Blake the satisfaction of eating his food? That stupid truck is the whole reason he ...

Grrr. "I'm fine, thanks." I cross my arms over my chest and

look away, back to the dance floor where Chloe and Frederick are slow dancing despite the crazy antics going on around them. It's sweet, how they've only eyes for each other, for this moment.

"Stop being so stubborn."

"I'm the least stubborn person on the planet." And I'm not being snarky or cute when I say that. It's the truth. People often say I'm *too* easy-going.

"Normally, yes," Elisse says. "Except when it comes to him. And why is that, I wonder?"

"You know why."

"I know what you tell us. But if Marilee can forgive him for his absence, why can't you?"

Because he abandoned his sister when she needed him most. And yes, I know he had to have been hurting too, but to stay away for six years? Doesn't he realize what he did to her? Especially considering everything she was going through with Donny.

So yeah. When someone hurts my friends—well, that's hard to forgive. Add in his other offenses, and Blake the Flake Moffitt is basically the worst.

But I can't say all of that, because if I do, then Elisse will just go down the "Lucy has a crush" rabbit hole again.

And that rabbit hole leads somewhere that couldn't be farther from the truth. Like, we're talking Narnia. Middle Earth. Better yet ... Wonderland. (You know, because there was an *actual* rabbit hole in that one.)

Words clearly won't work to convince Elisse that I don't have feelings for Blake. There's only one way to do that. "All right. Get me a grilled cheese and I'll try it."

"No way. Go get it yourself."

I scoff and set my champagne flute on a nearby table. "I have no desire to talk to him." Don't want to ruin this wedding for myself—or others—by forcing a conversation between the two of us. How completely painful. "And I know he doesn't want to talk to me." Why would he want to talk to someone he finds so annoying?

My hands fist at my sides.

Elisse notices with an arch of her eyebrow. "Mmm hmm. So you're going to give Blake the satisfaction of watching you starve?"

"Blake doesn't care what I do."

And he doesn't care what I say either. Doesn't care after the funeral that I begged him to stay, for Marilee's sake. That I told him Donny was no good for her, that I needed his help intervening.

He just left anyway.

And thankfully, after tonight, I won't have to see him again for a good long while.

"Come on," I say. "Let's dance."

But at that moment, Marilee approaches with a plate of sandwiches. And *sweet macaroni*—they look fantastic. Golden yellow cheese spills out from between two slices of crusty Texas toast, which are grilled to perfection and sprinkled with what looks like parsley. I can practically taste the butter and cheesy bread melting in my mouth.

"Here, Luce," Marilee says as she holds out the plate. "I noticed you hadn't eaten yet."

Ugh, fine. At least I didn't have to schmooze Blake to get one. And I can be certain he hasn't spit on this one either. "Aw, you're the best," I say with false brightness. "Thank you." So I take one. Just to be polite, of course.

Elisse snags one too, and Marilee takes the third.

I bite into mine and it's like nothing I've ever tasted. Yes, my palate is limited to what we offer in Hallmark Beach, because I rarely travel anywhere else, but Tiny at The Green

Robin cooks up a mean burger and basically anything else I crave.

But this ... this really *is* gourmet.

And fine, maybe gourmet is sexy.

Because I want the sandwich, not the man who cooked it. Just clarifying.

What's not sexy is the way I devour the thing, licking the dripping cheese from my fingers.

Elisse looks at me with far too much satisfaction. "Good, right?"

I shrug and take a napkin from Marilee's plate. "It was okay."

Marilee just laughs, and then her face brightens. "Oh, hey. I was talking to April, and she mentioned that you were sleeping on the couch. Do you need a place to stay?"

"Yeah, I'm thinking it's time to move out. I just haven't had a chance to look yet. Why?"

"Sarah and Mandy are moving out next month," she says. Marilee still lives in her three-bedroom childhood home, but she rents the other two rooms to a pair of sisters who came last summer for jobs at Jordan's adventure tours company and never left. "They decided to get an apartment together. Wanna be my roomie?"

"Wait, are you serious?" I jump up and down. "So we could like, actually live together?" We always dreamed of that. But then she and Donny got married pretty much right out of high school and we never had the chance.

"We could indeed. If you want to."

"Of course, I do." I sling an arm around her shoulder. "I can't imagine anything better than living with my best friend."

Other than her terrible brother, there's not a thing about Marilee Moffitt that I dislike. As long as he stays far, far away, this is going to be—as my new friend Chloe would say—completely brilliant.

Quick Author's Note

Thank you so much for reading *Beachside Kisses With My Bodyguard*. Chloe and Frederick first appeared in the California Dreamin' series (starting with *Saving the Secret Prince*, but Chloe was more prominently featured as a side character in *Needing the Next-Door Neighbor*), and so many readers commented that they'd love to see their story that I just had to write this one!

This book is also special because it's the first book of the Hallmark Beach Small Town Romance series. I'm planning to give each of the women in this friend group a story, so I hope you got invested in each one of them and look forward to reading those.

As you can see from the epilogue, I'm continuing the series with Lucy and Blake's story. There's definitely some history there, right? I can't wait for you to find out what it is.

If that sounds right up your alley, you can order Beachside Kisses With My Enemy right now. It should release in 2024.

Also, if you want a little sneak peek of Chloe and Frederick beyond this story, you can download a bonus epilogue at kristincanary.com/bodyguard.

AND FINALLY, turn the page to check out a FREE

PREQUEL to the California Dreamin' series, which you should definitely read while you wait for Lucy and Blake's book. This series is all about the San Diego friend group you get a brief glimpse of at the end of the book you just read, and includes all the best tropes, friendship goals, and swoony book boyfriends you could ask for!

a free story for you

Enjoyed *Beachside Kisses With My Bodyguard?* Not ready to quit reading yet? If you sign up for my newsletter at kristinca nary.com/freebook, you will automatically receive *Enamoring Her Amnesic Ex*, the love story of Connor's brother Kevin and his wife Lola (who you briefly met if you've read Book 1 in my California Dreamin' series, *Loving the Ladies' Man!*). This is just a gift from me to you as a thank you for choosing to hang out with me.

Enamoring Her Amnesic Ex:

Two years ago, he broke my heart—and now he's forgotten all about it.

When my sister goes into labor, what are the chances that the nearest hospital would be the one where my ex, Kevin Bryant, is a surgical resident?

You know—the man who decided being a doctor was more important than love and left me reeling. Hard.

But when we run into each other—quite literally—he falls, hits his head, and wakes up with amnesia.

And he still thinks we're together.

His brother Connor asks me to pretend we're dating, just for a little while, so we can ease Kevin into the truth.

But the real truth is that being around this strong, capable man again is making me remember things *I* would rather forget.

Yeah, hi, my name is Lola, and I'm clearly a glutton for punishment. Because here I am. Pretending with him. Taking care of him.

Kissing him.

Just waiting for the bubble to burst.

Because as soon as Kevin snaps out of this and remembers the past, there WILL be another heartbreak.

And all I'll have is the memories of what was.

Read on for a sneak peek of the California Dreamin' prequel novella, Enamoring Her Amnesic Ex...

sneak peek

ENAMORING HER AMNESIC EX

Of all the hospitals in San Diego, my sister had to pick the one where *he* works.

Fine—if we're being technical, she didn't really have a choice. Her water breaking in the frozen foods aisle of her grocery store wasn't exactly Theresa's plan.

But come on, universe. Did the closest hospital have to be *his*? I feel I have a right to be upset by this, but since I can't be mad at Theresa, here I am with the biggest bouquet of flowers I can afford (hint: it's not THAT big) obscuring my face as I slink down the brightly lit hallways. And you'd better believe that anytime I see a tall doctor with brown hair, I hug the wall like it's wool and I'm static, baby.

But I'm not letting a potential encounter with my ex stop me from meeting my newest niece. Because family trumps everything—even if being in the place where Dr. Kevin Bryant is a surgical resident is giving me sweaty pits and an itchy nose. Or hey, maybe that's the flowers shoved in my face.

Wiggling my nose like that girl from *Bewitched*, I book it in my jeweled wedges down the hall, almost to the magical door where Theresa and Jake await with their new bundle of joy.

299

And then, I hear it—that voice I'd know anywhere, even though it was only part of my life for five months.

And yeah, they might have been the most intense and wonderful five months of my life, but phantom whiplash still hits me when I think about them. Because all the intensity, all the wonder, came to an abrupt halt when Kevin figured out I didn't fit into the picture he had for his life.

Now, I can't help the yelp that comes from my mouth as I stop and peek through the flowers. My traitorous heart—which shouldn't care one fig about the man standing at the nurses' station after he broke my heart into a million pieces nearly two years ago—thumps a happy jig against my chest.

Down, girl.

Because he may have the same high brow, the same tousled dark hair, the same strong arms and lean body that suggest he still runs and lifts weights every morning like clockwork, but the harshness in his tone, the rigidness of his stance as he yells directives at the nurses and disappears behind a set of doors are proof that he's not the man I thought I knew.

My Kevin was sweet. A little uptight, yes, but considerate and generous. My Kevin would never treat people like that.

But maybe I just saw what I wanted to see back then.

"Lola?"

I turn to find my brother-in-law standing in the hall outside my destination door, his brown-gray eyebrows raised. Jake's eyes are a bit red, probably from crying—he's a freaking waterspout, I tell ya—and his clothing is rumpled, I assume from the long night at the hospital.

Striding forward, I raise on my tiptoes and brush a kiss against his cheek. "Congrats, Daddy."

"Thanks. How's Sami?"

After Theresa went into labor and Jake joined her at the hospital yesterday, they asked me to pick up my five-year-old niece Sami from kindergarten and keep her at my apartment overnight.

"Wonderful and precocious as always." In fact, the girl asked me a million questions about birth and babies that started making me sweat. Thankfully, I was able to distract her with a Disney movie and pizza night. This morning before grabbing the flower bouquet I'm now holding, I dropped Sami back at school, where Jake will pick her up this afternoon so she can officially meet her baby sister.

"That's my girl." A grin sweeps his face and he pushes glasses up the bridge of his nose. Then he scans the hallway. "By the way, why were you standing there like Harriet the Spy just a minute ago?"

Note: Sami is obsessed with Harriet the Spy, so it's completely adorable that Jake uses it as a reference point in conversation. Not so adorable is the fact he caught my strange behavior upon seeing Kevin.

"No reason." I straighten and tug at the hem of my aqua-colored blouse. "How are Theresa and Baby Girl? Did you guys come up with a name?"

"Not yet."

"All right, all right. You twisted my arm. I guess I don't mind."

"Mind what?"

"Sharing my name with her. Lola Warren's got a great ring to it, don't you think?" I wink and breeze past him. As I step inside the room, my sister's tired voice wades out from the other side of the privacy curtain—and an older voice responds.

Mom.

Ugh. Is it too late to escape? I turn on my heel, but Jake shakes his head. He juts his chin toward my sister's bed. "I need you to stay with her. Theresa's craving a breakfast burrito from Dos Brasas."

"Fine," I hiss out. "But I expect one too. As payment."

"Payment for spending time with your sister and adorable niece?"

I stick my tongue out—not so mature for a twenty-four-year-old, but when did I ever claim to be mature? "For forcing me to talk with my parents."

"She's already been on the phone for fifteen minutes." There's a bit of sympathy in Jake's voice now. He knows why this is hard for me. "I'm sure you won't have to talk long."

"Still, you'd better throw in a Diet Coke to revive my energy when you return."

He chuckles, pats my shoulder, and leaves.

Groaning inwardly, I brace myself for the inevitable. Then I throw on a happy face and walk around the curtain, ginormous bouquet in tow.

Theresa's blonde hair is a bit grungy, tossed up in a messy bun on the top of her head—stay-at-home mom style, as she'd say—and her face is devoid of makeup like always, but the tiny smile lines around her lips are on full display as she snuggles her infant daughter against her chest with one arm and holds up her phone with the opposite hand.

When she sees me, Theresa turns the screen my way. "Look who's here."

I wave at the grainy image of my parents, who are squeezed in front of their computer in Zambia, where they teach English to underserved communities. Apparently they do a lot of good in the village where they've lived for more than a decade.

I hope so, considering what it's cost them—what it's cost all of us.

Stuffing down the bitterness, I set the flowers on the windowsill of the small room. "Hi, Mom. Hi, Dad."

"Lola! So good to see you." My mom looks older every time I see her on-screen—her hair a little grayer, the wrinkles around her eyes a little more prominent—but maybe it's just the terrible Internet connection. I wouldn't know, since they haven't been back to visit since Sami was about six months old and I've never been to Africa.

"You too, Mom." I move to the head of the bed, and Theresa flips the phone back around so it's fixed on her youngest daughter, who is sleeping and breathing in and out with an adorable little mew. At 8 pounds, 6 ounces, she's bigger than Sami was, though her legs are scrunched up like a little frog. Theresa has dressed her in pink footy pajamas that are just about the cutest thing I've ever seen.

Bending down, I kiss her sweet downy cheek, then the top of Theresa's head. "Good job, Sis."

"She's pretty great, isn't she?" My sister yawns and nearly drops the phone. "Sorry. Long night."

"We won't keep you, dear." Mom clicks her tongue. "Oh, I just wish I was there to hold my grandbaby."

"You could come home, you know." The words are out before I can call them back. I know better. Nothing is going to change. At this point, why would it?

"Lo ..." Theresa warns.

Dad sighs deeply, taking his glasses off and rubbing his chin with a big meaty fist. "You know we would, Lola, but the people here need us."

We *need you.*

They're the words I've longed to say for eleven years since they left a thirteen-year-old me in the guardianship of my twenty-three-year-old barely married sister because their new life was "too unstable for children." But I don't say those words, because they're not true anymore. Nope. Theresa and I have learned to rely upon each other. We are all the family we need.

I force another smile. "I know."

After a few more pleasantries, my sister says goodbye and

hangs up the phone. "That wasn't so bad, was it?"

"Torture." I tilt my head. "But worth it to meet this sweet girl."

Black-as-night curls stick out the bottom of Baby Girl's white cotton beanie with a pink satin bow. Apparently all Flanagan girls are born with dark hair that eventually falls out and comes back in nearly white blonde. At least, that's what happened with me, Theresa, and Sami. "Can I?"

"Of course."

My long hair falls forward over my shoulder as I gather the tiny bundle in my arms and get her situated. Her button nose and rosy lips remind me so much of her older sister, it's uncanny. "The Flanagan genes are strong with this one."

"Right?" Theresa pours a glass of water for herself from a pale pink jug. There's only enough to fill half her cup, and she downs it quickly. Then she relaxes against the bed. The room is small but thankfully private, and it smells like a mixture of baby formula and lemongrass. A large window lets in the morning light of another gorgeous mid-September day in San Diego.

As Baby Girl coos and inhales, I sigh in contentment. This is where I belong. With my family, who need me. I'll never regret choosing this life.

"So." Theresa studies me then tugs at the thin sheet covering her. "Did you see that job opportunity I sent you yesterday? You know, before I made a complete mess in Aisle 3." She hangs her head. "I'll never be able to show my face in my favorite grocery store again. Can you imagine the person who had to clean that up?"

"Oh, stop it. The staff will take one look at this sweetness and forget all about how she came hard and fast into the world." I run a fingertip along her forehead, tracing her cheeks, her nose. "Although maybe it wouldn't hurt to get them all gift cards as a thank-you. I'm definitely glad the manager acted quickly when she realized your contractions were coming so close together."

"Me too. And so grateful Jake made it just in time." Theresa, who is not the crier in the family, sniffles despite herself. "Find yourself a nice guy like him, Lo. It may have taken me a few years to see him as more than my nerdy lab partner, but now I find him the most handsome man alive. There's nothing sexier than watching him hold our daughters. Daughters. As in, more than one." Tears start streaming down her cheeks at an alarming rate. "Oh my gosh, I'm sorry. These postpartum hormones are something else."

I reach across to the counter and snag a few tissues, shoving them into her hand. "You definitely scored one of the good ones."

And once upon a time, I thought I'd done the same. From the moment I met Kevin at the diner where I still work—and accidentally served him a hamburger instead of his requested pastrami sandwich—things were like lightning between us. Hot and charged, yes, but deep too, leaving a lasting trench, a mark, on my heart.

Theresa blows her nose and then fixes her eyes on me again. "You didn't answer my question."

My nose scrunches. "What question?"

"The job opportunity. Did you look at it?"

"Oh." I kind of want to ask her which one she means, since she sends me several each week. But I'm not sure if she's in a teasing mood, given the sheen of tears still coating her eyeballs. "Um, no, haven't had a chance yet."

"Well, I think it's perfect for you. Assistant costume designer at a theater in Los Angeles." She straightens and I can tell she's about to go into teacher mode—I guess she can't help it after teaching science to middle schoolers for so many years. "Now, I know it doesn't pay all that well, so you might have to have a second job, but you're basically working two jobs now anyway. And this way, you'd get paid for the theater work. No more of this volunteer stuff. Which would be fine, but you have a bachelor's degree in costume design, for goodness' sake. You should be paid for your genius."

Baby Girl rustles and makes a sound like a grunt. *I agree, girl. I agree.* "It does sound like a great opportunity." I let my words trail off.

"But?"

"But you know how I feel about moving. I'm not going to be some distant aunt who never sees her nieces."

"Lo, Los Angeles is only a few hours away."

"I know, but—"

"And"—I hate how big-sister bossiness pervades her tone— "if you're ever going to go to New York and design on Broadway, then this might be a good step in the right direction."

"New York isn't happening, Reese." I try to infuse a lightness to my tone, as if my statement doesn't prick my insides.

"But it's your dream."

"Was my dream. In middle school. But now that I know what it would require ... well, I'm just not willing to make that sacrifice."

I refuse to abandon the people I love like my parents did.

Like Kevin did.

Not for a million dollars—and not even for the chance to design costumes on the Great White Way.

As if I've somehow summoned her help, Baby Girl opens her big beautiful blue eyes—and starts to wail. It happens so suddenly that I jump, but Theresa just laughs and holds out her arms. "Saved by the cry of hunger."

Standing, I hand over the hangry monster who has replaced my sweet little niece. But as soon as Theresa has her suckling— like a freaking boss, I might add—she turns her pointed gaze to me again. "Now, where were we? Oh, yeah. About to dissect the trauma our parents unwittingly unleashed on you by sticking you with me as a pseudo mom. Is that about right?

"I mean, when you put it like that ..." I tease.

Thankfully, I'm saved by yet another interruption when Jake waltzes through the door, a brown paper bag in hand and a soda. He wiggles them in the air and Theresa nearly leaps from the bed—but doesn't, of course, because I'm guessing Baby Girl would deafen us all if she unlatched. But when Jake places a foil-wrapped burrito the size of my forearm on the table in front of Theresa, she gives him the most solemn expression before saying, "I don't think I have ever loved you more than in this moment."

He turns amused eyes to me before handing me a burrito and the soda. "Do you feel the same?"

"Would it be weird if I said yes?" I grin. Living with him and Theresa for five years before living on campus at the University of San Diego for my undergrad gave Jake and me lots of time to perfect the brother-sister relationship. Even though I have my own apartment now, I still spend lots of my free time at their house, watching Sami and doing movie nights with my sis.

Theresa rips into her burrito, taking a bite and sighing with pleasure. The scent of sausage and cooked eggs makes my own stomach rumble, and I start to unwrap my burrito, which is warm in my hands.

"Do you have to work today?" Jake asks.

I freeze. Shoot, what time is it? My eyes land on the ancient clock above Theresa's head and the tension leaves my body. "Not for another hour." Which is good, because the lunch rush at Dom's waits for no one. Of course, I've told my boss that I might be switching shifts a lot in the next few weeks as Theresa might need me. And thankfully, the first costume fittings for

The Music Man aren't until this weekend, so I don't have any set times I need to be at the theater until then.

Before I can even take a bite of my burrito, Theresa has inhaled hers, all while Baby Girl happily nurses. Jake is watching in awe of them both, and suddenly I feel like the thirdiest third wheel ever. I should be used to it by now—it's basically been happening since my parents foisted me on the newlyweds—but I still can't seem to escape the ick swirling in my stomach at the thought that I'm more an invasion than a help.

I stand, set the burrito on my chair, and grab the now-empty water jug from Theresa's side table. "I'll get you a refill."

"Oh, thank you. That would be great." My sister strokes Baby Girl's back. Both of them look like they're in a food coma.

Hustling from the room, I quickly find the kitchen area where the nurses stash little packets of crackers, containers of applesauce, and sandwiches for hungry mamas. There's an ice and water machine and I use both to refill the container to the brim. Once I set the lid on top, I take my time moseying back to the room. I stop to study a wall papered with children's artwork from the pediatric wing, smiling at the crooked lines and creative shapes.

"Lola?"

For the second time in an hour, someone is calling my name. But this time, it isn't my brother-in-law.

It's *him*.

And his voice in my ear is so unexpected that I shriek and jump, forgetting that there's a full container of water in my hands.

Liquid careens out of the top—guess I didn't secure that lid as well as I thought—and all over Kevin. As if that wasn't bad enough, I drop the jug, allowing what's left inside to spill out onto the floor beneath him.

Eyes wide, he's staring back at me with a look that likely mirrors my own. Along his strong jawline is a dusting of stubble, which is kind of a surprise given his propensity to shave every day. He always said doctors should present themselves as professionally as possible.

I lift a hand and give him the tiniest wave known to mankind. "Hi, Kevin."

"What ..." He looks down at his green scrubs, which are drenched. Then his gaze moves back to me. "What are you doing here?"

The once-bustling hallway is now strangely devoid of people, as if the universe knows this moment is embarrassing enough. "I didn't come here to see you, that's for sure." I cross my arms over my chest.

"That's not what ..." Kevin tugs at the badge on the pocket of his scrub pants. "Sorry. It's, um, good to see you."

"Sure it is."

Kevin shifts from one foot to the other. I'm shocked he's still standing here, to be honest. Maybe he's expecting me to go quietly like I did the last time we spoke. But I've got two years' worth of pent-up anger and hurt just begging to be unleashed on him. The only reason I'm keeping them in check? I don't want my sister's care to suffer. Not that a surgical resident would have anything to do with Theresa. But still.

Oh, yeah. And I guess I also maybe feel like he wouldn't care one way or the other. He was so clinical when he dumped me.

No feeling. No heartache.

It was so ... *easy* ... for him to let me go.

So sue me if I'm relishing his discomfort in this moment just a tad.

A pager on his belt goes off and visible relief finds the

cracks in his face. "Well, I'd better go. I hope ..." He swallows. "I hope everything is okay."

Dang it. There's a sliver of the Kevin I knew—the one who understands what it is to lose someone and works desperately hard so others don't have to. I can't leave him thinking that there's something wrong with my family. Or me. "Theresa had a baby."

"Right. Of course. That's why you're in this wing."

"Yep." My smile hitches one corner of my mouth at his logical brain at work. "Why are you here though? Doing a rotation in OB?" While dating him, I acquired quite the medical vocabulary.

"Just covering a shift for a colleague." He checks his watch. "Speaking of."

"Right." I bite the inside of my cheek, because the idea of saying goodbye ... "Well."

"Well." His eyes connect with mine and spear me right there on site. I can't move, can't breathe. Their deep chocolate tones wash me in their sweetness, in the depths of what was. What could have been. If only ...

Then the connection is severed when he pivots quickly.

But instead of moving away, he slips in the puddle of water that—until this moment—I'd forgotten completely about.

Apparently he did too.

His head bangs against a medical cart behind him. Before I know what's happening, his eyes loll back into his head and close.

"Kevin?" I drop to my knees, and my jeans are soaked in an instant—not that I care. He looks really pale, though I don't see any blood and his breathing seems okay. I pat his cheek but he doesn't wake up. Turning my head toward the nurses' station down the hall, I cry out. "Help!"

A few people come running and they push me aside while I

watch them take stock of the situation. They call for a bed and a woman in a white coat hurries over and examines him. It's all happening so quickly and my own breath is coming in short bursts. I clench my fists at my sides.

Finally, as they lift him onto a bed, his eyes flutter open.

"Thank you," I whisper as I step forward.

But the doctor gives me a side-eye. "Sorry, miss, you need to step back."

"Don't talk to my girlfriend like that," Kevin says before his eyes roll back into his head and he passes out again.

Did I miss the "ex" in ex-girlfriend? Maybe I'm the one who hit my head. And no, it's NOT wishful thinking, thank you very much.

The doctor and team start wheeling him away and I realize I'm biting my lip so hard that I taste blood. One of the nurses—a sweet older woman with a white poof of hair—puts her hand on my lower back. "We're taking him to the emergency department to get a full workup. Don't worry, we'll take good care of him."

And I do the only thing I can do. Because this is Kevin, and even though he is the absolute last person I wanted to see today, this is kind of all my fault and I owe it to him to make sure he's all right.

After shooting Jake a quick text, I follow the nurse down the hall.

Enamoring Her Amnesic Ex is ONLY available by signing up for my newsletter. Grab it here: kristincanary.com/freebook

Kristin is a wife and boy mom who functions best on peach tea and cookie dough ice cream. A desert dweller, she always has her eye on the next trip to a beach somewhere—and if she can't travel there in person, then you'd better believe she's going to write about it. Kristin is never fully satisfied with a movie, TV show, or book without a hefty dose of romance in it, and she's grateful to be living a true-life love story with her own crazy little family. Connect with her at KristinCanary.com.

 facebook.com/kristincanary

 instagram.com/kristincanaryauthor

* 9 7 8 1 9 6 1 2 2 3 2 1 9 *